CASSIE'S RETURN
Bradford Hall, Book One

BARBARA MCMAHON

Cassie's Return
Copyright © 2023 Barbara McMahon
All Rights Reserved

Prologue

Twelve years ago

"Come on back to my place," Travis said, revving the car and careening recklessly down the narrow road. The trees crowding the edges of the country lane whipped by in a blur.

"I need to get home," Cassie said, nervous about the speed.

Today had been a mistake. Cassie had known that almost the moment she'd agreed to go with Travis, but she couldn't back out. Getting even with Matt should have made her feel better, but she'd been annoyed with Travis all day. She should never have given in to him and played hooky from school to go to New Orleans. She was tired and hungry and feeling more than a little guilty.

Now she had to sneak back into the house so Margaret didn't give her grief for skipping school.

Piper was supposed to tell Matt that Cassie had cut classes to go to New Orleans, and with whom. If Matt could fool around with Evelyn, Cassie was justified in having some fun with Travis.

Only she hadn't had fun. Travis had been all over her, and fighting him off had become a full-time task. Now they were almost back in Bradford, and Cassie was counting the minutes until she could shake off this loser.

"Come on, baby," Travis said, putting a hand on her bare thigh.

The guy never gave up. She slapped his hand away. May in Mississippi was warm, but she'd also worn the shorts to make a statement. Pulling her leg away, she glared at him.

"I need to get home. Margaret will skin me alive if she finds out I skipped school."

"If? You mean *when*," Travis said, sneering. "Like old man Douglass isn't going to tell at some point?"

For sure the principal would call and complain about one of Margaret's foster children again. He called so often, she was sure he had her number programmed into his phone. Usually it was about Fiona, but once in a while about Piper. This would be the first call about Cassie.

It didn't matter. Her foster mother would be infuriated.

Still, it'd be worth it if Matt got the message. If he could play around, so could Cassie.

"Damage has already been done," Travis said, smirking at her. "Might as well go all the way."

"Stop playing games and get me home," she ordered.

If he didn't turn at the intersection that led to

Bradford Hall, she'd jump out at the next stop sign and get there on her own.

Which was exactly what she ended up doing.

Travis scoffed at her request and cruised past the turnoff. As he slowed for the next stop, never quite coming to a complete halt, she snatched her purse and flung herself from the car. He called after her, but she turned and began walking.

The car roared away.

It took her more than forty minutes to walk home.

The old house stood on a rise overlooking the sleepy Mississippi town of Bradford. It had been in Margaret's family since before the turn of the last century. A big brick house with eight bedrooms and a large old-fashioned kitchen, it provided ample space for a family.

Margaret Nunes had opened her home to three foster girls many years ago. Cassie resented the fact she had to live in foster care, but with both parents dead and no known relatives, she had no choice.

She stormed into the back of the house. Amazingly, no one was around. She walked through the kitchen to the front, then up the stairs to her room. The silence was spooky.

Opening her door, she tossed her purse on the bed and went back down the hall, peeking into Fiona's room. When she heard soft sounds coming from Piper's, she knocked on the door, opened it and stuck her head inside.

"You're back," Piper said, lying on her bed. She

scooted up to lean against the headboard. "The you-know-what hit the fan today."

Satisfaction coursed through Cassie.

"Matt wasn't happy to hear I went out with Travis, I take it."

"Oh, that. Yeah, he was totally pissed. I'm talking about Fiona. Someone beat the crap out of her and she blamed Margaret."

"What?" Cassie couldn't believe it. "Fiona's two inches taller than Margaret and athletic as all get out. Margaret talks tough, but she's never so much as slapped any of us. How could she beat up Fiona?"

"Fiona showed up here this morning black and blue with blood oozing from several cuts on her face. The cops came and took her to the hospital. She claimed it was Margaret."

"She's lying." Cassie went to sit on the bed. "What really happened?"

"I don't know the whole story. I was sent off to school before I could find out more. When I got home, the place was empty. I don't know where Margaret and Fiona are right now. Your plan worked, by the way. Matt had a fit when I told him you took off with Travis."

Cassie nodded, her own situation taking second place to the news about Fiona.

"I bet it was Jack. She should have dumped him weeks ago. He's bad news."

"Maybe, but she was mad as all get out and kept glaring at Margaret, saying it was all her fault."

Who would have beaten a sixteen-year-old girl? She would never believe Margaret would lay a hand on any of them. It had to be Jack. He was a classmate from the wrong side of town. He'd been in and out of trouble as long as Cassie and the others had known him. He and Fiona had a thing going—against Cassie's advice and Piper's. But Fiona was headstrong. No one could budge her when she made up her mind.

"So spill, how was Travis?" Piper said.

"Not as hot as he thinks, though his car is cool," Cassie told her. "The day was a drag."

She'd only gone to get back at Matt for his defection. Could she have found another way?

The phone rang.

Piper leapt up and ran down the stairs. The only phone in the house was located at the base of the stairs. Margaret had a cell phone, but none of the girls did.

Cassie followed right behind her.

"Hello...? Oh, yeah, she's here." Piper turned and held out the receiver. "It's for you. Sounds like Dolores."

Cassie hesitated a moment. She didn't want to talk to Matt's sister. Dolores had been the one to tell her about Matt seeing Evelyn again. Cassie hadn't wanted to believe her—Dolores was known for being a class-A liar—but she'd gone to Evelyn's house when Dolores had told her.

And sure enough, when Matt had rung the bell, Evelyn had opened the door and flown into his arms and kissed him. Cassie had seen it with her own eyes.

The boyfriend she'd dated exclusively for months had been kissing another girl.

"Hello."

"So you dumped my brother," Dolores said. She sounded worked up, talking fast.

"If going out with Travis is dumping, then I sure did."

"Ha, you'll be sorry."

"Yeah, how? Dumping a two-timer is the only way to go." No matter how much it hurt. "You might consider that yourself."

"What are you talking about?"

"Come off it, Dolores, the whole school knows Stewart's cheating on you."

Matt would be furious that Cassie had told his sister her boyfriend was seeing someone else. They'd argued over whether to tell her or not.

But Cassie no longer cared what Matt thought. Maybe telling Dolores some home truths would show her she couldn't have everything her own way.

"He is not. He's *my* boyfriend!"

"Whatever. Why are you calling?"

Cassie had no desire to prolong the conversation.

"Matt wants to talk to you."

"About what?" Cassie asked. "There's nothing to say. You were right, I saw him kissing Evelyn."

So much for trust and loyalty. The pain struck again. How long would it be before she got over the betrayal?

"I expect he wants to talk to you about your

behavior," Dolores said with a syrupy tone.

"Mine? What about his?"

"You going to make up with him?"

"No."

"Good."

"You going to make up with Stewart?" Cassie asked.

"You're wrong about him. There's nothing to make up."

"Ask your brother if you don't believe me. He knows it as well as I do. You two deserve each other."

Dolores hung up.

"She's so weird."

Cassie placed the receiver on the hook and told Piper what Dolores had said.

"She's obsessed with her brother," Piper observed. "She doesn't want him to see anyone, just to pay attention to her."

"That's creepy. Besides, she's been going out with Stewart Palmer. Now he's going out with Patti."

"Yeah, well I think Dolores is a nut," Piper said. "No wonder Stewart found somebody else. Look at all the times she's called to get Matt home on some pretext or other. You'd think the guy would get wise."

Cassie felt she had to defend Matt.

"He's the man of the family. He feels responsible for her and his mother."

"For a crazy sister and a drunk mother? He'd better get that scholarship to Tulane and get the heck out of town when he graduates."

"We all want to get out when we graduate," Cassie said. "This is a dumb town."

She sat a few steps above Piper on the staircase.

"I want to know about Fiona."

"As far as I can tell, we have to wait until they get home to find out the scoop," Piper said. "I already called some of Fiona's friends to see if they knew anything. No one did."

By six o'clock, neither Margaret nor Fiona had returned to the house. Piper and Cassie fixed sandwiches for their dinner, eating in the kitchen, speculating about the different scenarios that would explain what had happened to their friend.

The phone rang again.

"Maybe that's them now," Cassie said, dashing out to the base of the stairs to answer.

"Cassie?" It was Dolores again.

"What?" Cassie said in exasperation. "I need the phone. I'm expecting a call."

"Matt hates you. He never wants to see you."

Dolores was gloating, no doubt about it.

"Fine. I'll stay out of his way. I'm not feeling too positive about him myself!"

"I lied. My brother would never cheat on you. You're the fool. Now he won't forgive you. You're history. But he'll always be here for me, no matter what. He's my brother, and we don't need you pushing your way in, trying to take him from me."

"Dolores, you're crazy. I wasn't trying to take him from anyone."

Cassie felt her heart drop. Had Dolores really lied about Evelyn? Or was she lying now? Cassie had seen Matt kissing Evelyn with her own two eyes.

"Forget him, he's not for you." The words were full of venom. "I'll make sure you never get your hands on him again."

Cassie slammed down the receiver. She'd known Dolores was a little wacko. She was also a drama queen. But she was Matt's sister, and Cassie had always tried to be polite to her. If Dolores had lied—

The implication struck Cassie with full force. Matt hadn't cheated—but she had. He'd never forgive her. She should have asked him for an explanation, not gone off for the day with Travis, the guy with the worst reputation in school.

Well, not the worst. Jack had that honor. But Travis was trouble from way back. His hands all over her today had proved that.

Piper came into the hall.

"Was that Fiona or Margaret?"

"Dolores again. She said she lied about Matt and Evelyn."

Piper gave a whistle.

"But I saw them together."

Doubt niggled at Cassie. What if she'd made a mistake? She loved Matt. He was the best thing ever to happen to her. He was due to graduate in another few weeks and she'd follow the next year. They'd been going together for months. He was kind, caring, sexy.

But she had seen him kiss Evelyn.

"So talk to the guy," Piper suggested.

They heard a car in the driveway and hurried to the back door. Margaret got out of the old sedan. She seemed surprised to see the two girls at the door. A deputy's car turned in behind hers.

"Where's Fiona?" Piper asked from the doorway.

"She's in the hospital."

The older woman walked to the back door, looking ten years older than when they'd seen her that morning.

"She won't be coming home."

"What? She's going to die?"

Cassie couldn't believe it. Fiona had been healthy that morning. How badly was she hurt?

"No, not that." Margaret walked past them and went to sit at the kitchen table. "She's being taken to another home."

She looked at each of them. "You two are being reassigned, as well. No one believed me when I swore I hadn't touched Fiona."

The deputy stepped inside the kitchen and stood near the door.

She stared at her hands.

"How could they think I would strike a child?"

"What do you mean, we're being reassigned?" Cassie asked.

Margaret raised her eyes.

"You and Piper are to pack and be ready to leave by nine in the morning. Social Services will be taking you to another foster home after the sheriff asks you both some questions. The deputy is here to make sure you two stay safe until morning."

Margaret's voice was strained.

Stunned, Cassie looked at the cop. What had Fiona told the police?

Piper touched her arm. They left the kitchen together, not speaking until they were in Piper's room.

"We have to find out what's going on," Piper said. "And just where they plan to send us. Margaret didn't hit Fiona. She couldn't possibly have caused the damage I saw. Why would Fiona say she had?"

"I don't know. Why would Dolores lie about Matt and Evelyn?"

"It's hardly the same thing," Piper snapped.

"It is to me. Both lies are changing my whole life."

Cassie headed for the door.

"Where are you going?"

"To find out something."

She sneaked down the stairs. There was only silence from the kitchen, so she picked up the phone and dialed Matt's number. She would talk to him as Piper had suggested. And tell him she was being reassigned.

Where would they go? She couldn't think of an available foster facility in town. But Social Services wouldn't assign them out of town, would they?

The phone rang and rang. Finally Dolores picked up.

"Matt, please," Cassie said.

"He's gone to work. He's so angry. I've never seen

him so angry before. He hates you." Dolores was practically shouting. "I'll make sure he always hates you. You can't have my brother!"

"Shut up, Dolores. He's your brother, not your boyfriend."

"He's *mine*. He loves *me*. You tell him I never lied to him."

"Tell him yourself."

There was a pause. Then Dolores said, softly, almost in a singsong voice, "I won't be here to tell him. But he won't ever forget me. Or what you did."

"Where are you going?" Cassie asked despite herself.

"Nowhere. I'll be dead."

The receiver slammed down.

Cassie couldn't believe Dolores would ever even think of such a thing. How like her to be so melodramatic. How Matt stood it was beyond her.

Cassie listened for a moment. No sounds came from the kitchen. Slowly she walked to the front door and eased it opened. She had to talk to Matt. Had to hear his side of things and explain her own.

And what was she going to do about Social Services? He had to help her or she was going to lose her home. Dolores couldn't be right. He would forgive her. Nothing had happened between her and Travis. It was Matt she loved. She couldn't lose him.

1

Cassie Hodges swore again as she shifted to balance her dripping, overstuffed handbag, stack of damp mail, twisted skeleton of an umbrella and soggy bag of food, all the while trying to unlock her apartment door.

"Blast it all!" she muttered through clenched teeth.

The perfect ending to the day from hell. She hated days like this. She was wet from head to toe and had a raging headache to boot. Sometimes it didn't pay to get out of bed.

"If anything else goes wrong, I'm wiping the date off the calendar for years to come," she muttered, finally succeeding in opening the door.

She burst into her apartment, dropping the handbag and remnant of her umbrella onto the hardwood floor.

She kicked off her sopping shoes and tossed the mail on the counter separating the kitchen from the living room. She was freezing. The month of April was supposed to be the beginning of spring, not the tail end of winter.

The forecast had been for a little rain—ha! If the storm that now raged over Boston had arrived after midnight as predicted, instead of twelve hours earlier, she wouldn't have been caught in it at all. She glanced at her watch. It was not quite eleven-thirty. Too bad the storm hadn't listened to the weatherman.

Every cab in the city had been elsewhere, leaving her to trudge the twenty blocks between work and home in the pouring rain. The wind had laughed at her paltry umbrella, twisting it inside out within seconds of leaving the safety of the restaurant.

"If I ever win the lottery, I will hire my own chauffeur," she vowed as she traipsed into the kitchen. She turned the faucet on high, blasting water into the teakettle, which she quickly set on the gas range. Hot chocolate or tea would help to warm her up along with a hot shower.

Impatiently waiting for the water to boil, Cassie turned her phone back on and saw there was a message. She needed to get out of her wet clothes. The rain had soaked through her jacket and even her sweater was damp. Yet she pushed the play button.

"Hello, Cassie," a familiar voice said. "I know you're still at work, but call me when you get home no matter how late."

Cassie frowned, checking her watch. It was late, but she'd still call.

Stephen would wait up until she did.

He didn't like the fact she worked until after eleven most nights, and after midnight on Fridays and Saturdays. But as a sought-after chef in one of the hottest restaurants in Boston, Cassie was used to the long hours. Stephen knew working late came with her job. There was no need to have her check in every night.

Guilt tugged at Cassie. She was tired and cranky. She should appreciate that Stephen cared enough for her to want to know she was safe. It was nice to feel cherished. She shouldn't take out her bad mood on him.

She started to call him when the teakettle screamed. Cassie quickly made a cup of tea, then punched the speed dial for Stephen's number.

"What are you doing still up?" she said when he answered.

"Waiting to hear from you. You're later than I expected." He sounded worried. "Are you all right?"

"Sopping wet. There were no cabs so I had to walk."

"In this downpour at this time of night? You should have called me."

She smiled, feeling warmed with his concern.

"I'm fine," she assured him. "I wouldn't have asked my worst enemy to come out on a night like tonight."

"I wish you'd quit that job," he said. "Find something that has daylight hours. Or open a business of your own. You know I'd back you in a New York minute."

He'd suggested it before. Maybe it was time she gave the idea some serious thought.

"After this walk home, I'm closer to starting that catering business we've talked about," she murmured, taking a sip of the warm tea.

More days like this and she'd take the plunge. She'd never thought of herself as an entrepreneur, but she had menu ideas for special events bubbling around in her mind.

"You'd still be working evenings, but with a better clientele," Stephen said. " And you could take off when you wanted. Let's get married right away, sweetheart."

He'd been patiently waiting for her to pick the right time to get married.

She loved Stephen, but was not quite ready to make that final commitment. What was wrong with her? Or was she still adjusting to the fact they were engaged? It had only been a few weeks. She needed to get used to the idea.

"Maybe I could work from home and we could spend all our time together," he said facetiously.

Cassie laughed.

"Sweetie, I can't see your clients coming to our flat. Besides, we'd be tempted to do a lot more fun things besides work."

His chuckle warmed her even more. She did love him. She wished she had called him for a ride, just so she could have seen him this evening.

Why was she dragging her feet about setting a wedding date?

"Okay, so open a bakery. At least you'd keep more normal hours."

"Something to think about, but bakers have to start work about four in the morning. I'm not sure that's for me."

Baking was fine, but she loved the challenge and range that creating main courses offered.

"You could do charity work," he suggested. "You know Mother would love to have you on some of her committees."

Cassie wrinkled her nose, not that he could see.

"I don't think that's my thing."

They'd had this discussion once before. She thought she'd made her position clear. Sometimes Stephen heard what he wanted to hear, not what she said.

As for Stephen's mother—Cassie adored Adele Cabot. She was all Cassie wished her own mother had been—loving, elegant, devoted to her only child. And she was more than welcoming to Cassie.

At one point Cassie had wondered if her feelings for Stephen had grown out of her liking for Adele and her hopes to have her for a mother-in-law.

"It beats working nights and never having time for a normal social life," he said easily. "Speaking of which, Mother is having some friends down at the Cape this weekend. I told her we'd join her."

This wasn't the first time he'd made plans for them without consulting her. She wasn't up to dealing with it tonight.

"Stephen, you need to check with me before accepting invitations."

"This is just a weekend at home. No big deal."

"I'm working Friday and Saturday nights, but I could make it there Sunday in time for brunch," Cassie said.

She loved spending time at the old Cabot family home on Cape Cod. It was totally different from what Cassie was used to. She'd been a foster child in a small Mississippi town—no family, no background, no money. But her lack of background hadn't stopped Stephen from proposing or Adele from accepting her into the family with welcoming arms.

Cassie's childhood seemed distant—as if it had happened to someone else. Twelve years since that fateful night. She'd never gone back. After graduating from high school, she'd left Louisiana behind for good. Boston had been her home for the last ten years.

"Switch with someone like you did two weeks ago," Stephen suggested.

"I can't do that very often. That was for that special opening at the museum you wanted us to attend. I traded with Paul, but I can't keep asking him. He has his schedule and I have mine. Once in a while maybe."

Didn't Stephen realize that many people came to the restaurant solely because of her?

"It'd give us time together," he said in that sexy Bostonian accent that still sounded exotic to her ear.

"I'll see about switching Saturday night. Then I could get there Saturday morning, but I can't switch two nights." Cassie was firm.

"Deal. I'll take what I can get. We're leaving Friday afternoon and will return Monday morning. Shall I drive back and pick you up?"

"No, I'll get there on my own."

"I'll drive Mother's car and leave you mine. That

way you and I can come back together."

"Sounds like a plan."

"And maybe while we're there, we can discuss setting a date for the wedding," Stephen suggested.

"We'll see." Cassie hated to feel pressured, but she was too tired to argue tonight. "I've got to get out of my wet clothes. I'll talk to you tomorrow."

Her bare feet felt like blocks of ice. She had plonked the bag of food on the counter beside the mail. Thankfully the soggy paper sack had held up. She didn't know what she would have done if she'd dropped her dinner in some puddle blocks from home. She popped the meal into the oven, set on a low heat, and headed for the bedroom and some warm clothes.

A quick *hot* shower and sweats, that's what she wanted. That, plus peace and quiet for at least twelve hours!

Ten minutes later she was toasty warm in fleece sweats and thick socks. Her hair was slightly damp, but she hadn't wanted to spend a lot of time drying it. She was starved!

Passing through the living room, she picked up the ruined umbrella and stuffed it in the trash. She ran a practiced eye around the room. It was tidy. Immaculate, actually. Just the way she liked it.

She returned to the kitchen to eat a late dinner. People sometimes teased her about being a neatnik, a control freak. But she liked order. She felt able to cope with anything as long as there was a certain amount of harmony in her life. In Cassie's mind, order equaled harmony.

Sitting at the breakfast bar, she riffled through the mail as she ate the warmed roasted squab. She could almost feel the storm even inside the eighth-floor apartment. Rain sheeted down her windows, the wind howled. She pitied anyone still out in the tempest.

Once she'd finished eating, she took her hot tea and the newspaper that had come in the mail and went to sit in her cozy chair in the living area. The *Bradford Bugle* arrived weekly—a hometown paper for a woman who hadn't been to Mississippi in ten years.

Boston had been her home since her second set of foster parents had moved to the city a couple of years after she'd graduated from high school. While Cassie was not technically a part of their family, they'd invited her along and she'd gone. After high school she'd tried a semester of college, but it wasn't what she'd wanted. She had felt restless and had had no direction, so had been happy to move east. She'd lived with the Johnsons until they'd been transferred to California six years ago. Cassie still missed Dottie and Al and kept in touch.

A couple of years ago, before she'd met Stephen, Cassie had given in to a bout of nostalgia and had begun a subscription to the weekly paper from her hometown in a vain hope of feeling connected to her past.

At first, it had been strange reading about places and people she remembered but hadn't seen in so many years. But as the months went by, she began to feel a tenuous connection.

She had even taken a chance and contacted her former foster mother, Margaret Nunes. Margaret's house in Bradford was the closest thing to a real home Cassie had ever had.

She thought about the old brick house, Bradford Hall. In her mind it was still the stalwart building standing in lonely splendor atop a small knoll on the outskirts of the sleepy southern town. It had been her home for so many years.

For a moment a kaleidoscope of images flooded her mind. The shock of losing her mother when she'd been only four. The uncertainty and fear when she'd suddenly been thrust into foster care at Bradford Hall to live with strangers.

People often said young children didn't remember much, but she recalled every day at Margaret's with her foster sisters.

Piper, Fiona and Cassie. Wild girls with no place else to go, they'd carried chips on their shoulders the size of elm trees as they'd grown into rebellious teenagers. But they'd ended up closer than sisters. There had been laughter and shared confidences, plans and dreams.

Fiona dealt with her anger at the world by challenging authority every chance she got. Piper seemed vain and conceited to those around her, but underneath was a girl desperate to know something about her family. Cassie's own insecurity had been covered by a brash bravado and clinging dependence.

A jumble of images from those days—poignant, funny, bleak—flashed through Cassie's mind now.

Their lives together had ended abruptly when Cassie was sixteen. In the space of two days, the world as she'd known it had changed.

Nothing had ever been the same.

She shook off her somber mood and scanned the front page. Opening up the paper, she stopped in surprise. There in a sidebar column on page two was a report of Margaret Nunes's stroke and hospitalization.

For a moment, emotions swelled in Cassie. She felt like the uncertain sixteen-year-old she'd been all those years ago—alone, adrift, afraid—after being forced from Margaret's home. The last twelve years might never have been. She was transported back in time to the last day she'd seen her foster mother.

The older woman had seemed indomitable. She'd been the strength of that household, caring for the girls, making ends meet on a limited income and the small stipend from Social Services.

Cassie had written to her frequently since that initial contact two years ago, sending her cards at Christmas, even calling her a couple of times to chat on the phone. They'd made tentative plans more than once about getting together, but Cassie hadn't gone back to Mississippi and Margaret hadn't come to Boston.

The news of her stroke shocked Cassie. She couldn't imagine Margaret sick at all, much less gravely ill.

Checking the date, she saw the paper was only three days old.

She picked up the phone and input Bradford hospital into Google so she could get a phone number. It was now after midnight, but a hospital was staffed twenty-four hours. There'd be someone on duty who could give her an update on Margaret's condition.

Several frustrating moments later she hung up. No one would give her any information. She wasn't a relative. Margaret didn't have any relatives after her father had died. That had been one reason she'd opened her home to foster children in need of family.

There had to be someone in town who could find out how Margaret was doing and let Cassie know.

The first name that came to mind was Matt Bennett's.

The old hurt resurfaced. Cassie knew he wouldn't give her the time of day. Not after those hateful words he'd said to her that last day in Bradford.

If Piper or Fiona were still in town, she could have called one of them. The only person she could come up with was Edith Harper, Margaret's best friend. But when she called Information, there was no number listed for her. Was her phone unlisted? Or had she switched to a mobile phone and disconnected her land line?

Surely Margaret would have written if anything happened to Edith.

Darn it, who could she call?

Not for the first time, Cassie felt the aching loss of

her best friends. Sisters united, they'd called themselves. She rubbed the small scar on the tip of her index finger. She remembered the day the three girls had pledged undying friendship and sisterhood. Blood sisters.

It had been Fiona's idea. They'd been thirteen at the time. Three girls with no family to call their own banding together. Cassie's parents were dead. Fiona's mother was too caught up in drugs and abusive men to care about her only child. Piper's parents were unknown.

To solidify their bond, they'd each cut a fingertip and mingled their blood. What a mess they'd made, cutting deeper than necessary. Blood had spattered their clothes and the bedspread.

Margaret had been upset with the mess they'd made, but the bond had never wavered until the day they were sent to different foster homes throughout the state of Mississippi.

It was all because of the accusations Fiona made. Angry at Margaret for reasons Cassie never knew, Fiona had accused their foster mother of beating her, and she'd had the injuries to prove it.

Social Services had stepped in immediately after the sheriff had interviewed Cassie and Piper the next morning, swiftly taking each of the girls from Margaret's home and placing them elsewhere.

By the time her junior class in Bradford had held its prom that spring, Cassie had been living in Biloxi with the Johnson family. She never knew where Piper and Fiona had been sent. In the twelve years that had followed, she'd never heard from either of them. Nor, as far as she knew, had Margaret. She'd asked in earlier letters, but Margaret had said neither had ever contacted her.

Losing touch with Fiona and Piper had been devastating. Cassie had tried to find them but ran into brick walls at every turn. She'd kept to herself at her new school and was grateful her second set of foster parents had invited her to remain with them when she'd turned eighteen. They'd helped her far more than she'd deserved.

It wasn't until she'd left Bradford that Cassie realized how much living with the other girls meant to her. Margaret, too, though at the time Cassie had often thought her rules too strict.

As time passed, however, she recalled happy memories. Laughter as well as tears.

The three girls had made plans to go to college together, to get a large apartment in New Orleans. They'd been united in their desire to leave Bradford and take their chances in the world.

Homesickness grabbed hold of Cassie, surprising her. She suddenly yearned to see Piper and Fiona with a fierceness that startled her. How could they have let the years go by without finding each other?

Had Piper or Fiona learned of Margaret's stroke? Would either of them consider returning to Bradford?

Cassie sat on the sofa for long moments, lost in memories and indecision. But the idea forming in her mind grew stronger the more she thought about it. She hadn't left town under the best of circumstances. But time healed old wounds.

And she owed Margaret.

She could make a quick visit. See Margaret. Reassure herself her former foster mother was going to recover.

Cassie rose and went to the window. The rain continued its assault. The Charles River glittered in the distance, light reflecting from the choppy surface. The asphalt below gleamed beneath the streetlights. The few cars on the road splashed through the puddles, coating the sidewalks with their spray.

She leaned her forehead against the cold pane. She wanted to go back. She wished she could see the others, discover what they'd done with their lives.

Maybe she could recapture that ephemeral feeling of family she'd had so long ago.

Her fear for Margaret grew. What if she didn't recover? What if the stroke put an end to the Margaret she knew?

A sense of impending doom grew. She had to get to Mississippi. She'd let things go far too long without making a real attempt to reconnect with Margaret and revisit her childhood home. It was too bad it had taken a tragedy to prompt the thought.

Cassie had spent so many years alone. It was one thing to vow to remain aloof, to protect her heart from further bruising, but the reality had led to a solitary existence. She had made a mistake as a teenager and it had left her wary of getting close to anyone—afraid of hurting and of being hurt herself.

Margaret had done her best for her girls. Cassie appreciated her even more now that she was on her own. She couldn't imagine taking in three young girls and raising them alone as Margaret had done.

Was this the end? Was Margaret alone in the hospital, living her last few days with no one to visit, to talk to her, to love her?

Cassie couldn't allow that. It was said that you could never go home again. But for her entire childhood, Margaret had given Cassie her best. She was the only mother Cassie remembered. And now she needed Cassie.

What was she waiting for?

In less than two minutes she punched in the reservation line of an airline.

2

Cassie's high heels clicked on the polished linoleum floor the next day as she followed the directions the nurse had given her to the ICU waiting room. She looked neither left nor right, but focused on getting to the end of the corridor.

She tried not to breathe deeply, She didn't like the smell of disinfectant and sickness and fear. She hoped by this time Margaret was out of immediate danger and on her way to a quick recovery.

Cassie's dove-gray suit, dark-gray shoes and soft white silk blouse looked out of place among the gaily colored uniforms the nurses wore. It had still been raining in Boston, with the temperature in the low fifties, when she'd decided to wear the wool gabardine suit. How could she have forgotten that here in Mississippi it would be pushing the high eighties, with humidity to match?

She wanted to strip off her panty hose, tear the sleeves from her blouse and drop her suit jacket in some trash can. Then bundle her hair up on top of her head to cool her neck. Instead it was tied back neatly, primly, at the nape with a clip.

The last time she'd been in a hospital it had been for Dolores. They'd arrived too late. She'd already died. Cassie shivered at the memory, fervently hoping that would not be the case today.

Now as she reached the ICU nursing station, she asked where she would find Margaret Nunes.

"Are you a relative?" the nurse asked.

"Sort of, I was one of her foster children."

"You'll have to talk to the doctor to get an updated prognosis."

"Will I be able to see her?"

"I guess that relationship is close enough to visit. Rules are one person at a time every two hours for a few minutes." She glanced at her watch. "No one else has been to visit Miss Margaret so you can come with me."

Cassie followed the nurse, sad to hear no one had come to see Margaret. So glad she'd made the trip. As they walked through the doors into the unit, the nurse took a folder from a rack. Scanning the notations, she glanced at Cassie.

"Dr. Pendarvis will be finishing his rounds in a few minutes. He already checked Miss Margaret earlier. I'm sure he'd be happy to talk with you and answer any questions. There's been no change in her condition. We're monitoring her closely. There's a nurse on duty here at all times."

As the woman turned to leave, Cassie peered around her, shocked at the frail-looking figure lying so still on the high bed. She was hooked up to tubes, a large machine monitoring her vital signs. It was Margaret.

Cassie almost didn't recognize her.

Her hair was covered by wide strips of gauze holding a bandage over the left side of her head. What few strands escaped lay against the hospital pillow, gray and lifeless in the subdued light. Her determined blue eyes were closed. She seemed shrunken, smaller than Cassie remembered.

Cassie tiptoed closer, her eyes filling with tears at the sight. Until that moment, she hadn't understood the reality of Margaret's situation. There really was a distinct possibility she'd never leave the hospital.

Cassie couldn't stand the thought. Her heart ached for the woman who had spent so many years raising three orphans and was now so alone. Cassie should have contacted her as soon as she had turned eighteen. She should have done more for her over the years. How could she have ignored the woman for so long?

What if she hadn't subscribed to the paper a couple of years ago? What if she hadn't written and renewed communication? Would Margaret have died without Cassie ever knowing?

Dashing away the tears, she wanted to reach out and force Margaret to sit up and recognize her. She wanted to ask Margaret to tell her all she'd been doing since they'd last seen each other. She wanted the foster mother she remembered.

No matter how things had ended with Matt Bennett, Cassie should have made contact with

Margaret earlier. Insisted she come visit her in Boston. Or Cassie should have come back to Bradford sooner. How could she have let so many years go by?

The attendant nurse stepped up to the bed, gently laying the back of her hand on Margaret's cheek while scanning the monitors. She mouthed, "No change." Then she moved back to her seat a short distance away.

Cassie pulled an empty chair next to the bed and sat. Could Margaret feel her presence? Did she know Cassie had come as soon as she'd learned of her stroke? Would Cassie's own silent demands for her to wake up penetrate somehow and trigger an awareness?

She knew what loss felt like and hated it. The death of her mother when Cassie was four had shaken her world. It had been shaken again that terrible day Matt's sister had died and Piper, Fiona and Cassie had been separated.

When she'd moved to Boston with her new foster family, Cassie had given up hope of returning to her childhood home. After so many years in Boston, she felt as if her life was centered there now. She'd made friends, established a place of her own. She was even planning to marry a seventh-generation Bostonian.

Cassie thought back to the previous night. Although she'd booked her flight to New Orleans, the nearest large airport to Bradford, as soon as she'd decided to make the trip, she'd waited until just before leaving before calling Stephen.

He had not been happy with her plans.

"What do you mean you're going to Mississippi? You said nothing about this last night."

"I only found out after we spoke. It was too late to call you after that. I'll just be gone a few days. But I have to see Margaret. She could be dying."

"What about your job? I thought you couldn't get time off this weekend."

She was surprised at his reaction. Visiting someone who was gravely ill didn't compare with going to a weekend house party.

"It's not exactly a social occasion. Margaret had a stroke. She's in her seventies, which isn't young. I need to see her."

Stephen had been annoyed she hadn't consulted him earlier, and for that she felt guilty. Didn't she often have the same complaint about him?

At the end of the conversation he'd eased up and had even offered to drive her to Logan Airport.

"I'll take the T," she'd said.

She was used to taking public transportation. No sense in disrupting his day.

"Shall I call you once I know what's going on?" she'd asked.

"Of course. And I want to know when you'll be returning so I can meet your flight. Maybe you'll be back by the weekend."

He'd sounded hopeful.

"You never know," she had said, irritated he was still focused on his mother's house party.

Margaret was the person who had raised Cassie.

They weren't as close as they might have been, but Cassie owed her a great deal. Going to see Margaret when she was so ill was the least Cassie could do. Stephen should understand that.

Cassie sat lost in thought now as she watched Margaret's chest slowly rise and fall. She felt so helpless. Surely there was something she could *do*.

Endless minutes slipped by. The left side of Margaret's face was badly bruised. The nurse had told Cassie that Margaret had hit her head when she'd fallen after suffering the stroke. One hand was bandaged, lying lifelessly on top of the light bedcover. Tubes hung from multiple IVs connected to Margaret's arm.

"Ms. Hodges?"

Cassie looked up at the doctor who approached. He appeared to be in his mid-fifties and his warm, intelligent eyes inspired confidence.

"Yes?"

"I'm Dr. Pendarvis. Are you a relative of Margaret's?"

"I was one of her foster girls years ago. I just found out last night she'd had a stroke. Can you tell me about her condition?"

He gave her a brief rundown. Cassie let the medical terms swirl around her. When he finished, she asked for the bottom line.

"Basically, I can't guarantee anything. Her age is against her, of course. But she's in pretty good health considering everything. It's up to Margaret."

"So we wait and hope?" she asked.

He nodded. "A prayer or two would be helpful. We're doing all we can. She's on blood thinners, and we've relieved the pressure on the brain caused by the fall. She's also on antibiotics, and we're keeping her hydrated and nourished. The rest is up to her."

"The longer she's unconscious, the worse her chances, right?" Cassie asked.

She dreaded confirmation of her fears, but needed to know the facts.

"Usually. But we think she was found very soon after the stroke. We administered the drugs immediately. Those first six hours are crucial, so we're hopeful. Sometimes people wake up and it's as if they took nothing more than a long nap."

"Is there anything I can do?"

The doctor studied her for a moment.

"Try talking to her. Coma patients often respond to familiar voices. If you notice any change, any agitation, notify one of the nurses at once."

Cassie nodded. "Thank you."

When he left, she drew her chair closer to the bed.

"Hi, Margaret. It's me, Cassie. It's been a long time. I bet you're surprised I'm here. I read about your accident last night and I came right away. Wake up so we can visit, can you?"

Cassie swallowed. This was harder than she'd expected.

"Wake up, please. I want to tell you all my news. Since I wrote last, I've become engaged. His name is

Stephen Cabot. He's a Yankee, but you'd still like him."

Cassie didn't know if Margaret would or not. The woman had had some odd notions. Cassie and the other girls had laughed at her old-fashioned ideas. But Margaret had always been fair. She'd give any Yankee the benefit of the doubt.

"I'm sorry I wasn't better about keeping in touch. Wake up so we can tell each other all we've been doing lately."

Ten minutes later, Cassie was talked out. Discouraged at the lack of response, she brushed her lips against Margaret's pale cheek.

"I'm going now. They let me stay longer than I was supposed to. But I'll be back soon. Wake up, Margaret, please."

She patted her hand, lying so lifeless on the sheet, then turned, blinking back tears. She'd hoped the sound of her voice would work a miracle. She should have known there were no miracles left, especially in Bradford.

Cassie went to the hospital cafeteria in a small building adjacent to the main facility. It was early afternoon in Bradford. She was hungry, yet she wanted to stay nearby in case Margaret woke. She'd left her phone number and the nurse said they'd call if there was any change. She had also told her she could return in a couple of hours to visit.

After buying a large latte and bagel with cream cheese, she went to an empty table and sat down. She took her cell phone out of her purse and punched in Stephen's number at work.

"I'm here safe and sound," she said when she got through to him.

"And how is Margot?"

"Margaret. She's still in a coma. She may not come out of it, or she could recover with no harmful side effects. The doctor wasn't sure. I'd think they'd know more than that."

She felt frustrated at the lack of a definitive prognosis.

"If she's in a coma, she doesn't know you're there," Stephen said.

"No. But the doctor said maybe a familiar voice would help her wake up. I talked with her the entire time I was allowed in to see her. Now I have to wait another hour or two before I can visit again. Stupid rules," she added in frustration.

"I'm sure the hospital has rules for a purpose."

"I don't want to be logical," Cassie said. "I'm frustrated, cranky and scared."

"Honey, you said she was in her seventies. It may be her time to go."

"Gee, you're a world of support. Seventy is not that old."

She shouldn't blame Stephen for his pragmatic view. In other circumstances, she'd probably agree with him. But with Margaret, she didn't want pragmatism; she wanted hope.

"What do you want me to do, paint a pretty picture that has no relation to reality?" he asked gently.

"No."

Stephen was much too realistic for that. He was an attorney; he dealt in facts.

"I just hate the thought of her dying. I should have done more over the years. I owe her a lot."

"She was paid by the state to take care of you," he reasoned.

"But she did a lot more than just feed me and give me a warm bed. I guess it's too much to expect you to appreciate that."

As soon as the words were out, Cassie regretted them.

"I think you'd better wait and call me once you've had a good night's sleep."

Stephen hung up.

Cassie swiped off her phone. She wished she could tell him being cranky didn't have anything to do with lack of sleep. She feared things were spinning out of control and she hated that.

She bit into her bagel. She needed all the energy she could get to make it through the next few hours.

If there was no change in Margaret's condition by night, she'd have to check into a motel to get some sleep or collapse in sheer exhaustion. Worry took as great a toll as hard work.

She fervently hoped Margaret would regain consciousness soon. It had been less than twenty-four hours since she'd learned of Margaret's stroke and she was already going crazy. How did people stand it when loved ones remained in a coma for weeks on end?

Cassie sipped her latte, her eye caught by a tall man

in uniform, hat held in hand, striding into the cafeteria. He looked to be in his early thirties, dark hair and dark eyes. His gait was long and firm and he was heading toward her table.

Cassie's instincts went on full alert. Was he coming to talk to her?

He stopped at the end of the table.

"Sheriff Samuel Witt. Are you Cassie Hodges?"

"Yes."

She gestured to the chair opposite and the sheriff sat down, placing his hat on the seat next to him. He was nothing like the sheriff who had held office when she lived in Bradford.

"The nurse upstairs told me you might be here. I'm the person who responded to the call and got Margaret to the hospital."

"I'm one of the foster children she raised. I just read about her condition last night in the paper and got here as soon as I could."

"Do you live nearby?" he asked.

"Boston."

"You get the *Bradford Bugle* in Boston?"

His incredulous look was almost amusing.

She nodded. "A bit of home."

She felt foolish once she said it. Stephen had laughed at her sentimentality. How must it seem to a tough cop?

"Who found her?" she asked, realizing she knew no details beyond the bare facts reported in the paper.

"Henry Vetter had an appointment with her that

afternoon. He waited for a while after knocking on the back door. Her car was in the driveway. When she didn't answer, he tried the knob. Found it unlocked and Margaret at the bottom of the cellar stairs. We don't know how long it was between the time she fell and the time she was discovered. It could have been several minutes or several hours. The doctors suspect it hadn't been too long, however. The emergency medical team diagnosed a stroke and took appropriate action."

"Who's Henry Vetter?"

"Hank's a handyman around town. Margaret wanted him to do some cleanup in the yard."

"Hank? Tall and painfully thin? No hair?"

Cassie remembered the man. He'd had a crush on Margaret way back when, though Margaret had done nothing to encourage him. Cassie remembered the jokes she and the other girls had shared at the thought of Margaret having him as a boyfriend.

"One and the same," Sam confirmed. "You know him?"

"He used to come around and help out when I lived at Bradford Hall. I thought he was ancient back then, I can't believe he's still working."

"Hank's about seventy-six now," Sam said. "But he looks older. Probably looked ancient to a teenager."

"I guess."

"I'm surprised you came," Sam said.

"Why?"

"I've only been in town for a couple of years, but

even I've heard about the situation that got you pulled from the foster home. I wouldn't think there'd be much love lost between you girls and Margaret."

"Margaret never hurt any of us. Fiona blamed her at first, but later when she tried to explain and tell the truth, no one listened."

And the accusations Matt and his mother had made about Cassie hadn't helped the situation, either.

"Seems Sheriff Halstead thought he had enough evidence to get you girls removed from the home," Sam said.

"Fiona's accusation never even got as far as an arrest."

Cassie hadn't found that out until she'd made contact with Margaret a couple of years ago.

"The fallout resulted in the three of us girls being yanked from the only home we knew and separated from each other. Margaret never did anything but take good care of us."

"Going out to see the house?" he asked, ignoring her passionate conviction.

"I may." She wondered if she really wanted to see the old place. There were so many memories. Would stirring them up do any good or only open old wounds?

3

It was late afternoon by the time Cassie turned onto the once-familiar white crushed-shell driveway at Bradford Hall. Visiting the place had been a spur-of-the-moment decision. Once it was made, it hadn't taken her long to drive from the motel where she'd checked in. Every mile had been crowded with memories.

Driving down Main Street, she'd seen the courthouse where she and Piper had been taken for questioning the morning after Fiona had spun her outlandish story.

And where Sheriff Halstead had interrogated her about Matt's sister, Dolores Bennett, only hours later.

The old theater was still in business on the next block, a new Disney film showing. No multi-theater complexes for Bradford.

The five-and-dime was gone. A coffee shop flourished in its place. Looking down Center Street, she'd caught a glimpse of the old brick high school. Memories swept through her at the familiar sights and sounds.

The sultry weather zapped her energy. She should

have changed into something more suitable for Mississippi in late April than the sophisticated suit that had been perfect for Boston, but she'd been too impatient to take the time to change once she'd checked into the motel. She'd wanted to see the house. Not stay in it. Not spend a lot of time there, but see it.

The crushed shells crunched beneath the tires as she drove the short distance up the hill to the back of the house. Huge oaks lined the winding drive, leaves drooping in the afternoon heat. The familiar gray Spanish moss dripped from the branches in ghostly decoration.

A battered pickup truck and a sleek sedan were parked at the top of the hill, bumpers almost touching the detached garage.

She pulled her rental car in beside the truck and stopped, staring at the house.

Little had changed. She could almost imagine Margaret coming to the back steps to yell at her for being late. Or see Fiona sneaking off behind Margaret's back.

The house had been painted in the intervening years. The curtains replaced. The Victorian architecture still looked out of place in a state more used to antebellum homes along the river. Yet its familiarity tugged.

A mingling of delight and sorrow filled Cassie. She took a breath. Could she go in?

The sloping yard was a riot of colors. Flowers grew haphazardly in beds adjacent to the house, around the old oak that shaded the front lawn and in scattered sections along the edges of the grass.

Margaret's doing, Cassie knew. Margaret had always loved beautiful flowers.

After her second visit to see Margaret, the doctor had told Cassie he'd have the hospital call her cell phone immediately if there was any change in Margaret's condition—either way—and he'd urged her to go get some rest.

But the sheriff's question had plagued at her, and she had to finally admit she was anxious to visit Bradford Hall, her home for twelve years.

Cassie climbed from the car and headed for the back door. It stood open, the screen door standing guard against insects. Obviously the owners of the vehicles were inside.

She stepped in and listened, her eyes scanning the room. The linoleum flooring was worn and faded, having been installed long before she'd first arrived.

The counters were still narrow—never providing enough room when preparing meals for four. The refrigerator looked newer than she remembered, as did the range. But the cabinets needed to be painted. And the window over the sink still looked as if it couldn't be budged. She'd have expected Margaret to have had that fixed.

It was a huge old house and must have taken an enormous amount of upkeep. No money for extras— that had always been a problem when Cassie had lived here.

The sound of angry masculine voices came from the front of the house. Hesitating only a moment, Cassie headed in that direction.

"Hello?" she called.

As she walked through the dining room, memories assailed her. The faded wallpaper hadn't been changed—the rose pattern ancient even years ago. The huge table was surrounded by a dozen chairs. They'd eaten every dinner there and often had guests on Sunday.

Margaret had done her best to teach the girls manners, from the proper fork to use to how to converse with visitors.

The voices grew silent. Cassie continued toward the living room. She stopped in the wide doorway. Two men turned to look at her.

She only glanced at the man on the left before her eyes latched on to the one person in the world she'd never thought to see again.

Matt Bennett.

She shivered and stepped back, remembering the hateful words he'd flung at her the last time she'd seen him. He had blamed her for his sister's death. Nothing Cassie had said had made a difference. He had called her a liar and, worse, a murderer. He'd been upset, but there had been a kernel of truth in his accusations.

Cassie had been the one to tell Dolores her boyfriend was seeing someone else. Cassie had known Matt's sister was unstable, but she'd done it out of spite for the hateful things Dolores had said to her.

That didn't excuse her and she still carried a certain amount of guilt even after all these years. It had also made her very careful about what she said to others.

The older man spoke.

"Who are you and what are you doing here?"

She looked at him, recognizing the town banker, Allen McLennon. He'd aged over the years, but was still a fine-looking man. He'd been dating Margaret the last Cassie had seen him.

When Margaret had been accused of abusing her charges, had he stopped seeing her? Margaret had never mentioned him in any of her letters. Cassie hadn't thought about him in all these years. She'd have to ask Margaret what had happened, when she was better.

"I'm Cassie Hodges. I used to live here. I'm in town for a few days and came by to see the place."

Much as she wanted to focus on the banker, her eyes were drawn back to Matt.

He was as tall as she remembered, lean and muscular. He wore faded jeans, work boots and an attitude that didn't quit. The chambray shirt emphasized the width of his shoulders. His dark hair was worn a little long and looked thick and wavy. Dark eyes clearly displayed the anger that simmered. Twelve years hadn't softened him at all, it seemed. If anything, he looked harder than ever.

Cassie felt a shiver of trepidation. Tilting her head slightly, she glared at him. She was not some sixteen-year-old anymore, needing approval and acceptance.

If he couldn't handle her being here, that was his problem, not hers.

"Vultures circling the kill?" Matt suggested.

Cassie's temper flared, but the intervening years had taught her well. She kept it under control.

"I came as soon as I learned about Margaret. I've already been to see her. What's going on here?"

She glanced around at the old living room, wondering what the two men were doing.

It was Allen who answered. "The bank has a loan against the property which is in arrears. Matt and I were discussing the next step. Just because you once lived here doesn't give you any rights. This meeting is private."

"What's it about?" Cassie asked.

"Foreclosure and sale of the property," Matt replied. "Which I will fight in every way possible."

He glared at Allen McLennon.

"You can't sell Margaret's house," Cassie protested. "She needs it to come back to when she's out of the hospital."

"Allen's the one talking about selling," Matt said. "I'm trying to talk some sense into the man."

The two men glanced at each other.

Cassie's suspicions rose.

"What's the real issue?"

"The bank holds a note," Allen explained tersely. "Margaret took out a loan and put the house up as collateral. If the note isn't paid up, we have no choice but to force a sale to recoup our loss. Matt is interested in buying the property. However, there are other companies making offers. I suggest it should go to the highest bidder."

Cassie glared at Matt.

"You can't buy Margaret's home."

"If she can't meet the payments, the place goes on the block. Why shouldn't I be the one to buy it?"

"But—"

If the house was sold, did it really matter who bought it? For some reason, Cassie didn't want it to be Matt.

The mere thought of the house being sold startled her. Somehow she had thought it would always be here, waiting for her and Piper and Fiona to return someday.

"Why the concern? What fond memories could you possibly have of this place?" Matt asked.

The strain of the past twenty-four hours finally caught up with her. She'd had a miserable day yesterday, topped off by terrible news about Margaret. Then a fitful night's sleep, followed by the rushed trip to New Orleans and the drive to Bradford. Suddenly it was all too much.

"Doesn't sound to me like I'm the vulture here. Margaret will get well and return home. You two stop fighting over her property. It will remain with her!"

She turned and headed back through the hall to the stairs. She quickly climbed the steps and made her way to the room that had been hers.

Pausing in the doorway, she stared in disbelief.

Nothing seemed to have changed. There was her bulletin board on the wall, faded pictures and pages held with thumbtacks. The blue gingham coverlet still covered her bed. The dresser looked as if it hadn't been touched in a dozen years. But the room was tidy and clean. There was no dust anywhere.

She heard a phone ring. Moments later footsteps sounded on the stairs. Cassie wasn't surprised to see it was Matt.

"If you can do anything to help Margaret save her house, do it now, or get out," he told her bluntly. "Allen's planning to force the sale. He said the bank will ask a steep price because of all the land. I hope I can meet it. But if it goes to auction, it's anyone's guess."

"Then why don't you pay off the loan and give Margaret a chance to get back on her feet?" Cassie asked, doubting Matt really wanted to help.

He probably wanted an inside track to getting the house and land. Property values weren't as high in Mississippi as Massachusetts, but the twenty-five acres Margaret owned had to be worth a lot.

"Cassie, Margaret Nunes has been in a coma for almost a week. She's unlikely to wake up, and even if she does, she'll probably have to live in an assisted-care home the rest of her life. Whatever happens, I think it's certain she's not coming back here. If that's the case, then I mean to have the house and the property."

He glanced around the room and looked at her.

"Was this your room?"

Cassie nodded, moving into the room. She lightly touched the bed. It brought a flood of memories.

The house was old, with many rooms, all of them high-ceilinged and spacious. There was even a third story, which Margaret never used. The once-white Priscilla curtains on her own high windows drooped, the starch long ago leached out.

She felt sad that the bedroom she'd occupied for so long looked tired and lifeless. She never expected that Margaret would have kept it exactly the same. Why had she? In case Cassie returned?

They'd all been told that last day that they would not be coming back to live with Margaret. Cassie had believed Social Services. Hadn't her foster mother? She wondered how Margaret had dealt with their departure. They'd never discussed that in their recent letters.

"Don't let me keep you from anything," she said, studiously avoiding looking at Matt.

Her heart pounded, and memories crowded her mind. They had been high-school sweethearts. As close as two young people could be, spending every waking moment outside of school together.

At one point, Cassie had suggested they run off and get married. Matt had refused. Had her love been stronger? Or had it been one-sided?

After Dolores had died, Matt wanted nothing to do with her. He blamed her for his sister's death.

Sometimes Cassie wondered if he was right.

As an adult, she knew no one was responsible for another person's suicide. Still, telling Dolores of her boyfriend's betrayal had been more than the teenager could deal with. The guilt had faded over the years. Now it surged back as strong as ever.

"You're not keeping me from anything. Can't do much more today. I'm making sure nothing happens to the house."

He leaned negligently against the door-frame.

"I'm not here to damage the house or steal anything, just to walk through," she said.

Even if he wrongly blamed her for Dolores's death, he had to know she wasn't a vandal. Those last days in Bradford remained crystal clear in her memory. Dolores's death wasn't the only problem between them. There was the lack of trust and the uncertainty of where she'd ever stood with him.

But she would never do anything to harm Margaret or her property. Matt knew that. Why was he baiting her?

"What happened to Piper and Fiona?" he asked. "Never figured any of you would come back.

The hard tone was unfamiliar. Cassie remembered his easygoing southern drawl. She'd loved to listen to him when they'd been dating. He didn't sound like the same person she remembered.

"Well, that proves you don't know everything, doesn't it?" she retorted. She didn't need to explain herself to him.

"You sounded like Fiona there. You used to act like

Miss Prim and Proper Goody Two-shoes in public."

She ignored the comment. She'd tried to be proper in public. But it was the time she spent with Matt that she remembered most and then she had been most improper.

"But not in private," he said, as if reading her thoughts.

Cassie glared at him. She'd never admit it to him, but she felt uncomfortable knowing he remembered everything she did about their time together.

Had Dolores lied about his involvement with Evelyn? Or had saying she lied been the lie? Cassie and Matt had never discussed that. The police had arrived before they'd gotten to the subject uppermost in Cassie's mind that night so long ago.

"Piper sure didn't worry about looking proper," he continued when she didn't speak. "As I remember, she worked her way through the football team."

"She did not!"

He was deliberately trying to provoke her. Cassie knew it and tried to keep her temper under control. Matt had always known how to rile her. But she wasn't a besotted teenager anymore.

He nodded, giving that damn smile again.

"Oh, yes she did. She was the neediest girl I ever knew. But banging every boy in high school wasn't the way to get what she wanted."

"I suppose you have firsthand knowledge," she said, hoping to call his bluff.

He didn't know her at all, much less Piper. If he

had, he could never have accused her of the things he had. Or Piper.

"Fiona was in trouble more than anyone else I knew," Matt said. "Yet she escaped jail. At least while living here. Is she doing time now?"

Cassie shook her head, not willing to admit she didn't know exactly what Fiona was doing. But it couldn't be time in prison. Fiona had been high-spirited and rebellious because of her mother. But she'd never do something that would land her in jail. At least Cassie hoped not.

She met Matt's gaze, refusing to give him the satisfaction of knowing he was getting to her. Tilting her chin defiantly, she said nothing.

"Too bad Fiona caused the breakup of your foster family."

That was too much for Cassie.

"Too bad the adults in charge didn't believe her when she finally told the truth," she snapped back. "Piper and I swore Margaret had never hurt any of us, but would anyone listen to us? No. They moved everyone out so fast we never had a chance—"

She closed her mouth. She was not going there.

"Chance to mess up more lives like you did mine?" he prodded.

"Never mind. I've seen and said enough."

She headed for the door. She hoped he moved before she reached it because she wasn't up to pushing him out of the way. She was not going to go over old ground with Matt Bennett. If she never saw him again, it would suit her fine.

Cassie remembered her frantic efforts to convince everyone that Margaret had not harmed Fiona. Cassie had repeated her argument a hundred times. To Sheriff Halstead. To Edith Harper, Margaret's best friend, when she'd helped a stunned Cassie pack for the trip to Biloxi. To the new foster parents who had taken her on.

Being removed from Bradford had been a terrible blow to Cassie. But she couldn't change the past. She'd survived. Hardships survived made one stronger, she remembered Margaret saying more than once. Living on her own in Boston had shown her she could cope with whatever came her way. Better than cope—succeed.

"I'll be spending most of my time at the hospital until Margaret recovers. I'm staying at the motel in town. I'd suggest you and Mr. McLennon wait for her to recover before making any plans about her property."

She'd make sure she kept her distance from Matt. He knew he made her uneasy, and seemed to relish the knowledge. She was not responsible for Dolores's death. She had told him about the call. It wasn't her fault Dolores had overdosed and died.

And Matt saying it was didn't make it so.

Matt's narrowed gaze held hers for a long moment before he stepped aside and let her leave the room.

Without another word, she returned to her car, shaken. After twelve years, she had thought she'd be immune to the man. She was wrong.

A half hour later, showered and dressed in cooler clothes, Cassie stood by the window of her motel room, feeling refreshed. She idly watched some children play in the park across the street. How they had the energy to run around in the heat was beyond her. Yet she remembered days when she and Piper and Fiona had played on the grounds of Bradford Hall—spraying each other with the hose, sliding on the wet grass. Or lying beneath the huge old oak, talking and laughing.

Cassie gazed at the children, wishing she could be as carefree as they were right now. She turned away, determined to do what she could to find out more about the situation with Margaret's house. How could Margaret be in danger of losing it? What would it take to bring the arrearage current?

Cassie didn't have a lot of savings, but she had some. It had taken years to accumulate what she had. Dare she give it all away? On the other hand, Margaret needed help if she was in danger of losing it. Cassie owed her.

Or maybe she could locate Piper and Fiona.

If they were together again, could they recapture the closeness they'd once had? Cassie thought it unlikely. Too much time had passed. They'd made new lives, had different experiences.

Still, she'd love to see them both again. She yearned for that special feeling of belonging that she'd taken for granted as a young teenager.

Even with Stephen and his family, she didn't feel the same bond. Being married to him would change that, she hoped.

She slipped on sandals and headed for the nearest restaurant. She'd eat dinner and get back to the hospital to see if there'd been any change in Margaret's condition. She was losing her optimism after her last visit, but the nurse had tried to encourage her.

One of the best things about Bradford was its size, Cassie thought as she strolled along the sidewalk. She could walk almost everywhere.

A few moments later she was standing in the blessedly cool café, grateful that the restaurant wasn't any farther away. She'd forgotten how heavy the air could be here. She glanced around.

Ruby's Café was a haunt from the old days. Many afternoons Cassie and her friends had shared milk shakes and fries, sometimes splurging on juicy burgers with the works. She almost expected to see the place full of high-school kids.

The café was comfortably full, but given the hour, there were few teenagers. The hostess seated her near the front and Cassie scanned the menu. Maybe she'd give in to nostalgia and have a hamburger with the works.

"Cassie Hodges?"

She looked up into the smiling face of Betsy Fellows, a former classmate.

"Betsy?"

"I wasn't sure it was you. Look at you with that sleek hairstyle and slim figure. Wow, you look great!"

Cassie laughed, standing to hug her high-school friend.

"I can't believe you recognized me. How are *you?*"

How cool to run into Betsy her first night here, Cassie thought. If she stayed in town long enough, she'd look up a few other classmates. Those she wanted to see, she qualified, thinking of Matt.

"Doing great. Waiting tables as you can see. How long are you in town? Let's get together and catch up."

"I'd like that. I'm here because of Margaret, so I'm not sure exactly what my plans are. It depends on her."

Betsy's smile faded. "That's a downright shame, isn't it? How is she?"

"Still in a coma."

"I hope she recovers." Betsy glanced at her pad. "It was awful what happened to you all back then."

Looking at Cassie again, she shook her head.

Although this wasn't the time or place to discuss it, Cassie hated to let the adults who'd been in charge all those years ago get off scot-free. They'd had the power and they'd abused it. If nothing else, maybe she could set the record straight while she was in town.

"Margaret was never the same," Betsy said. "It was months before she started going out in public again. I remember my folks talking about it. And now this. Just when I thought she was getting excited about life again."

"Why's that?"

"Because of the new center for pregnant teens."

Cassie frowned. "What center?"

"The one Margaret and Matt talked about building at Bradford Hall." Betsy seemed surprised that Cassie had to ask. "Matt's here now," she said, tilting her head to the left.

Cassie turned around and looked right into Matt's dark gaze. He was seated at a table behind her with two other men.

"I don't know about the project," Cassie said, turning quickly away and sitting back down in her chair.

Great, now the man probably thought they were talking about him. Which they were.

"I thought the bank was about to foreclose."

"I don't know about that. But I know Matt and Margaret discussed a home for unwed pregnant teens. Even brought it before the planning commission for approval. Which it got, provisionally. Margaret was most determined. You remember what she was like when she made up her mind about something."

Cassie nodded. So Matt and Margaret were partners in this scheme. Then why was he planning to buy her property if the bank sold it? To cut her out of the loop?

"I can fill you in, but not now," Betsy said, keeping a practiced eye on the rest of her area. "It's hopping tonight. Do you know what you want to eat yet?"

Cassie ordered and Betsy hurried off to the kitchen. She wanted to know everything, but for the moment would have to be patient.

Having Matt right behind her made Cassie feel self-conscious. His scathing comments after his sister's death still had the power to hurt. She pushed the memories from her mind. Their relationship had ended years ago. She wouldn't let his presence disturb her like this.

While Cassie was eating, another former classmate stopped by to greet her. That surprised her. Had she been close to other girls, not just Piper and Fiona? Were her memories warped because of the way she was removed from Bradford?

Bemused, she left the café once she'd paid her bill, and headed for the hospital. The evening had cooled slightly and the walk would be pleasant. Cassie drew a breath of the soft southern air. It felt good to be back. In a surreal way, it seemed almost as if she had never left.

"Going to the hospital?" a familiar voice asked.

She glanced over at Matt as he fell into step with her.

"Yes."

She thought he had left the café before her.

"I'll go with you."

"I know the way."

"What are you really doing here, Cassie?"

"I told you, I came to see Margaret."

"You've ignored her for years, why now?"

"I haven't ignored her. We've written, spoken on the phone a few times. Not that it's any of your business."

"Did she tell you about the plans she and I talked about for the house?"

Cassie shook her head, wondering why Margaret

hadn't mentioned that. Of course, the last time Cassie had heard from her had been Christmas. She had written twice since then, but hadn't received a letter in return. She wasn't going to share that information with Matt. She'd find out what she could from Betsy when they got together for lunch the next day.

"If you and Margaret made plans together, why are you siding with the banker?" she asked.

"I'm hardly siding with Allen."

"Seemed like it to me. He wants to sell, you want to buy."

"He and I don't see eye to eye on most things. But if the property goes up for sale, I'll do my best to buy it. Keep it in the family so to speak."

"Or cut Margaret out of the loop. It's not going to come to that," Cassie said.

"Oh no? Why not?"

"Never mind."

She could see the hospital now. Only a few more minutes and they'd be there.

He walked in silence as they approached the brick building. Cassie wished he'd leave, but he followed her in to the lobby. She wondered if he planned to accompany her all the way to Margaret's room, and when he stepped into the elevator beside her, she figured she had her answer.

She looked at him. "Visiting as well?"

"I need to know if Margaret's awake yet or not. Time's running out."

Cassie stared at the closed elevator doors. She

wished he was a thousand miles away. Feeling edgy, she willed the elevator to rise quickly. At last the doors opened and she stepped out into the hall of the intensive care unit.

Matt went a couple of steps before he realized she wasn't with him. Turning, he looked at her, one eyebrow raised.

"Cold feet?"

"I'm not going with you. You don't need or want me around. You made that clear years ago, Matt. Visit Margaret all you want. When you leave, I'll go in."

"If she's still in ICU, they won't let me see her," he said, ignoring her accusation.

She shrugged and leaned against the wall, prepared to wait forever if necessary, but she was not going with him.

Her cell phone rang.

"You can't have that in here," he said.

"I know the rules."

She fished the phone from her purse and checked the caller before switching it off.

It was Stephen. She turned and punched the button for the elevator. "I'll go back outside to call," she said as the doors slid open.

Alone on the front grounds a few minutes later, she quickly dialed Stephen's number.

"Hello, Cassie. I tried calling you just now."

"I know, Stephen. I was in the hospital and couldn't take the call. What's up?"

"I wanted to see how you're doing. How's

Margaret? Any change in her condition?"

"Margaret's still in a coma. I don't think the future looks all that good. The longer she's in the coma, the less likely it is she'll recover."

Cassie didn't like thinking about that.

"I'm sorry, sweetheart. I know that's disappointing. Is there anything you can do?"

"Not really. Be with her, I guess."

"Do you know yet when you'll be returning home? I'll be disappointed if you can't make it here this weekend."

"I was only planning to come out for part of Saturday and Sunday," Cassie reminded him. Why did she feel so cantankerous? She should be happy to hear from Stephen.

"If I can't make it, you'll still have a good time."

Her mood had to do with coming home to Bradford. Not coming *home,* she corrected herself. Coming back to visit. Bradford wasn't home.

"I can fly down to join you if you need me," he said.

He was sweet to offer.

"Thank you, but there's nothing you could do. Bradford's a sleepy southern town which hasn't changed much since I left. As soon as I know more about Margaret's prognosis, I'll have a better idea when I'll be heading back."

Much as she would like to see him, she knew he wouldn't fit in here. And then she'd feel responsible for entertaining him.

"Call me tomorrow," he said.

"I will."

She clicked off the phone when he hung up. She should also check in with her boss, she realized.

Matt strode from the hospital.

"No change," he said, not breaking his stride.

"Matt, wait," she called as he moved past her.

He stopped and turned to look at her.

"Tell me about the loan," she said.

"I don't know the particulars, only that Margaret was having difficulties lately. She mentioned it once when we were talking."

"When you two were planning that home for unwed teens?"

He raised an eyebrow. "What did she tell you about that?"

"Nothing. I heard it from Betsy."

"I thought we had a deal going, but if Allen sells the property, it'll change things."

"But you plan to buy it."

"If I can. But to recoup the costs, I'd have to develop at least part of the property. The house is going to take a lot of renovation to make it suitable for group living. If I have to purchase it outright on top of renovations, I'll have to find the money somewhere."

"What do you mean, develop the property?"

"Build some houses to raise cash."

Cassie thought of the woods and meadow area in the twenty-five acres Margaret owned. As children, Piper, Fiona and she had played freely there, their imaginations transforming the forest and fields into magical kingdoms.

"What are you talking about?" she asked. "Who would buy houses here?"

"Bradford is becoming a popular bedroom community of New Orleans. Lots of new houses are going up. Margaret's land is prime. I could build a development there that would cover the costs of buying the property and funding the home I want to establish."

"How could you?"

Cassie was outraged at the thought of losing all that open space.

Matt shrugged. "There's a consortium trying to buy up property around here for an exclusive golf and country club. Margaret's twenty-five acres would be prime land for that. It's them or me, and I'd rather it be me."

"The property is too hilly," Cassie protested. "It'd make a lousy golf course."

"But the house would make a terrific country club, and some of the back acreage could be leveled enough for a golf course. I met a lot of opposition with my proposal. Allen would love nothing better than to see it permanently squashed."

"A home for unwed teens. Was Margaret planning to go on living in the house?"

"She was going to run the place," Matt told her. "I guess her stroke puts an end to that idea."

"After losing her foster care license?" Surely they hadn't forgotten that, Cassie thought. "Who would let her?"

"It's a long story. In the meantime, I hope Allen won't try to push things through just because she's in a coma."

"They were seeing each other just before I left. I guess the romance died," she added, almost to herself.

"They stopped seeing each other the same time you girls left," Matt told her. "Guess he couldn't risk being associated with a child abuser."

Anger flared in Cassie.

"Margaret never abused anyone and you know it."

4

Matt watched Cassie walk back into the lit lobby. She'd changed in the years since he'd last seen her. She was tall and slim and carried herself with an air of assurance that had been lacking that last afternoon when she'd come to see him.

She'd been with Travis Montegue all day, then had tracked down Matt with some cock-and-bull story about Dolores lying. He'd never heard the real story from his sister. She'd been dead the next time he'd seen her.

If Cassie had told him about Dolores's call earlier, he might have saved his sister.

Or if she'd kept quiet about Stewart seeing Patti. Maybe he could have told Dolores in a way that would have been less traumatic for her. But how could Stewart's cheating not be a shock when Dolores had been pregnant with his baby?

He'd never forgive Cassie for telling his sister.

For a moment, the past caught up with him. He remembered the times they'd shared, the plans they'd made. His feelings for Cassie had been so intense. He'd never experienced anything close to them in all the years they'd been apart.

He turned and headed for his car. He had hours of work still ahead and no time to reminisce. Somehow he had to make sure Allen didn't jerk the property out from under Margaret and him. The proposed home for teens was too important to him. He was counting on its completion to bring some kind of healing to his life. Nothing else had worked.

Matt drove the short distance to the old house his mother had owned, which he'd inherited after her death. Pulling into the driveway, he tried to ignore the dilapidated state it was in. The place was in need of major repairs, repainting and some kind of landscaping. Hard to believe the owner was a successful builder. He should do something about it.

But he no longer lived in Bradford. His home was in New Orleans and he only used the house here when he stayed over. He'd been here a couple of weeks now to work on the Bradford Hall project and already felt itchy and anxious to leave.

Letting himself into the house, he paused as he always did, expecting to hear Dolores calling out, or loud rock music, or one of his mother's drunken soliloquies. But the empty walls echoed with silence. No one lived here anymore. Only the son, who came infrequently.

Matt went to the kitchen and quickly got a beer from the refrigerator. He took it to the back stoop and sat on the top step, gazing over the rapidly fading line of trees in the distance. It would be dark before long.

He'd liked the dark at one time. He and Cassie had

used it to sneak out and meet at the town park. No one had seen them. It had been their special time. He frowned, not wanting to take a walk down memory lane, but his mind seemed to have other ideas.

For a moment, he felt eighteen again, so caught up with the dark-haired beauty from Bradford Hall. He'd lived for the times they could be together, just the two of them.

If he'd kept his mind on his responsibilities to his family instead of being ruled by teenage hormones, his sister would be alive today. And maybe even his mother.

But they were both gone.

Once he built his home for unwed pregnant teens, he'd see about getting rid of the house. It would need work before he could sell it. Maybe he should rent it out. Even then, it needed major repairs. Time he made some long-overdue decisions.

After he finished the beer, he headed inside to the makeshift office he'd set up in the dining room. There were several emails waiting for him.

He called the foreman on the McIver job and discussed the progress. He knew Joe Randall was on top of things, but Matt hadn't built a successful business by leaving things to others. It was his company, and if he couldn't be there for the day-to-day operation, he'd keep long-distance tabs on the work.

The McIver project was a luxury apartment building with lots of green space. It was behind schedule due to delays in the delivery of cabinets for the kitchens. He hoped his crew could catch up soon and finish the project. Joe was optimistic.

Matt read the emails, jotted some notes. When he'd dealt with the pressing matters, his attention turned back to the group home he wanted to establish. Tilting back in the chair, he tried to think of ways to make sure Allen didn't get control of Margaret Nunes' property.

Much as he hated to consider it, one solution would be to enlist Cassie's help. Everyone knew she'd been raised by Margaret. She was the closest thing to a daughter Margaret had.

Could he get a judge to grant her permission to occupy the house? As for the delinquent payments, he'd try to float another loan. His cash flow was limited at the moment, but once the McIver property was completed, he'd receive a huge check, hefty enough for a sizable profit and operating capital for another year. He just wished that job wasn't still weeks from completion.

Matt brought the chair down on all four legs and rose. He was beat. Time for bed. Options would come or they wouldn't. He'd learned that over the years.

Could Cassie do anything? She owed him. He couldn't change the past, but he would use any means available to insure the group home was established. He needed to do that. For Dolores—and for himself.

Cassie entered the ICU and went straight to Margaret's bed. The nurse greeted her with a smile.

"No change. Have a seat. Talk to her again, maybe she'll wake up."

Cassie pulled the chair closer to the bed and sat down. She gently brushed back some of the gray hair from Margaret's forehead. It had been dark and thick all those years ago.

She took Margaret's hand. For a moment, time seemed to shift. She remembered Margaret taking her hand when she'd first picked her up. Where had that been? In an office? Cassie couldn't remember, only that her mother was gone and she was scared.

Then this stern-looking woman had reached out and taken her hand. Offered her home to an orphan who had nowhere else to go.

"I don't think I ever told you how much I appreciated you, Margaret," Cassie said in a low voice.

She didn't want the nurse to hear, but she had to tell Margaret.

"Where would I be today if you hadn't taken me in?"

Gently she stroked the worn hand. Their roles were reversed now. She was the strong one, and it was Margaret who needed her help.

"I can stay as long as you need me," Cassie said. "Wake up and we'll make plans. I'll find Piper and Fiona and it'll be the four of us again, if only for a visit. Do you know where they are? Did you ever find them? You said in your first letter that you hadn't heard from either one. I don't know where they were sent, but if I can locate them, I will. Wake up and tell me how to make that pecan pie of yours that was so good we almost got sick eating so much. Or how to make that honey ham we had on Sundays after church."

Cassie swallowed. She'd forgotten the attempts Margaret had made to give them the best possible home. Money had been tight. She'd told them that more often than not when they'd asked for things. Cassie had a much better appreciation now of how Margaret must have stretched every dollar.

"I'm getting married soon," Cassie said, hoping something would break through to Margaret. "He's a lawyer in Boston. Very successful. You'll have to come up to meet him before the wedding. You'll be the mother of the bride. We still have to set a date. We'll have to make it summertime. Boston in winter is too cold. You can't imagine the snow."

Slowly Cassie told Margaret more about her life in Boston, of her ambitions to one day open a catering firm. She wanted Margaret to know that her cooking had influenced Cassie's choice of career.

Glancing at her watch, Cassie saw it was after eleven. The nurses had completely disregarded the visitor rules. It would be close to midnight by the time she got to bed. She squeezed Margaret's hand slightly.

"I have to go now. But I'll be back tomorrow."

Margaret's fingers squeezed back.

"Margaret?"

Cassie's fatigue fled. Had she imagined it, or had there been a response?

She squeezed again. A moment later Margaret definitely squeezed her hand.

"Nurse!" Cassie looked around.

The young woman rushed to the bedside.

"Problem?"

"I don't think so. I think she squeezed my hand."

The nurse took Margaret's hand and gently gripped it. A moment later she smiled.

"She sure did. Let me call Dr. Pendarvis. He'll want to know immediately."

Patting Margaret on the shoulder, she headed for the phone at the desk.

"Margaret, wake up. It's me, Cassie. I've come to visit you but you're asleep."

The older woman's eyelids fluttered, and then Margaret slowly opened her eyes, gazing at Cassie.

"Hi."

Cassie felt overwhelmed. Did this mean Margaret would recover?

Margaret opened her mouth to speak, but a garbled sound came out. Panic flared in her eyes.

"Wait, you're all right. You're going to be fine. You had a stroke and you're in the hospital. But now that you're awake, you'll be fine."

Cassie hoped she was speaking the truth. Where was the nurse? Why couldn't Margaret talk?

She looked around and saw the woman heading her way.

"My goodness, Miss Margaret, you're awake," the nurse said. "I'm so glad to see that. I've called the doctor and he's coming right over. How are you feeling?"

Margaret tried to speak again, but it was still gibberish. She looked distressed.

"Don't try to talk just yet," the nurse said gently. "Aphasia is a common problem with stroke. It means there's a mix-up between your thoughts and your vocal cords. Wait for the doctor and he'll tell you more."

She turned to Cassie.

"I think that's enough excitement for one day. I'll be with her until the doctor arrives. Why don't you go home and get some rest? You can come back first thing in the morning."

Cassie knew she was being dismissed. At least Margaret had woken up. Smiling at Margaret, Cassie leaned over to whisper in her ear, "I'll be back early. We have lots to catch up on."

Margaret's eyes began to close.

"She's probably tired," the nurse said. "We'll take good care of her. See you in the morning."

Cassie left feeling elated. Margaret would be fine, she knew it. And she'd stay until she saw it for herself.

She seemed to almost float back to the motel, enjoying the coolness of the night air, fired up with happiness. She didn't feel nervous walking the dark streets. She had done it many times as a teenager.

When she drew near the park at the center of town, she could make out the gazebo in the dim lighting. Occasional band concerts were held there, but she and Matt had used it as their own special meeting place. She'd felt so daring in his arms, so alive.

Cassie shook her head. No more thoughts of Matt. She was here for Margaret.

Now that Margaret was awake, Cassie was more

determined than ever to locate Piper and Fiona. It was time they came back together as a family.

She briskly headed for the motel. In the morning she'd visit Margaret, get an update from the doctor and then see what she could do to find Piper and Fiona.

Cassie entered the cafe the next morning, ravenous. She told the hostess she'd eat at the counter and took one of the empty stools near the middle. After scanning the menu, she placed her order and then sipped the hot coffee the waitress had given her. Ambrosia.

"Good morning, Cassie Hodges."

She looked up at Sam Witt.

"Good morning, Sheriff."

"Mind if I join you?" he asked, indicating an empty stool to her left.

"Feel free."

She watched as he tucked his hat carefully on the stool beside him. He nodded at the waitress and she waved, then came over to pour him a coffee.

"I hear Margaret woke up last night," Sam said once the waitress had left.

"News travels fast," Cassie observed.

"She's always seemed to be a nice lady to me."

Cassie nodded.

"I looked into the file the previous sheriff had on the residents of Bradford Hall. It could be she got a rotten deal a few years back."

Sam's expression remained neutral, but Cassie knew he was probing for information.

"We tried to rectify that, only no one would listen," she said hotly. "And Margaret wasn't the only one who got a rotten deal. All three of us girls were sent elsewhere. We lost touch. Can you imagine what that was like? We were like sisters, but that didn't seem to matter to anyone."

It still rankled that no one had believed her and Piper over Fiona.

But she was older now, Cassie thought, and wiser. At least she hoped so. Would those in authority listen to her now?

"Maybe you can help me, Sheriff," she said with a flash of inspiration. "I want to find Piper and Fiona. They need to know about Margaret."

"You don't have any idea where they are?" he asked.

She shook her head.

"We weren't allowed to contact each other. I tried to find them when I turned eighteen, but was stonewalled at every turn. So I gave up."

"It might be hard to track them down after so many years," he said.

"Maybe, but I'm not prepared to give up so easily this time around. I thought I'd check the Internet and then question some former schoolmates."

Sam sipped his coffee. He was silent for a long time. Cassie's eggs and grits arrived before he spoke again.

"I could search for driver's licenses nationwide. Ask a couple of the Social Service folks if they'd check their records for me. Maybe get some leads. Of course, if they married, I won't find them using maiden names."

"I'd really appreciate your help," Cassie said, excited about the possibilities.

"What help is that?" Matt asked, suddenly appearing at Cassie's elbow.

She swung around and frowned.

"Not that you need to know, but the sheriff is going to help me find Piper and Fiona."

"Why?"

"They'd want to hear about Margaret, I'm sure."

She wasn't going to tell Matt how much she wanted to see her foster sisters again. That edgy feeling was back. She wished he would leave her alone.

"You can do that?" Matt asked Sam.

"I can make a few inquiries easily enough," Sam said. "You here for breakfast?"

Matt nodded, taking the empty seat on Cassie's right.

"I'll have the house special," he told the waitress.

He leaned one elbow on the counter and looked at Cassie. She took another bite of her eggs before they got cold, but felt too flustered to eat much more. Why didn't he leave her alone?

Although she knew the information must be in the files, she turned to the sheriff and gave him Piper's and Fiona's full names and ages. "Anything you can find would be terrific."

"Seems like they'd come back if they wanted," Matt muttered. "You did." He glared over at Sam. "Maybe you can help me out, too."

"Something on your mind?" Sam asked.

"Allen's trying to force the sale of Margaret's place. I want a way to counter him."

Sam shrugged. "I don't see that I can do anything. If Margaret didn't make her payments and the loan is in arrears, it's the bank's right to call the loan."

"She owned the house free and clear when we lived in it," Cassie protested. "I remembered her saying that was the only way she could afford to have foster children. Did she take out a loan after we left?"

"Maybe," Matt said. "She inherited the house from her father, didn't she?"

Cassie nodded.

Matt frowned. "Allen says the bank holds a substantial note. It's in arrears and he plans to collect however he can. Seems to me the least you and Piper and Fiona could do would be to help her save her house."

"So you can make it into a home for unwed teenaged mothers, which she's in no condition to run? Seems Margaret loses either way."

"Beats having the place razed to make way for a fancy country club that only a few people in town could use," Matt countered. "And she wouldn't lose with my plan. She's part of the package."

"Does Bradford need a country club? Who would join?"

"A lot of young urban professionals have bought homes in new developments on the south side of town," Matt told her. "You've been away a long time. Folks don't mind the long commute to New Orleans when they can get bigger homes for less money here in Mississippi."

Cassie considered the implications. Had the sleepy little town she remembered changed so drastically? Margaret never mentioned the town's building boom in her letters. Maybe after she visited Margaret today, she'd take a drive around town and see for herself.

"Unless you're not here to help Margaret," Matt said.

Cassie realized Matt had been speaking to her.

"I'm sorry...what did you say?"

"I was just wondering why you came back to Bradford after so many years. You three girls were the only family Margaret had left. Maybe you figure you stand to inherit something if she doesn't recover."

Cassie's temper flared.

"What a spiteful thing to say. But I guess that's the best I can expect from you."

She pushed away her half-eaten breakfast and drew some bills from her pocket, throwing them down on the counter.

"I came because I wanted to be with Margaret—to see if there was anything I could do to help."

"Like you helped Dolores?"

"Go to blazes!"

Cassie slipped down from the stool and headed to

the door, anger churning inside her. He hadn't changed one iota. He'd blamed her for Dolores's death twelve years ago and obviously still did.

"Well, that went well," Sam murmured, reaching for his mug.

Matt took a deep breath and shrugged.

"I shouldn't have said that last bit. It's ancient history."

"Who's Dolores?"

"She was my sister. She died a long time ago."

"And Cassie was involved?"

Matt nodded. "She told Dolores her boyfriend was cheating on her. Dolores was pregnant with his kid and went over the edge."

Sam studied the dark brew in his cup for a moment.

"Tough break. What happened?"

"Dolores killed herself."

The words were blunt. Matt found it hurt less that way.

"She wrote a note blaming Cassie. By the time I found out, Dolores was already dead. If I had reached her in time—"

He didn't want to think back to that awful day. He'd tried to keep his sister on an even keel, but she had been so mercurial. Today she'd probably have been diagnosed as bipolar and offered drug therapy, but back then, it was just passed off as teenage hormones.

His sister had been totally jealous of Cassie and the

time he'd spent with her. She'd threatened suicide more than once. But Matt had never really believed she would kill herself. He'd always thought the threats were merely her way of getting attention.

"I'm sorry about your sister," Sam said.

Matt nodded. What was there to say?

His cell phone rang. Reaching into his pocket, he pulled it out .

"Bennett here," he said.

It was his foreman.

"Trouble at the McIver site, boss. The load of tiles arrived but they're not what we ordered and the guy is refusing to take them back. I showed him the work order and the sample square we have but he's not budging."

"Let me speak to him," Matt said, wondering why nothing was easy these days.

That job should have been finished a week ago. They were still at least two weeks from completion and this screw up could put them even further behind schedule.

Sam rose and retrieved his hat. Giving a two-finger salute he strode off and left Matt to deal with yet another problem.

Cassie stormed down the sidewalk, filled with anger and also regret. She and Matt had been inseparable in high school. Dolores's death should have drawn them closer, not split them apart. How could he think such horrible thoughts about her?

It only showed her how little he'd been committed to their relationship, she told herself for about the millionth time. She'd been devastated when he'd accused her of contributing to Dolores's death. She'd only been sixteen herself and so mixed up with all that was going on. She'd gone to see him after she'd talked to his sister. Not that she had believed Dolores would truly kill herself. She'd talked about it before, but how could anyone have known that this time she'd meant it?

But Matt had refused to listen to Cassie—really listen—when she'd tried to explain. His view was black and white and that was the end of it.

Her cell phone rang. Cassie took a deep breath and reached for it. Was it Stephen again? She should have called him from the motel before she'd left this morning. Feeling mildly guilty, she answered, "Hello?"

"Cassie, my dear, this is Adele. I do hope everything is going all right down there. Is there anything I can do?"

Cassie felt relief it was Adele Cabot and not her son.

"Nothing I can think of, but how nice of you to call."

"My dear, when Stephen told me why you couldn't make it this weekend, I had to get in touch immediately. You know we worry about you and want to do anything we can to help."

"I know, and I appreciate that. Margaret was in a coma until last night, then seemed to come out of it, but she can't talk. I'm on my way to the hospital now to see her again."

"Men can be so insensitive—yes, even Stephen. He's annoyed because you can't be here this weekend. But I told him you feel a special bond with Margaret and you'll be back before he knows it."

Cassie glanced at her left hand, shocked to see her ring finger bare. Then she remembered she'd left her engagement ring on the bathroom counter in her apartment. She didn't wear it to work since it got in the way. What would Stephen think if he knew she hadn't remembered to put it on for this trip?

"Margaret was so strong all the time I was growing up," Cassie said, focusing on Adele's comment. "She looks frail now. No one knows the full prognosis yet. The doctor will be doing more tests now that she's awake again."

"Take all the time you need, Cassie. And when you have a moment, do call and let me know how she's doing. We love you."

Cassie hung up feeling marginally better. Adele was such a sweetheart. And so much more understanding of the situation than her son.

Maybe it was the difference between a woman's viewpoint and a man's. Stephen was annoyed. Matt thought Cassie had come back to Bradford out of self-interest. Only Adele seemed to understand why she had to be here.

At the hospital, Cassie went straight to Margaret's room. The lights were brighter today than they had been when Margaret was in a coma. She appeared to be asleep.

"Is she any better?" she asked the nurse in a soft voice.

"She had a restful night and awoke a little while ago, but has drifted back to sleep. I expect she'll sleep more than stay awake for the next day or two. But the doctor said he was pleased with her progress, so that's good."

Cassie went to sit beside Margaret's bed. She reached out to take her hand, squeezing it gently. "I'm back, Margaret. Wake up soon so we can visit."

She sat in vain for almost an hour. Finally Cassie slipped out to the waiting room. She'd go back in as soon as the nurse let her. Leafing through an old magazine, she tried to wait patiently.

A few moments later, a wheelchair glided into the waiting room.

"Cassie Hodges, I declare. Look at you, all grown up and pretty as a picture."

Cassie looked up and recognized Edith Harper, Margaret's best friend. She rose and crossed the small waiting room to give the elderly woman a hug.

"Edith Harper, I didn't expect to see you today. How are you?"

"As you can see, not as mobile as I once was. My arthritis is terrible. I can scarcely get out of bed some days. But I heard Margaret had regained consciousness, so I came to see if I can visit her."

"I was in to see her a little while ago, but she's still asleep."

"That's what the nurse said. Told me you were in here. Let me look at you, child. I declare, you grew up pretty. Shame on you for staying away so long. Boston isn't that far, not for you young things."

Cassie nodded. "You're right, I should have come to visit."

"Sit down. I hate the fact folks tower over me now that I'm stuck in this chair. Tell me about Boston. Margaret said you work as a chef in some fancy restaurant."

Cassie sat near Margaret's old friend and told her all about moving to Boston, her training at culinary school and the various positions she'd held over the years. She asked Edith what had been going on in Bradford and the older woman obliged with a lot of gossip, mostly about people of Margaret's generation.

"I heard that Bennett boy is back in town," Edith commented.

"Matt? I've seen him. Doesn't he still live here?"

She'd assumed Matt had never left Bradford.

"Oh, no, he lives in New Orleans. He has some big construction company down there, building homes, renovating some of the older ones in the Garden District. Making a name for himself, as I hear it. He talked Margaret into renovating her place for a home for unwed mothers. I declare, it's a crazy idea. I told her so. But she said she never felt as needed as when she had you girls living with her. She wants to feel needed again."

"I guess we all do," Cassie murmured.

"*Hmmph.* I'd just like to be walking again. Besides, Margaret's too old for such foolishness. Look at this stroke. I expect that'll end any such nonsense."

"You don't think Matt will go ahead without her?"

"She won't be the one running the place is what I think." Edith glanced at the doorway. "I hope I can get in to see her soon. My painkillers will wear off before long and I'll need to be getting home."

"I can go see if they'll let you in now," Cassie offered.

"That's sweet of you, girl. You staying at Margaret's?"

"No. I'm at the motel on the edge of town."

"Why there? Honey, Margaret will skin you alive if she finds out. If any of you girls were to come home, I know she wanted you to stay with her. I've heard her say it a dozen times if I've heard it once. 'Course, you're the only one who got back in touch with her. Don't know why you waited so long, but at least you did contact her. Besides, you'll be more comfortable at the house."

"I can hardly barge in if she's not there."

"Sure you can. I'm in charge with Margaret ill. I say it's fine."

"You're in charge?"

"Sure enough. We signed powers of attorneys for each other a few years back. If I get incapacitated, she's to tend to me, and vice versa. I thought I'd be the one to need the help, not the other way round."

"Do you know anything about a loan being in arrears?"

"Oh, blast. Is she behind on payments? She took a loan out a couple of years back and put up the house as collateral. I tried to talk her out of it. That place came to her from her father and it was paid for long before old man Nunes died. Times have been hard lately. I don't know why she took out the loan. She'd only say she had a special reason. But I can't imagine she's spent all that money already."

"Allen McLennon told Matt that the loan payments were long overdue and he plans to sell the house to recover the bank's money. If he does that, Margaret could lose her house."

"Nonsense. He must've been talking about something else. Margaret doesn't have a big enough loan against her house to lose the entire thing. Besides, she and Matt have that crazy scheme to turn it into a home for unwed teens, in honor of his sister." The elderly woman narrowed her eyes. "Of course, I wouldn't trust that Allen McLennon any farther than I could throw him."

"He and Margaret were an item when I was still living with her," Cassie said. "What happened?"

"I don't know the full story, but I remember Margaret stopped seeing him when you girls were taken away and never had a good word to say about him in all the years since."

Cassie leaned back in her chair, puzzled by this information. What had happened between them? The three girls had laughed and joked about Margaret's suitor when Margaret and Allen had been dating. Allen was a number of years younger than Margaret and always dressed well. They'd found it hilarious that he was interested in a spinster like Margaret.

How unkind, Cassie thought now. Margaret had deserved her chance at happiness. She'd only been in her late fifties at the time, and Allen in his late forties. It could have worked.

What had gone wrong?

Besides the situation with Fiona.

Fiona never revealed who had hurt her so badly, but Cassie and Piper suspected Jack. He'd been in trouble with the law more times than Cassie could count. Despite his bad reputation, he'd had a way with some of the girls in school—those who thought they could reform him, Cassie surmised. He and Fiona had dated for a while before she'd broken it off. He hadn't taken it too well.

"So you'll stay at Margaret's?" Edith asked.

"If you think it's okay, I'd love to," Cassie replied.

It'd save money and give her access to Margaret's papers. Maybe she could find an address for Piper and Fiona. And discover what she could about this loan that threatened to take Margaret's home from her.

Something Edith said suddenly clicked.

"If you have power of attorney, you can find out about the loan, can't you?"

"I can," Edith said. "I'll have to dig up the papers we signed, then I can go see Allen McLennon himself and find out what's going on."

"If I stay at Margaret's, I can search through her

papers to see if I can find out why she's behind in payments. I really need to know how much money we're talking about."

"Fifteen or twenty thousand, as I remember," Edith said. "I didn't have that much or I'd have lent it to her myself. But it's not enough to foreclose on her house. The land would be worth close to a million dollars, I'd think."

"We need to see how the loan was written. But whatever the terms, I won't let Margaret lose her home!"

"Me, either," Edith said.

Cassie stood up and gave Edith a quick kiss on the cheek. As she was getting ready to leave, another thought struck her.

"Was Dolores Bennett pregnant when she died?" Cassie asked, stunned at the possibility.

Hadn't Edith just said Matt had planned the group home in her memory?

"So it seems. It was hushed up at the time, but Matt told Margaret that was the reason he wanted to create a safe place for young girls to go if they got pregnant. I guess Dolores felt she didn't have anywhere to turn."

"I don't see why," Cassie said. "Her brother did everything he could for her and his mother. If she hadn't wanted the baby, she could have given it up for adoption."

Which would have been best for the baby, Cassie thought. Dolores had been too unstable to be a mother. Cassie remembered the number of times Matt had backed out of a date because Dolores had wanted him to stay home with her. Or how often they'd cut short their time together so he could rush home to deal with his sister and her myriad problems.

Who would have suspected Dolores had been pregnant? Was that the real reason she had taken her life when she'd learned Stewart was seeing someone else?

Cassie felt the old guilt surge anew. She should never have told Dolores about Stewart. But how could she have known what the girl would do? Cassie had been sixteen herself at the time, as upset and emotional as any other teenager.

5

He had no choice, Matt thought when he left the café. He had to return to New Orleans and get this tile mess straightened out. And if he drove back to the Crescent City, he might as well spend a day or two there and make sure the rest of the project was under control.

Why hadn't Margaret told him there was a loan against the house? If he couldn't raise the funds to pay off the arrearage, he'd lose what he'd already put into the project—and worse, he'd have to scrap the idea. At least until he found another facility large enough to accommodate several girls at a time.

Margaret knew how important the home for teens was to him. She'd said it was important to her, as well. He figured it had something to do with her three foster children being taken from her. Maybe she needed closure, as well.

He turned into the weed-filled driveway of his childhood home. At least he had a place to stay while he was in Bradford. He could also get started on repairing the house when he wasn't needed at Bradford Hall.

It didn't take him long to close up the place and change his clothes. Before heading out, though, he wanted to check on Margaret once more.

When he reached the hospital, he found Margaret had been moved out of ICU and was in a semi-private room. Edith Harper was seated beside Margaret's bed. And Margaret had her eyes open!

Matt headed into the room, only to be intercepted by the nurse.

"Sorry sir, we're limiting visitors to one at a time. Can you wait or return around two? Miss Margaret will be ready to see someone then. Miss Harper's time is almost up."

"I won't be here at two, I'm heading for New Orleans. I need to see Margaret now."

"She already has one visitor—"

Matt stepped around the woman and went into the large room. He stopped by Margaret's bed, ignoring the nurse's protests.

"Margaret, am I glad to see you're awake. I've been so worried about you. Thank God you're doing better."

She looked at him and smiled with one side of her face. She tried to speak.

"Shh, don't try to talk, you'll just get agitated," Edith soothed, patting her friend on the arm. She looked at Matt. "She's not talking so good just yet. It'll come."

"I know it will. We're looking for you to make a full recovery," he said.

He'd stopped by to ask about the loan, but was

finding that difficult in light of her inability to speak.

"I have a quick business question for you."

"She can't deal with business now," the nurse said firmly, taking his arm and trying to urge him from the room.

"A quick question is all," he said, refusing to budge.

"She's a bit foggy," Edith said in a low voice. "Cassie wants to know the same thing. She'll handle everything when she gets back."

"Where is Cassie?" Matt asked.

"Gone to move her things to Margaret's. She'll be staying there until she returns to Boston."

"Then I'll talk with Cassie," Matt said. "You get well, Margaret, okay? That's all you have to worry about right now."

Cassie walked down the hall to the linen closet. Everything was in the exact same place Margaret always kept it. She took out clean bedding and headed back to her room. It felt odd to be in the house alone. As if in a time warp, she kept expecting to hear Fiona running up the stairs or Piper on the phone.

After making the bed, Cassie put away her clothes. If she was going to stay longer, she'd have to buy a few things to stretch her wardrobe. Cooler clothes, for sure, to accommodate the sultry Mississippi spring.

The house phone rang. She dashed down the stairs to the small table near the base of the steps and scooped up the receiver. Just like it had always been.

"Hello?"

It was Betsy.

"I had to track you down, girl. Fortunately Bradford is small enough that everyone knows everyone else's business. Are we still on for lunch?"

"Sure thing. I thought we could meet at the café around twelve-thirty, or don't you eat there when you're off?"

"'Course I do. Food's the best in town."

"Sounds great."

There was a knock at the front door.

"Oops, someone at the door," Cassie said quickly. "I'll see you later."

Opening the door a moment later, she wished she'd peeked through the glass side panel. Matt Bennett stood in front of her.

"I don't need this," she murmured and shut the door in his face.

His hand caught the edge and kept it from closing all the way.

"We need to talk," he said.

"We have nothing to say to one another," she replied curtly.

He'd changed clothes since she'd seen him at breakfast. Instead of jeans and a T-shirt, he now wore crisp khaki slacks and an expensive polo shirt. Mirrored sunglasses hid his eyes, but nothing could conceal the stubborn determination in his jaw.

He pushed the door open and stepped into the entryway without a word. Slipping the glasses off, he stared at her, his dark eyes unreadable.

"What do you want?" Cassie asked.

Let him say what he'd come to say and then leave. She wasn't up to dealing with Matt and his moods. At least they had some privacy here, not like earlier at the café.

"Edith told me you were staying here."

"And why does that concern you?"

"You'll be in a prime position to check out this loan situation for me."

Cassie shook her head. "I don't think so."

"For Margaret, then."

"Margaret can handle her own affairs once she's well."

"According to the doctor, she might not be fully functioning for a long while. And she might never remember everything that happened before the stroke."

"Then you go to Allen and find a way to stop him."

"He's stonewalling. He's been against the idea of a home since it came before the planning commission. He has no reason to deal with me. He'd like nothing better than to have that consortium get the property for a golf course."

"Not my problem. I want the house for Margaret, nothing else."

His gaze narrowed as he studied her for a moment. Cassie resisted the urge to fidget. He had some nerve. Blasting her every chance he got about Dolores and then asking for help for his precious project.

"It's Margaret's problem. What if she can't pay the

balance due and Allen calls the loan? Where would she live? Forcing a sale means everything is sold. Once the debt and expenses are paid, Margaret would get the rest, but do you think she wants to lose her home and all its furnishings and pictures?"

"How much is owed?" Cassie asked.

"I don't know. I can't find out any of the details. Allen talks about confidentiality and all. If the bank forecloses, then I'll find out, but so will the other bidder. I don't want that. I went to see Margaret this morning because you said she'd regained consciousness, but she can't speak, and my being there upset her." Matt sounded both frustrated and remorseful.

"I think trying to talk and being unable to is what upset her," Cassie murmured.

She didn't want Matt to know she planned to do all she could to make sure Margaret kept her home.

"Whatever. You need to find out what is owed and how long I have to pay it off before Allen starts the proceedings."

"Maybe," Cassie hedged.

She wasn't so sure owing Matt would be any better than owing the bank.

"Darn it, now is not the time to play games. Either you help Margaret or you don't."

"I don't have a problem helping Margaret," she said.

"It's me, right?"

"Let's see, Matt. First you basically accuse me of

murdering your sister, and then you tell me I'm a liar to my face. Now you think I should help you out?"

He ran a hand through his hair and looked away for a moment, obviously clamping down on strong emotions.

"Look, let's make a deal. I won't talk about Dolores and you can help Margaret."

Cassie considered the suggestion. She wanted him to *believe* her. To trust that she had not known Dolores was seriously planning suicide. When she'd told him years before, he hadn't believed her. But at least this would be a step to regaining that trust.

"I'll think about it on one condition," she said.

"What's that?"

He looked forbidding, standing squarely in front of her. He was several inches taller and broader than she remembered. For a moment an image of the teenager he'd once been danced in front of her eyes. She wished they could return to those days, recapture the special feeling that had been theirs alone.

"You give me a fair hearing about Dolores—the events of that day and evening. You listen to me without interrupting and then decide how guilty I really am."

"And if I choose not to do that?" Matt asked.

Cassie shrugged, hoping he wouldn't call her bluff.

"Then you're on your own."

She'd longed for a chance to explain everything to Matt and have him really listen to her. If he'd agree to give her that much, she'd be happy to do almost anything he wanted.

The muscles in his cheeks grew taut. She knew he was holding back the vitriolic words that had spewed forth in the past.

"When did you want this discussion?" he asked.

"Not today," she said, stunned he was actually going to listen to her. "I have too much on my plate as it is, and I have to leave to meet someone in a few minutes."

"I'm on my way to New Orleans, but I'll be back in a few days."

"I'm sure we'll find a time to talk,"

Cassie said, suddenly wondering if talking would be enough. Would telling her side give her the relief she wanted if he didn't believe her?

"Then I'll get in touch when I get back."

Cassie leaned against the door and watched him walk back to his truck.

She was uncomfortable around the man. At one time she had counted the moments until they could be together. Now it was as if they were strangers—no, even worse. Enemies.

She regretted Dolores's death as much as anyone. She had done her best that last year to avoid Dolores and her manipulative lies, but she had never wished her harm. If only she'd taken Dolores seriously when she'd said she'd be dead before Cassie could talk to her brother again that fateful day.

Cassie wondered if she should have insisted she and Matt have their talk before she agreed to help.

Not that it made any difference. She'd do whatever she could for Margaret, whether it helped Matt or not.

Once on the highway heading for New Orleans, Matt set the cruise control and let his mind wander back to Bradford Hall and Cassie Hodges. It seemed strange after all these years to see her there again. She looked totally different from the girl he'd once thought he loved. Her hair was shorter, and she wore it pulled back from her face. Her clothes were a casual chic she never would have considered a dozen years ago.

She also seemed much more confident than he remembered. She'd been so anxious to please when she was younger, afraid of being rejected. Was that the reason they'd resonated with each other when they'd been teens? He was used to needy women—his mother and sister were classic examples. Maybe he liked the role of white knight.

What did that say about him?

He'd changed since his mother's death. He was no longer anyone's knight in shining armor and had no wish to be. He'd been a failure anyway—with Dolores, with his mother, and maybe even with Cassie.

He'd also made up his mind long ago to stay out of the marriage stakes. He enjoyed the company of a variety of women, but refused to get serious about anyone.

Yet Cassie's face seemed to hover in front of him. Cassie had wanted to get married when she was sixteen. Yet she was still single as far as he knew. Why?

She'd been so desperate for a family of her own when he'd known her. He'd have thought she'd have married right out of high school and had a half-dozen kids by now.

At the time, he'd refused to marry her. They had both been far too young. And after her role in Dolores's death, he wondered if he could ever look at her without a feeling of hurt and betrayal.

Matt tapped the navigation screen and in seconds a rollicking Zydeco tune distracted him. He had problems facing him in New Orleans; he didn't need to dwell on the situation in Bradford. Either they'd be able to fend off a sale, or the house would go on the market. Win or lose, Cassie Hodges would be back in Boston before long.

Betsy was sitting at a booth along the side wall when Cassie entered the café just before twelve-thirty. Smiling at her friend, she hurried to join her.

"I'm having the burger and fries,"

Betsy said a moment later when the waitress came to take their order.

"Me, too. They're still the best, right?" Cassie asked, closing the menu. She grinned at her friend. "Besides, it's what we always used to order when we could scrape up enough money. Is that why you got the job here? To have all the burgers you want?"

Betsy laughed. "Actually, I rarely eat the food when

I'm working. Probably because I'm around it all the time. But I do enjoy the burgers when I splurge. So tell me all about what you've been doing since you left."

"I live in Boston now," Cassie said.

"No kidding. Wow, a Yankee. Margaret must love that," Betsy teased.

"She's never said anything."

It was true. In her phone calls and letters, Margaret had never expressed an opinion one way or the other about Cassie living in New England.

"Did you go to college?" Betsy asked.

"For a semester, then I decided it wasn't for me. I ended up going to culinary school. I'm a chef."

"How cool. I remember you loved to cook when you lived with Margaret. Did you get your love for cooking from her?"

Cassie shrugged. "You could say that."

"What a hoot. What's it like to cook for so many people every night?"

"Fun, challenging, tiring. I'm on my feet for eight or nine hours every day."

"Tell me about it," Betsy groaned. "That's the worst part of waiting tables. But I like the people contact. And the perks when I get home."

"What perks?"

"My husband rubs my feet. He says I work so hard I deserve a little pampering."

"You're married?" Cassie smiled her delight. "Who to?"

"Dexter Bullard. Remember him? He was in Matt's

class, a nerd to beat all nerds, if you can believe it. He's in insurance now, and doing well. I think people trust men who wear glasses."

"Or are just plain trustworthy. How terrific. When did you get married?"

"Six years ago."

"Any kids?"

Betsy shook her head. "We wanted to have time to ourselves first, but we're thinking about it now. I'll be twenty-nine on my next birthday, you know. I think I'd like to have one baby before I'm thirty."

Cassie nodded. She would turn twenty-eight on her next birthday. Where did the time go?

"Tell me all about your job and where you live," Betsy invited.

The burgers arrived, and while they ate, Cassie told her friend about her apartment, the restaurant where she worked and the difficulties she'd faced getting used to Boston's cold winters.

"You're not married then," Betsy said at last.

"I'm engaged," Cassie said slowly.

Betsy's eyes widened. "And you're just telling me now! Give! Who is he? What does he do? What's he like?"

Cassie took a sip of her cola, stalling for a moment. What was Stephen like?

"He's probably the nicest man I'll ever know," she said. "He's an attorney with an old law firm in Boston. He does wills and estate planning. And his mother is a love. Adele is a widow, but she's so active in civic events it's amazing. And she throws the most fabulous parties. She and I go shopping sometimes, just to look at things, not to buy, and we have so much fun together. At Christmas, she helped me decorate my apartment and it was the most elegant Christmas I've ever had."

Betsy sat back and listened as Cassie continued talking. From time to time she frowned, but never said a word until Cassie wound down.

"Sounds to me you like Stephen's mother more than the man himself," Betsy said.

"Of course not. Stephen is... Well—" Cassie floundered, realizing she was having a hard time picturing Stephen.

Instead, Matt's image sprang to mind.

"I always thought you and Matt would marry and live happily ever after," Betsy said. "You two were so crazy about each other in high school. I thought it would be so cool to have childhood sweethearts marry."

Cassie pushed away the remainder of her burger.

"He blames me for Dolores's death," she said softly.

Betsy sat up at that. "No way!"

Cassie shrugged. "She called me several times that day, and the last time she hinted at death. But I never thought she was serious. Matt believes I deliberately goaded her into committing suicide by telling her Stewart Palmer was seeing someone else. Nothing I said got through to him."

"I remember how much she resented you. But Matt was her *brother*. And everybody knew Stewart was seeing someone else."

Cassie thought back to those wild teenage years. Dolores had had an obsessive fixation on Matt. Had he not seen it?

"Now that I look back, I think Dolores was insecure," Cassie said. "She needed the reassurance that she was important to him. Their father deserted the family when she was a baby, and their mother didn't offer much in the way of support."

"The town drunk, you mean," Betsy said bluntly.

"Sounds awful when you say it aloud," Cassie observed.

But it had been true. She'd never seen Matt's mother when she hadn't been drunk.

"She died about two years after Dolores," Betsy said. "Liver problems caused by excessive alcohol."

"Poor Matt," Cassie murmured. "He had a tough time."

"So did you and Margaret's other girls. The official story was she was abusive. Is that true?"

"Never!"

Cassie flared at the accusation.

"I told the sheriff over and over that next morning she never raised a finger to any of us. He refused to listen. We didn't have a lot of time to discuss anything. When he finished his interrogation, I was on my way to a foster home in Biloxi."

Dolores had died, Matt had turned on her and her entire world had shifted on its axis.

"What happened after we left?" Cassie asked. "I didn't write to Margaret for the longest time. When I finally did, I had moved to Boston and settled there."

"I only remember a little," Betsy said. "My folks didn't know Margaret well, different generation and all. The scuttlebutt around school was that she was taken off the lists of eligibility for foster care. But no charges were filed that I remember. I didn't pay too much attention. Mostly I missed you. And Piper. What is she up to these days?"

"I was hoping you might know. I lost touch with both Piper and Fiona. Apparently Margaret did, as well. I asked a couple years back when I first wrote her for their addresses, but she said she hadn't heard from either one. It's sad. I was the only one to keep in touch— and I waited so long to make that contact."

"You should have come back sooner for a visit."

Cassie nodded, knowing she wouldn't be here today if not for Margaret's stroke.

"Well, I'm here now," she said. "Where do you and Dexter live? Tell me all about what being married is like."

"We live in the new section of town. The yards aren't very big, which suits us fine. We'd rather spend our free time doing other things, like boating on the river, not yard work."

Betsy told Cassie about Dexter and how they'd fallen in love. Then their talk turned to vacation spots they'd been to over the years, different movies they enjoyed and books they liked.

Betsy had to leave at two and Cassie returned to the hospital. She wanted to see Margaret, then track down Edith Harper and get some information on how to acquire copies of Margaret's loan papers. Edith should be able to do something. If not, there would be other ways to find out what she needed to know. Cassie wasn't giving up.

6

Margaret was awake when Cassie went in to see her.

"Hi," Cassie said, smiling.

She reached for Margaret's hand and squeezed gently. The older woman squeezed back.

"Did Edith tell you I'm back at the house? I'm in my old room. Nothing's changed. I can't believe you left it that way. I wish I'd come back to visit before now."

Regrets crowded. She should have done more, and sooner.

Margaret looked at her, blinking slowly.

"Feeling better?" Cassie asked.

She sat on the chair next to the bed, Margaret's hand still in hers.

Margaret looked away, then back at Cassie. Her eyelids were beginning to droop.

"If you're tired, go on back to sleep. I'll stay with you awhile. I'll come back when the nurses say I can. Did I tell you I ran into Betsy Fellows? She's Betsy Bullard now. We had lunch together."

Cassie told Margaret about Betsy until she realized

the older woman had fallen asleep. Slipping her hand from Margaret's, Cassie stood up to leave.

Time to find Edith and whatever information she could on the delinquent loan.

By nine o'clock that night Cassie was bone tired, but not ready to go to bed yet. She sat in the dining room of the old house, going through the piles of papers in the drawers of the old Victorian breakfront that Margaret used as a desk. She'd never had a proper desk.

And judging from the jumble of papers Cassie found, Margaret didn't have a filing system, either.

Electric bills from two years ago were mixed up with recipes from friends at church. Cassie couldn't stand the disorganization. While she searched for the loan papers, she also sorted the papers into separate piles. She wondered how long it would take to make her way through the six giant drawers.

Edith had agreed to go with Cassie to the bank first thing on Monday morning to exercise her power of attorney and find out the details of the loan. But Cassie hoped to learn something before that.

As she sifted through the documents, she was also looking for any clues to Fiona's or Piper's whereabouts. If Margaret had any information, it'd most likely be in one of these drawers.

Cassie scanned another invoice, this one for water. It was quite recent. She placed it in yet another pile. First thing after she saw Margaret in the morning, she was going to buy file folders and a cabinet and get this place organized.

The top drawer yielded no answers.

She pulled open the second drawer. A faded scrapbook was stuffed to one side. Papers were piled high in the drawer, but Cassie pulled out the scrapbook first.

When she opened it, she was startled to see pictures of the three girls when they were small. Piper had been the first of Margaret's foster children. Baby pictures were carefully labeled. Cassie had arrived when she was four. There were several photos of her and Piper together. Fiona had been in and out of Margaret's care, depending on the situation with her mother, but Cassie thought she and Piper had already started kindergarten when Fiona had come. They seemed to be the right age in the first picture with Fiona. Three five-year-olds, how young they seemed.

And three of them were in the playground at the elementary school. Cassie couldn't remember the picture being taken.

Slowly she leafed through the scrapbook. There were many more photos. Margaret had jotted notes beside some. On another page was the first report card where Cassie had made straight As. Fiona's showed high grades in most subjects and a failing mark in math. Cassie smiled. She remembered how Fiona had hated that math teacher.

Sighing softly, she went through the entire scrapbook, page by page. The final pages were empty. The last photo in the book was of Fiona, looking angry and put out. When had Margaret taken that one?

She closed the book and placed it on top of the breakfront. She'd look at it again later, but there were still five drawers to go through.

When the second drawer yielded no information on the loan, Cassie glanced at the clock. Maybe she should go to bed and start again in the morning. Tired as she was, she couldn't resist peeking into the next drawer to see how many papers were there.

The top invoice was dated four years ago. Next was a magazine from the previous month. Cassie scooped out the jumble and found another scrapbook. Pulling it out, she expected more pictures from their childhood, but this book was devoted to Piper. A grown-up Piper. Had Margaret located her?

There was a newspaper article Cassie had never seen, reporting the marriage of Piper Jeffries to Billy Bob Thompson in Jackson, Mississippi. Cassie read the announcement, stunned to learn Piper had married right out of high school.

Turning the page, she found another article about Piper winning a local Mississippi beauty contest. This was followed by a newspaper clipping of her at a county fair. The next page showed a picture of Piper modeling clothes for a catalog. Then one with her on the runway at some fashion show. This last article was written in French.

Fascinated, Cassie turned page after page. As far as she could tell, the scrapbook followed Piper's career for almost ten years. The last page was a color shot of Piper by the sea. The most recent captions were in

French. Obviously Piper was living in France these days and had become a model. Cassie couldn't understand French, but the photographs told a story.

Margaret must know where Piper was if she kept the album. Had Piper sent her the clippings? Did Margaret have an address or phone number for her?

She searched through the book, looking for a personal note—anything that would let her know where Piper was. There was nothing.

Tomorrow she'd ask Margaret. Maybe she could communicate somehow.

She put the book aside and prepared to close the drawer when another invoice caught her eye.

Drawing it out, she was surprised to see it was a bill from a private investigator in New Orleans for search fees for Piper Jeffries and Fiona Hunter.

Margaret had hired someone to look for Fiona and Piper. Cassie looked at the date. Two years ago. Margaret hadn't said a word to Cassie at the time. Had the investigation been successful?

Cassie put the invoice aside. Chances were good the investigator wouldn't be at work on the weekend. Now she would have to wait until Monday to call the firm, but she could ask Edith about it in the morning. Maybe she knew something. Or maybe Margaret would start talking and could answer all her questions.

Tired and a little disheartened, Cassie went upstairs to bed. Turning off the lights in the hall, she quickly closed her door. She'd never stayed in the house all alone before, and she wasn't looking forward to it.

Not that there was any danger, but it felt odd.

When the phone rang, Cassie debated answering it, then realized it could be the hospital. That decided it for her. She flicked on the lights and ran down the stairs.

"It's Matt," a familiar voice said when she answered.

"Is something wrong?"

Why would he be calling her at eleven o'clock on a Friday night? The thought jogged her memory. She hadn't called Stephen tonight. Was it too late? Blast it, how could she have forgotten? He'd be upset he hadn't heard from her.

"Nothing's wrong," Matt said. "Maybe we should have that talk now."

"Now? It's after eleven."

"No time like the present."

She sighed and leaned against the banister. She didn't plan to talk to him about Dolores over the phone, but there were other things they could discuss.

"I looked through some of Margaret's papers tonight. She doesn't have a very organized filing system and I didn't find anything about a loan. Did you know she hired a private detective to find Piper and Fiona?"

"No. I thought you'd all keep in touch."

"I didn't know where they were sent when we were separated. We weren't allowed to contact each other. I tried to find them later, but had no luck. Margaret said she hadn't heard from them, either."

"Did the detective locate them?" he asked.

"Apparently not. I only came across one invoice and it's old. Margaret might have their addresses in a book somewhere, but I think she would have told me. I did ask when I first wrote her a couple of years ago, so she knew I wanted to get in touch with them."

"You think either of them would come back to help?"

The skepticism in his voice was strong.

"She was our foster mother. The only mother Piper and I really knew. Why wouldn't they?"

"I remember hearing complaints all through school from you and Fiona about how strict she was, how unfair. I didn't know Piper that well, but I didn't get the feeling there was a lot of warm fuzzies between all of you."

"Maybe not, but a lot of teenagers have problems with their parents when they're growing up. You sure did."

"With one, anyway."

"Did you ever find out what happened to your father?"

Matt had talked a couple of times about trying to find his father when he grew up. Find him and beat him to a pulp.

"No. Didn't seem much point in it after Dolores died. And my mother was no help. I suspect her drinking is what drove him away."

"That doesn't excuse him from not keeping in touch with his own children," Cassie said.

"Some men aren't made for families. Me included."

Cassie didn't have a ready answer for that comment and she suspected he wouldn't like a platitude.

"I feel just the opposite," she said. "I want a large family, to feel connected. To be part of something that can never go away."

Stephen was an only child, so she wasn't marrying into a large family. But she wanted them to have half a dozen children. Funny, they'd never discussed the subject. She made a mental note to bring up the issue before setting the wedding date.

"So why haven't you married and had a dozen kids?" he asked, echoing her thoughts.

"I'm engaged," she said quickly.

She really needed to call Stephen. First thing in the morning. If Stephen had to call her, he'd be more than annoyed.

Cassie became aware of the silence on the other end.

"Are you still there?" she asked.

"I didn't know you were engaged."

"Since last month."

"You aren't wearing a ring."

"It's in Boston. I don't wear it to work and I left it behind in my rush to get here."

"Who is the lucky man?"

"Stephen Cabot. He's a lawyer in Boston. He's very nice."

Cassie winced. Was that all she could say about

him? Stephen had complained once before about her calling him *nice.*

"So you plan on a huge family and living happily ever after, huh?" Matt said. "It's more than Dolores got."

"Stop it, Matt! I was not the reason your sister died. Her suicide was horrible and your accusations only made it worse. You said we'd discuss the matter, but I don't want to do it over the phone. Call me when you get back here and we can arrange a meeting."

With that, Cassie hung up.

She was shaking from the conversation. All roads led back to Dolores. Was she deluding herself to think that after all these years she could make Matt understand that she was not to blame? Maybe the best thing to do was get things cleared up for Margaret and return to Boston and Stephen as quickly as she could.

Matt clicked off the and tossed it across the sofa. So much for finding out what excuse Cassie had come up with to erase her blame. He leaned back against the cushions and gazed at the ceiling.

Learning Cassie was engaged bothered him. He wondered why it had taken her so long to find a man she could love.

Or had it? Maybe she had married and divorced in the years since he'd seen her.

But he didn't think so.

He headed to the kitchen to get something to

drink. He felt restless. What was her fiancé like? he wondered. Rich and stable was his guess. After growing up in foster care, he was sure she'd want security. She'd yearned for it so much when they'd been going together. Security and trust.

Not that she was a shining example. He drew out a can of cola and popped the top, taking a long drink. He had thought they'd had an exclusive arrangement in high school. He'd believed the sun rose and set with her back then. But that was before he'd discovered the real Cassie.

It was bad enough she'd cheated on him, even worse that she'd ignored his sister's suicide threat.

He finished the cola then crushed the can in his hand, staring at the bent and twisted aluminum.

Then reason took hold. Nothing he could do to Cassie would bring Dolores back. The law had found nothing illegal about her actions. But he knew. And he'd never forget.

Early the next morning Cassie called Stephen at the Cabot home on Cape Cod. Adele answered the phone.

"Cassie, dear, how lovely to hear from you. I know this is Stephen's phone, which he left behind. You've just missed him. He and Tim Warner went out to play a round of golf. They wanted an early start to beat the weekend crowd. I'll have him call when he gets back."

"That would be great. I wanted to hear his voice. How's the weekend going?"

"We miss you, of course. How are you doing? What's the latest word on Margaret? I wish we were closer to lend support."

"I'm fine. Margaret's doing better. And while I appreciate the thought, there really isn't much you or Stephen could do here."

"We could be there with you. Of course, I would have to get rid of my guests and all. But maybe we should think about coming down after the weekend, if you're still there."

"I'm doing fine. I grew up here, remember? But is everything okay at the Cape?"

Cassie wanted to change the subject. She couldn't imagine Stephen or Adele in Bradford.

"Everyone is having a good time, I believe. There's so much to do down here, sailing, golf, or just lounging in the hammock with a good book. Tonight we're having dinner catered by a new local firm. I'm expecting a wonderful meal. The menu is to die for."

Cassie felt a pang. She'd love to cater one of Adele's parties, but Adele had yet to ask her.

At work, Cassie needed approval from the head chef to try anything different. Sometimes he took her suggestions, but Thomas had the final say over the menu. She'd love the chance to cater an event completely with her own creations.

When Cassie hung up from talking with Adele, she called the hospital. The nurse on duty told her Margaret had spent a restless night but was now sleeping soundly. She suggested Cassie visit later in the morning to allow Margaret to rest.

With unexpected free time, Cassie plunged back into the drawers in the breakfront.

The hours passed swiftly as Cassie sorted through years of papers, and as she did, she found herself learning more about Margaret and her recent life. She also felt a sense of control in creating order from chaos, and it kept her mind from dwelling on things best left in the past.

She discovered several more invoices from the private detective. The most recent, dated several months ago, showed he was looking only for Fiona. Did that mean he'd found Piper? She rummaged further, hoping to find a letter or report that would provide more information. But it looked as if most of the documents in these drawers were bills.

On impulse, she dialed the number on the invoice. The phone rang and rang. Apparently the private detective didn't work Saturdays or have an answering service.

Cassie returned to the stacks of papers. She couldn't find the original loan papers, but did come across two payment stubs from the previous year. The payments weren't huge, but if Margaret was several months in arrears, the total would be a considerable sum.

The second drawer on the right side yielded the information she wanted. Three dunning letters from the bank stated the amount owed. It was higher than Cassie expected. More than she had in her bank account.

She tucked the letters in her handbag when she headed for the hospital. After she visited with Margaret, she'd go to Edith's house and fill her in on what she'd discovered.

Margaret was still sleeping when Cassie arrived. She sat quietly beside the bed, hoping Margaret would wake up and show some improvement. But as the minutes slipped by, it seemed that Margaret needed her rest.

When the visiting time was up, Cassie headed for Edith's house. Just as she left the hospital, Matt walked up to her.

"What are you doing here?" she said, surprised to see him. "I thought you weren't coming home for a few days."

"I stopped by Margaret's place first but it was empty, so I tracked you here. I heard from my lawyer this morning. Allen is filing for a forced sale on Monday."

"He can't do that. I found some letters from the bank demanding payment. The total is more than I have, but I can come up with some of the money. If I pay down the debt, can't he grant an extension?"

"How much?"

She told him the amount. Matt whistled. "Not as high as I expected, but still a chunk of change."

"I have several thousand in my savings."

"Come with me and we can discuss this."

He took her arm and led her away from the hospital.

Cassie jerked free.

"What's to discuss? I'll pay what I can and ask Allen to hold off on the sale."

"I have a vested interest in the house, if you'll remember. I want to help save it for Margaret, as well."

"So you say. How do I know you plan to let her stay there now that she's been incapacitated by a stroke?"

"Some things you just have to take on trust," he said.

"You might follow your own advice," she murmured, falling in step beside him as he headed for the center of town.

If he had an idea on how to save the house, she wanted to hear it. She'd worry about his future plans for Margaret's property later.

"I can pull together almost half the amount of the overdue payments," Matt told her. "I'm a bit strapped for immediate cash now, but if we can stall for a couple more weeks, I'll have the funds."

"I can come up with at least half, so together we'd have the full amount to bring the account current. Wonder how much the entire balance of the loan is."

"I'm not sure we'll find out asking Allen. Don't forget he's taking a hard line against the home for pregnant teens. I suspect he gets a cut or something if that golf course gets in."

"Maybe a lifetime membership," she suggested cynically. "Anyway, I found out Edith Harper has a power of attorney for Margaret. She and I plan to visit Allen first thing Monday morning. As soon as I can open an account and get my bank to wire the money, I can pay down what's due."

"Coffee?" Matt said as they drew near the café.

"Okay, but I want to talk to Edith as soon as I can— see if she knows anything about this detective and if he was successful in finding Fiona."

"Not Piper?"

"The most recent invoice I found from him listed searching fees, but only for Fiona. Either Margaret gave up on Piper, or he located her. I'm hoping for the latter."

She told Matt about the scrapbook she'd found with pictures of Piper. "How else would she have known to look in French papers for articles and photographs? Wish I could read French."

"Take the papers to the high school and see if the French teacher there will translate," he suggested.

"Brilliant idea." Cassie smiled at him.

The first genuine smile she'd given him in too many years to count.

Matt felt it to his soles—and against his will. Scowling, he opened the café door, stalling for a moment, trying to catch his breath. He'd forgotten how beautiful Cassie could be when she smiled. At one time he'd hoped to have her with him forever.

Circumstances and her own selfish actions had ended that possibility. The fact he could still be affected by her smile upset him.

He resented the fact she was engaged. If Cassie were to remain single, it would be some kind of retribution for Dolores's life being cut short. But now she was headed for a happy ending his sister would never have the chance to experience.

Nothing had changed, he thought, feeding his anger and ignoring the feelings her smile aroused. He had to remember why he didn't trust this woman. Didn't want to be around her.

They found a booth near the front of the café. He sat across from her, as he had so many times when they'd been in high school. Only now he saw her for the cruel, selfish, egocentric person she truly was.

"Coffee?" the waitress asked.

"Yes." Cassie smiled up at her. "When is Betsy coming on duty?"

"She has the evening shift," the woman said. "She'll be here around four."

"Why do you want Betsy?" Matt asked impatiently when the waitress left.

He wanted to finalize the loan repayment plan and get out. Too much time around Cassie wasn't doing him any good.

"In case she knows anything that can help. It's a long shot, since I've already talked to her, but she might remember more if I ask the right questions. I tried the private investigator's phone number this morning, but didn't even get a recording. He has a post office box in New Orleans on the invoice, so I don't know where he's located or I'd go and see if he was working today."

"Unlikely. Most people take Saturdays off. Or maybe he's out on surveillance somewhere."

The coffee arrived. Cassie poured a healthy dose of cream in hers. Matt remembered he used to tease her that she liked milk flavored with coffee rather than the other way around.

He scowled at the memory. He didn't want to think of the past. His plans for the future were all that mattered now. And those plans did not include Cassie.

"How soon can you transfer the money?" she asked.

"Monday afternoon at the earliest. Remember, it still won't be enough to pay off the balance, even with your share. We'll have to worry about making payments in the months to come."

"I know, but I told you I'm planning on talking to Allen McLennon Monday to see if I can convince him to hold off on any legal action. Maybe change the terms for repayment of the loan, considering Margaret's stroke."

"Oh? And you know him well enough for that?" Matt was skeptical.

"Not really. I only know him because he was dating Margaret when I lived with her. But don't you think a banker would be concerned about bad publicity? Foreclosing on an elderly woman who is temporarily incapacitated is rather heartless. And it's not as if the total amount comes close to the value of the property. Seems like a rip-off to me."

"I'm sure he'd give Margaret the difference between the amount of the loan and the sale price of the property," Matt said.

"That doesn't matter," Cassie replied heatedly. "She wouldn't have her home."

"Rumor has it bankers have no hearts."

"But this isn't Boston or New Orleans. This is a small town where people know each other. I'm counting on the threat of bad publicity to give us a chance to come up with a plan to repay the rest of the money. It's one thing to sweep the transaction under the carpet, with no one knowing, but it's something else entirely if everyone knows you forced a sale when the owner was in the hospital seriously ill. You said we only need a few weeks until you'll have more money. I'm hoping I can stall the bank long enough for that."

Matt nodded. He considered pushing his crew to work overtime to get the McIver project completed. As soon as it was signed off, he should have more than enough to pay off Margaret's debt and get started on the renovations Bradford Hall needed. Time enough to worry about the rest of his plan later, when Margaret was well again. Cassie was out of the picture.

"Tell me about Dolores," he said.

Cassie believed she wasn't to blame for his sister's death. And technically she wasn't, he had to admit. Dolores had taken the pills herself.

But Cassie had heard his sister's threat and had done nothing to stop her or alert anyone in time to save her.

She looked at him warily. For a moment Matt wanted to change the subject. He had no desire to bring up the painful memories or think about what he and Cassie had shared all those years ago. He'd trusted her more than life itself back then, only to be betrayed in the worst possible way.

"Dolores had problems," she said slowly.

"She was working on them."

"Really? Didn't seem like it to me."

"Cassie, cut to the chase. Tell me about that last day."

She picked up her coffee and took a sip, stalling. Then she shrugged.

"I played hooky from school and went to New Orleans with Travis, based on what your sister told me. And what I saw," she began.

Slowly she recounted the events exactly as they'd happened. Everything was so fresh in her mind.

He shook his head when she came to the part about his kissing Evelyn, but remained silent, letting her talk.

"So I slipped out that last night and went to the service station where you were working. If you remember, you didn't want to talk to me."

"Because you'd spent the day with Travis."

"I know."

She remembered how cold and angry Matt had been. By that time she was beginning to suspect Dolores had lied about Matt's involvement with Evelyn. She'd been panicked about having to leave Bradford and Margaret, scared for Fiona and so mixed up about Matt. When he wouldn't listen, she turned to leave, shouting that his sister was up to her tricks again and threatening to kill herself.

"Honestly, Matt, think back. Dolores had threatened suicide before and never carried through. She was always trying to break us up. When she said it that day, I thought it was just another one of her tricks—to get you to rush over, only to find she was fine. I was more upset that she'd lied about you and Evelyn."

"There was no me and Evelyn at that stage. She and I broke up before I started dating you."

"She's pretty. You two were close. And I didn't imagine the kiss."

"Evelyn had a block about math. I went to tutor her a few times—I needed the money. That particular afternoon, she was thrilled about the B she'd just got on a math test."

"I saw the two of you earlier that week, and you had your arms around her."

The memory still burned.

"There was nothing between us," Matt insisted. "She gave me a kiss in her excitement. I didn't kiss *her*."

"Not according to Dolores. Then why would I have gone out with Travis? The guy was like an octopus, hands everywhere."

"Where was your faith in our relationship?"

"Your own sister told me you were two-timing me. What was I to think? You can't have it both ways. Either I should have taken Dolores seriously or I shouldn't have. I told you initially I thought her telling me you were back with Evelyn was a trick. But think about it, Matt. She manipulated you the entire time we were dating. I thought this was another ploy— until I saw you and Evelyn. Then I was hurt and angry. I wanted to pay you back. So I went out with Travis. I was sixteen. Who thinks at sixteen?"

He studied his coffee.

She leaned closer, wishing he'd look at her.

"I was mad at Dolores, too. That's why I told her about Stewart. I didn't know she was pregnant. I never suspected she was serious about suicide. Ten minutes after I got to the garage, that cop came by to tell you about your sister. If there was any delay, it was on the police's part. They tried to find your mother first, and then they came to get you. We arrived at the hospital, found out about Dolores. You read the note the cop had seen and closed up on me. You never really listened to my side of it.

"Matt, I know I was often annoyed by Dolores, but every time she threatened to harm herself, we were there. We'd drop everything and hurry over to make sure she didn't actually do anything. I told you what she'd said to me that afternoon. I didn't know it was too late. To be honest, I never truly believed she would do such a thing. But I went to find you to tell you just the same."

"If I had gotten to her sooner, she wouldn't have died," Matt said angrily. "They could have pumped her stomach and gotten rid of most of the drugs before they entered her bloodstream."

"Is that true? Or was it already too late? You can't

blame yourself. There was no way you could have known."

"I should have been there for my sister," he said. "She needed me. I knew she had serious problems. I should have been there."

"She should have been there for you," Cassie countered.

"What are you talking about?"

He glared at her.

"You said once that Piper was a needy person, but Dolores was worse—she focused all her attention on you. She couldn't stand to share you with anyone. She wanted you all for herself. She hated me."

"She did not."

"Yes, she did. You were too blind to see it, but it was true. Looking back now, I don't think it was personal. If you'd still been seeing Evelyn Montgomery, Dolores would have hated her."

Matt looked away, thinking back to those tumultuous times. He had tried so hard to keep his sister happy and safe. She hadn't liked Evelyn, he remembered. And she'd asked him what he was doing with a loser like Cassie when they'd started to go out. Why hadn't he seen the pattern then?

"And there was your mother," Cassie said slowly.

"Leave my mother out of this," he snapped.

"Why? She was the adult in that household. She was the one ultimately responsible. She should have done something with her daughter and her own life."

"She's dead."

Cassie pressed her lips together and glared back at him.

"Not talking about it doesn't change anything. I thought we were going to discuss the situation. Clear the air. We can't do that if every topic is off-limits."

The events of that night replayed in Matt's mind as they had hundreds of times over the years. One of the local deputies had shown up at the filling station where Matt had worked after school just moments after Cassie. The man had been trying to find Matt's mother, but with no luck. Matt and Cassie had been driven to the hospital by the deputy. Dolores was in the emergency room, already dead, a sheet completely covering her.

Matt had identified his dead sister. He'd been the one to deal with the deputy. He'd been the one to tell his mother later that her only daughter was gone.

He didn't want to remember her stricken expression, the wails of anguish.

Cassie was right—his mother should have been there for both her children. Instead, he had been forced to assume the role of parent. His mother hadn't been capable of raising two children. He'd known that at the time. But a child always tried to cover for a parent, hoping things would work out.

Cassie spoke the truth. He'd been seventeen years old at the time. His mother had been the adult, she should have dealt with everything. But she had been drunk all the time.

He had seen to meals. He had urged Dolores to do

better in school. He had been the man of the house from the time he'd been a little boy.

Anger burned in his gut. Despite all his efforts, he hadn't been able to keep his family safe.

He blamed Cassie, because if he didn't have her to blame, he'd have to admit he should have handled things better.

"It wasn't your fault," she said.

He looked at her.

"She was my sister."

"But you weren't responsible for her life. We were only teenagers, but you know how grown up we all felt back then. I was pushing for us to get married, remember? I thought I was old enough, and believed I could do what I wanted. Dolores was the same. She wanted you at her beck and call, because that was the only way she could feel in control of her life. She needed professional help, but no one seemed to recognize that. I'm so, so sorry she died, Matt. She didn't deserve that. But I don't deserve your blame, and neither do you."

He made no response. He'd feel guilty until the day he died. The fact was his sister had needed him and he hadn't been there for her.

The silence stretched out. Cassie pulled her wallet from her purse and laid down a couple of bills.

"I'm going back to Edith's. I'll let you know what happens after I talk to Allen McLennon on Monday."

He watched her leave, still feeling caught up in the past. At least she wasn't crying today the way she had been all those years ago. Of course, this meeting had been much more civilized.

He hadn't called her a murderer.

His mother hadn't come rushing in to hurl expletives at her.

But the past hadn't changed.

He thought about what she'd said.

Maybe in other circumstances, he, too, would have figured it was one more empty threat in a long line of Dolores's histrionics. Cassie had come to the gas station to tell him. He'd been on the phone to home trying to reach his sister when the deputy had shown up. Dolores had been troubled all through adolescence. How many more problems had being pregnant caused?

"Want a refill?" the waitress asked, stopping by the table.

"No."

He got up and fished out a couple of dollars, tossing them on the table. They floated down and rested beside the money Cassie had left. He stared at the bills for a moment, then turned and headed back to the empty house, all the old guilt laying heavily on his shoulders.

7

Cassie tried to keep from rehashing her meeting with Matt. What had she expected? That he'd immediately see how wrong he'd been and forgive her? Want her back?

Whoa! Where had that thought come from? She was engaged to Stephen. There was no question of Matt and her getting back together.

She tried to ignore the nagging thought as she hurried through the familiar town. Since she'd walked to the hospital that morning, she had plenty of time to think about what Matt had said.

The house seemed lonely when she walked up the driveway. The curtains hung limp at the windows. The grass needed to be mowed. She'd see to it all. Cassie looked around, suddenly feeling more at home than she ever had in Boston.

What a silly thought. She'd been gone for years. Her life was in Boston now.

When she and Stephen got married, she hoped they'd buy a house, not live in an apartment. She'd like to have a big kitchen, like Margaret's, only with lots of counter space and a state-of-the-art range. She'd also like to have a flower garden, with all different kinds of flowers, like Margaret's.

Funny, they'd never talked about where they'd live. When she returned to Boston, they needed to sit down and discuss the future.

Cassie entered through the back door just as the house phone rang. She rushed to pick it up.

"Hello?"

"Cassie, thank goodness you're home. This is Betsy. I desperately need a favor. It's asking a lot, I know, but we've got a real problem."

"What's up?"

"You said you were a cook and that you were toying with the idea of going into catering. We need someone to help out at my mother-in-law's bridge club tomorrow. Her regular caterer came down with Covid and is sick as a dog. Can you do that? There'd be about twenty-eight women."

"What were they planning to have?" Cassie asked.

She felt a thrill that Betsy had asked her. She'd love to help out. It'd give her some hands-on experience to see if she really liked catering.

"I have no idea. Ida Mae came down sick yesterday and is worse today. My mother-in-law said she hadn't planned anything herself and was leaving it all up to Ida Mae. So you'd have to do the whole thing from start to finish."

"I can handle that, no problem," Cassie said confidently.

It was something she'd dreamed about doing for a long time.

"Thank you, thank you, thank you. Lucille Bullard is my mother-in-law. Can you call her to talk to her directly?"

"Sure, let me get a paper and write down her number."

A couple of minutes later, Cassie was discussing the menu with Lucille. She arranged to run by Lucille's house that afternoon to look at the kitchen setup and pots and pans, and to finalize the menu.

Cassie felt a warm glow at the heartfelt thanks she got from Betsy's mother-in-law. She figured she should be thanking Lucille.

With a menu to plan, food to buy and prep work to start, Cassie had enough on her mind to keep from thinking about Matt and their discussion.

She'd given it her best shot. Either he believed her or he didn't. She wasn't going to give the matter another thought.

By the time Cassie visited Margaret that evening, things were well underway for the luncheon the following day. Lucille's kitchen was more than adequate, and she was delighted with the menu Cassie proposed—a quiche Lorraine, cranberry gelatin salad, Chinese green salad and assorted finger sandwiches. For dessert, Cassie suggested decadent chocolate truffle cookies. It was an easy, light lunch, perfect for a bridge club.

Bubbling with excitement, Cassie told Margaret all her plans. She detailed each step of her preparations and described how she would serve the luncheon.

When she had finished, she sat back in her chair and smiled at the older woman. Margaret's eyes looked brighter tonight, Cassie thought. But she still couldn't communicate. Yet Cassie knew she understood every word spoken to her.

"So that's my news. Oh, and Matt and I have a plan to keep the bank from foreclosing on your loan, so that's another worry you can do without."

Margaret frowned and tried to speak.

"Now, you know the doctor said you'll get better faster if you don't try to push yourself too hard," Cassie admonished, patting her arm. "Time enough when you're better to discuss that situation. Just rest up."

The nurse came to the bed.

"Feeling better?" she asked Margaret, giving Cassie a small nod. "Time for your visitor to leave so you can get your beauty rest."

"I won't be able to get here until late afternoon," Cassie reminded Margaret. "Then I'll be able to tell you how the luncheon went. Wish me luck!"

She kissed Margaret on the cheek, noting how soft her skin was, and how wrinkled. The strong, indomitable woman of Cassie's past was gone. She felt a pang at the ravages of time and gratitude she'd seen the article in the paper and come back to Bradford.

Cassie was almost home when her cell phone rang. She recognized Stephen's number.

"I tried to reach you earlier," he said, "but your phone was out of service."

"I was in the hospital again. Can't talk on cell

phones there. Was your golf game enjoyable?"

"Mother said you called. When are you coming home?"

"I'm not sure. Things are a bit complicated."

"Complicated how?"

Cassie hesitated. She knew what Stephen would say if she explained. Easier to be vague.

"Just complicated. Margaret is doing better, so that's a relief."

"Prognosis look good?" he asked.

"I think so, though the doctor refers to it as cautiously optimistic. She's started physical therapy already, can you believe it? She still can't talk, though."

"So there's really nothing for you to do there. She's getting good care. Recovery will take time."

He was right. Once the business of the loan was settled, there would be little need for Cassie to stay here.

"There are a few things I can do for her. I'm trying to find the other girls Margaret raised—Piper and Fiona. I know they'd want to know what happened. Maybe they can come visit, as well. It's been years since I've seen either one of them. So I don't know when I'll be back in Boston."

"We miss you this weekend. The Faulkners are here and they won't stop talking about their latest trip. If you were here, I'd have an excuse not to listen to Vern go on about the temples in Kathmandu."

Cassie laughed softly. "So I'm only a buffer, huh?"

"You know you're more than that to me," he said.

Why couldn't her heart skip a beat when he said such romantic things to her?

"Tell me about your day," he continued.

"I visited Margaret, and... Oh, and I got a catering job."

"A job? What are you talking about?" His voice changed slightly.

"A friend's mother-in-law needed someone on short notice when her regular caterer got sick. This will give me a chance to see if I actually like catering. We've talked about it before."

"There's no point doing it down there. You need to start here in Boston."

"It's a practice run, nothing more. Anyway, I visited the home where the luncheon's being held and the kitchen's well equipped. It should be fun, and it'll give me something to do. I can't stay at the hospital all day. Visiting times are strictly regulated."

"If Margaret's getting better, why stay at all? What does your boss have to say about missing work?"

Cassie grew defensive. She wanted to stay and make sure Margaret was going to get better. Her own job was not an issue.

"I called earlier this week and arranged a leave of absence for a little while. I know Thomas wants me to come back as soon as I can, but I'm entitled to family emergency leave."

Sometimes family took priority over a career.

Family. That's what Margaret really was. And Piper and Fiona.

She wanted to reconnect with her foster sisters, with people who had known her when she was a child. Who had shared the ups and downs of growing up in a small town in Mississippi. Boston didn't give her all she needed.

Stephen wouldn't understand that.

"Cassie?"

"Sorry, I zoned out for a moment. The restaurant will hold my job a little longer, I'm sure. If not, I'll find something else. I should have a better idea next week about when I'll be ready to return."

"I don't like you being so far away."

"I'm fine. I've already reconnected with a high school friend and moved back into my old room. I'm also checking out all the changes around town. My visit is turning out to be a lot different than I expected."

"Just don't get any ideas about staying there," he said.

Cassie laughed softly, then wondered if she ever could return to Bradford to live.

Not if she married Stephen. He was seventh-generation Bostonian and she knew he'd never consider leaving.

"I'll call you soon," she said as the house came into view.

Seeing it, she felt a welcoming warmth that was missing from her austere apartment building near the Charles River.

Or was it the Mississippi heat that made her feel so cozy?

She slipped her phone in her pocket as she walked along the driveway. Matt's truck was parked near the house. What was he doing here? Hadn't they said all they needed to say to each other earlier?

He leaned against the porch support, watching her walk up the drive. She felt a fluttering sensation. Nerves, of course. Was he going to start in again on Dolores's death? She'd told him she was sorry about his sister's death, but life moved on.

She had moved on.

Had Matt?

"Might as well turn in that rental if you're going to walk everywhere," he said when she drew nearer.

"I'm thinking about getting a van," she told him, climbing the steps to the porch. "What are you doing here?"

"Came to pay a neighborly call." He shifted slightly to watch her.

"I doubt that."

"I've been thinking about what you said about Dolores."

"And?"

She almost held her breath.

"The thing is, it's hard to know how to react. I've been angry at you for a lot of years."

She nodded, hope building.

"You were a kid yourself and had false information."

She wanted to remind him who had given her the false information, but she held her tongue.

"Heck, I was a kid myself. We can't change the past, Cassie. Dolores was responsible for her own death. Let it go at that."

It wasn't all she'd hoped for, Cassie thought, but it was all she was going to get.

"Is that it?"

"What more do you want?"

"To be believed when I tell someone something," Cassie said. "But beyond that, I guess you're right.... What does it matter? In a short while I'll be returning to Boston and we'll probably go another twelve years or so without seeing one another."

She nodded. "Okay, then."

"I have to get back to New Orleans. I wanted to see if you needed anything from me for your meeting with Allen on Monday. Margaret and I presented our proposal to the planning commission a few weeks ago. The town council gave tentative approval, pending some further analysis. Allen is against the project and will try to block us any way he can. So if you need other ammunition, I'll try to come up with something."

"I think the publicity angle will be my best bet. Should I call you and tell you how it goes?"

He nodded. Straightening away from the post, he reached into his pocket for his wallet and extracted a business card. "My cell number's on the card," he said, extending it toward Cassie.

She took it. Bennett Construction. No fancy company name for him.

"Okay, after I see Allen, I'll call you."

Cassie expected him to leave, but he remained in the same spot.

"Is that all?" she asked.

"Pretty much." He hesitated a moment, then looked directly at her. "Want to go to the barbecue place for dinner?"

"What?"

The last thing in the world she'd expected was an invitation.

"I have to eat, you do, too. Might as well eat together."

She stared at him, wondering what the catch was.

"Eat in peace?" she asked.

He nodded. "No talk of the past."

Cassie hesitated. She had a million things to do to get ready for the catering assignment. But she couldn't resist.

"Okay. Let me run inside and freshen up a bit."

A half hour later Matt turned his truck into the parking lot of Benny's Best Barbecue. It was already crowded.

"Saturday nights draw a big crowd," he said, pulling into a parking spot some distance from the main building.

"When a place has the best barbecue ribs in six counties, it's always crowded," she teased. "At least I assume the food's still as good as I remember."

"Last time I ate here, it was," Matt said.

Cassie wondered when that had been and who he'd been with. It had been forever since she and Matt had dated—teenagers in the throes of first love. She'd spent almost half her life, all of her adult life, away from Bradford and Matt. Still, there was a connection she couldn't deny.

She was glad she'd taken time to change quickly into a skirt and blouse and brush her hair out. It flowed around her shoulders, very different from her usual low ponytail, but it was fun once in a while to go with something different. She wasn't cooking tonight; her hair could go any which way.

They had to wait for a few minutes to get a table. Cassie studied the restaurant from a new perspective. She'd been a teenager when she'd eaten here before, but now as a chef, she was interested in how the restaurant functioned. She looked at how the tables were placed, how the place settings were arranged. She timed how quickly the food came from the kitchen, what the plate presentations were like.

"Do you think they'd let me see the kitchen?" she asked.

"No. They're too afraid of someone stealing their secret recipe." Matt grinned. "Besides, aren't you on a kind of vacation from work?"

"Not as of today," she said, and proceeded to tell him about the catering job at Lucille Bullard's.

Matt listened to Cassie explain about the luncheon Betsy had asked her to prepare. Sounded awful to him—lunch for twenty-eight picky middle-aged women. But Cassie sparkled with enthusiasm. Her eyes glowed and she seemed more alive than he'd seen her since she'd arrived back in Bradford.

He wondered what else would ignite a spark in her besides cooking.

Once he had, he thought dispassionately. Long ago.

He'd never found that special feeling with anyone else in the years since. Now he doubted he ever would. He wasn't cut out to be a family man and he knew it.

He'd spent the afternoon going over budget projections to make sure he could handle his share of the loan payment. And thinking about Dolores and Cassie and all that had gone on that last year Cassie had lived in the Bradford Hall house.

It could have been as she said. Dolores had lied as easily as others breathed. He hadn't liked that about his sister, but had tried to put enough trust in her so she'd feel more confident and not find the need to lie.

He remembered her animosity toward the girls he'd liked. It could have been as Cassie said—maybe Dolores had lied about him and Evelyn to cause trouble. If so, she'd succeeded in spades.

"I have a table for you now," the waiter said, appearing through the crowd. "Thanks for waiting."

The table was in the center of the room, almost jammed against the one next to it, where a family with three children were already enjoying the ribs.

Matt was glad for the noisy atmosphere. He'd had doubts after inviting her as to whether this was really a smart idea or not. But there was nothing romantic about the restaurant or the boisterous crowd. Cassie could hardly get the wrong impression about his invitation.

"Tell me about Bennett Construction," she said once they'd ordered. "I remember you liked building things, but I thought you wanted to be an architect, not the actual builder."

"Life doesn't always turn out the way we want. Money was tight. I got a partial scholarship to Tulane, but had to work my way through, and construction paid the best. Once I got involved in the actual work, I found I liked it and had an aptitude for it. I dropped out of college for a year to earn as much as I could. Never went back."

Sometimes he wished he'd switched his major to engineering and completed his degree. But the construction business had kept him too busy to return to college. And he'd done all right without the degree.

"So you stayed in New Orleans after attending Tulane?" she asked.

"There was nothing for me back in Bradford," he said. "My mother died a couple of years after Dolores. Besides, there's lots of building going on in New Orleans. I like the energy and opportunities."

"The restaurants are fabulous. I think it would be fun to work there. Think how I could advertise for my catering business after a stint at one of the more famous ones."

"Be a long commute from Boston."

She nodded. "It'll never happen, but sometimes I just think, what if?"

"I imagine Stephen would object."

There, he'd said the man's name. Would she get all starry eyed now and rhapsodize about her perfect fiancé?

"He would. He didn't even want me to come here. He offered to come down but there's nothing for him to do here."

"Hang out with you," Matt said, wondering if he wanted to do just that himself. Being with Cassie jarred loose so many memories—a lot of them good ones.

"No, he's very focused on his work and doesn't take a lot of time off."

Matt wished he knew what she was thinking. She had such a wistful expression, it tore at his heart.

"I don't, either, as a rule," she continued. "I worked hard to get hired at the restaurant I'm at now. And I spend a lot of my free time testing recipes for the catering company I hope to run one day. I know owning a business is harder than it seems on the surface, but do you find it worth all the extra paperwork and worry?"

"I think so. I can't imagine working for someone else."

"It does have its drawbacks."

"Don't you want to run your own restaurant?"

"No, I really want to have a catering service. I'd love to do wedding receptions, fiftieth anniversary parties, birthdays, special events, you name it. It's the variety that really appeals to me, finding different themes and creating menus."

"So you'll start with a luncheon for Lucille and move on."

She smiled and shrugged.

"Maybe. Or maybe I'll find it's more difficult than I thought and be thankful for the full support of a kitchen staff."

"Hire help."

"One day."

Their ribs arrived, and the next few moments were devoted to devouring the excellent meal.

The conversation after that was impersonal, almost as if they were strangers sharing a table, instead of former lovers. But given their past, Matt was surprised the meal wasn't more awkward. After all, he had accused Cassie of killing his sister.

When Matt drove back to Bradford Hall after dinner, he felt an odd sense of déjà vu. How many nights had he and Cassie spent studying together at the library, sneaking kisses, then hurrying to get her home before curfew? He'd always gotten her back before Margaret's deadline, usually feeling both guilty and resentful. Guilty for what they'd been doing between the library and home. Resentful because their time had been so limited.

The house was dark when he pulled in near the back door.

"I'll go in with you and make sure everything is all right," he said.

"I'll be fine. What could happen here in Bradford?"

"Probably nothing, but I'll check just the same."

He took a quick walk through the ground floor. Nothing was out of order. With the lights on, he could see how many repairs the house needed. It would take a lot of work to convert it into a suitable home for unwed pregnant teens. Matt was anxious to get started. If he could just get the town's planning commission to give the final go-ahead, he could order supplies, and once the McIver job was signed off, his crew could come up to Bradford for a few weeks.

Would Cassie want to help? Or did she still think he was intending to exclude Margaret since she'd had the stroke. He wished Margaret would regain her speech and tell everyone what she wanted.

"Thank you for checking," Cassie said, walking beside him back to the kitchen. "I told you everything would be fine."

"Call me after you talk to Allen."

"I will. And thank you for dinner."

She smiled politely.

Matt would never know what prompted him. Maybe the memories or maybe the polite smile that was at odds with the longing in her eyes. Before he had second thoughts, he leaned over and kissed her.

Cassie lifted the last of the grocery bags from her car and carried them into Lucille Bullard's kitchen. She had a thousand things to see to before the first guest arrived, yet her thoughts revolved around Matt's unexpected kiss last night. She'd had trouble going to sleep because of it, and had awakened with the taste of him on her lips.

It meant nothing! A brief touching of the lips. A gesture between two people who'd been close long ago.

But what kind of gesture? she wondered as she began to grate the cheese for the quiches she was preparing. A casual end to a pleasant evening? A maybe-I'm-softening-toward-you kiss?

Darn, she was tired of dwelling on it. She needed to concentrate on her cooking, not daydream about hidden messages.

Cassie finished preparing the pastry for the quiches by the time Betsy breezed into the kitchen.

"I'm here to help," she said, giving Cassie a quick hug. "Just tell me what you need and I'll do it."

"I didn't expect you, but thanks a million. I was wondering how I was going to get the food prepared and set all the tables before the guests arrive."

"Ah, my area of expertise," Betsy said gaily. "I'll set the tables, and then help serve the meal when the ladies get here. And I'm a terrific dishwasher."

"You're a lifesaver."

Cassie felt responsibility of the luncheon lighten slightly.

"Lucille is my mother-in-law. I want everything to be perfect for her."

The two women worked harmoniously together. By the time the guests began to arrive, everything was ready. Cassie and Betsy were kept busy during the luncheon, but the pressure eased by the time they were cleaning up.

"That was fun," Betsy said. "Even more fun than working at the café. Let's do it again."

"Two women did ask me if I was available for garden parties in May. Too bad I won't be here."

"Why not? Margaret won't be one hundred percent by next month. Stay until she's on her feet again. You can certainly make enough money to get by while you're here. I heard Suzanne Canaday say she wanted to talk to you about catering some business dinner her husband wants to have in a couple of weeks."

Cassie carefully dried the dish she'd been holding, thinking about the possibilities.

"I do have a life in Boston," she said mildly.

"But Margaret's here," Betsy argued. "She needs you. Stay a little longer."

"I'm not sure my boss would see it that way."

Still, the thought tantalized. If she did stay, she could help Margaret when she got home. She could also continue searching for Piper and Fiona, and try out some of her catering ideas. How long could she stretch out her leave of absence?

"With food like you served today, you'll get a job anywhere," Betsy encouraged her. "People around here would be lucky to have you! And besides, this catering business could really take off and you'd never have to go back to working for someone else."

"You forget. I have a fiancé waiting for me in Boston. If I venture into catering, I need to do it there, not Bradford."

"Well, sure, for a real business. But this would just

be a test run. Look how everything fell into place today. And with three more bookings, you're on your way! After your events here, you'd have references when you open in Boston."

Although she appreciated Betsy's confidence, Cassie couldn't help laughing.

"And if I fall on my face, I can always return to Boston and forget the catering idea with no one the wiser."

"You're not going to fall on your face. You will need help. And I'm your girl."

"You want to work with me? What about your job at the café?"

Why was she even talking about this, Cassie wondered. She couldn't stay away from her own chef's position much longer.

"I'll work around that initially. Who knows, you may end up having to hire more than just me."

Cassie looked at Betsy. Would she really have enough work to need actual staff? Excitement licked through her. She knew word of mouth was the best way to expand a business and, if today's success was anything to go by, she was off to a great start.

Not that she would open a business in Bradford, but a few events to gain experience wouldn't hurt. Especially with the variety talked about today.

She needed to talk to Stephen about it. He would have words of wisdom, she knew—if he could get beyond her wanting to stay a few weeks longer in Bradford. She had to be careful how she presented it to him.

"I can't stay long term," Cassie hedged. "I have responsibilities in Boston."

She'd give the matter some serious thought. On the plus side, it would fill the hours she wasn't at the hospital and bring in some needed income.

"But you're going to be here for another couple of weeks for sure," Betsy said. "I'll tell Suzanne you'll do that dinner in two weeks. And maybe we'll get another gig before then."

She set down her dish towel and headed for the living room.

"And so a business is born," Cassie murmured, once again giving in to the excitement of starting a new venture.

She wouldn't be able to run the business quite the way she wanted. A lot of the work would have to be done on-site at the customers' homes since she didn't have all the equipment she needed at Bradford Hall.

Or did she?

She thought of the large old kitchen at Margaret's. She had yet to go through the cupboards and pantry to see just what was there. Maybe Margaret had enough pans and dishes for the short-term. She couldn't wait to get home and take inventory.

Betsy hurried back, business cards in hand.

"All set, boss. We have a small dinner party next Saturday, Suzanne's business dinner the following Saturday, and a garden party the next day." She shuffled the cards. "And Mabel Truscott wants us to prepare a luncheon Thursday of this week for her niece's engagement. The announcement will be in tomorrow's paper. We're practically the first to know MaryLynne is engaged. I got all the particulars so you can get started ASAP."

Cassie took the cards and looked at them. Betsy had scribbled down the number of guests, contact phone numbers, dates and times. Cassie figured she could put the money she earned toward Margaret's loan payments.

"You'll have to talk to each woman individually about the menu," Betsy said, her eyes sparkling. "I should probably go with you to learn what I can. I'm ready to rock and roll. This is going to be so much fun!"

Cassie laughed aloud. "It sure is. Okay, then, we're in business—at least temporarily."

She didn't even want to guess what Stephen would say.

8

Cassie was totally energized as she headed for the hospital. A brief visit with Margaret had her feeling even better. She could tell Margaret liked listening to all the details about the luncheon. She seemed to get visibly brighter when Cassie said she was staying for a few weeks and going into the catering business with Betsy.

She still hadn't brought up the scrapbook she'd found with the clippings about Piper. She didn't know why. Somehow the time didn't seem right. So far Margaret was holding her own, but Cassie didn't want to upset her. Maybe when she knew more, she'd broach the subject.

Promising to visit again the next morning, Cassie headed for home. She was too full of energy to sit still, so she headed for Margaret's bedroom to see if there was an address book or any papers that might give her a clue to finding Piper and Fiona.

It felt awkward to enter the bedroom without Margaret there. Cassie couldn't remember ever doing so before. Margaret had respected the girls' privacy and expected the same from them.

The old-fashioned furniture was heavy and dark, and the cover on the bed was worn. There were landscapes on the walls, long curtains flanking the tall windows. The middle of the patterned rug was faded from the sunshine, but still rich in colors near the edges.

Walking around, she studied the things Margaret had on display, stopping when she realized the gold painted box was one she'd made for her foster mother in fourth grade. Each child had glued various shapes of macaroni on a small box, then spray painted everything gold. She was touched Margaret even had it, much less kept it in a place of honor in her bedroom.

Moving to the next shelf, she saw the plaster hand-print Piper had made in kindergarten. Tears began to blur her vision. Margaret had treasured these childish gifts, keeping them long after the children who made them had gone.

The framed drawing hanging over her bedside table was one Fiona had sketched—a rudimentary house with four stick figures, Margaret being the largest, Cassie suspected. Her own dark hair identified her, with bright yellow for Piper and brown for Fiona.

"We were a family," Cassie said softly, touching the drawing. "Why did you break us up, Fiona?"

There was a small secretary desk in one corner. Cassie hesitated about prying into Margaret's personal things, but she needed to know as much as she could. Opening the drop front, she saw stacks of papers much like the breakfront had held.

Sighing at the lack of order, she began to sort the clutter of papers. Her reward was the original loan document, dated three years ago. The $50,000 was more than Cassie had expected. Margaret had done a good job of paying it down—until the last few months. What had happened to change that?

She read the document through, not understanding all the terms and conditions, but getting the gist of the deal. The house had been used as collateral for the loan. If she fell into arrears, the bank had the right to foreclose.

Cassie already knew that. Somehow, she'd hoped for a clause that would be more favorable to Margaret. Even more discouraging, there was nothing in the pile of papers about Piper or Fiona.

After organizing the desk to her satisfaction, Cassie still felt restless. She went to the door that led to the attic stairs. It would be hot and dirty in the old attic. But she wondered if Margaret had kept any of her other things. She'd been whisked away so quickly she had taken only her clothes and a couple of treasures. A lot had been left behind.

Opening the door, she switched on the light and headed up the stairs. The light was dim, and dust covered every surface. The faint daylight allowed in through the small windows gave the place a spooky, haunted feel.

Cassie shivered. Dumb idea, but now that she was here, she wasn't backing out.

Old furniture was piled around the attic walls. She

and Piper used to sneak up here and rummage around the old trunks for dress-up clothes when they'd been preteens. Near the top of the stairs were several cardboard boxes taped shut.

One said simply, Cassie.

She opened it and looked inside. On top were some of the dresses she'd outgrown. Carefully lifting them out, she saw they were the ones Margaret had made.

A memory of Margaret seated at the old sewing machine late at night, patiently making clothes for "her girls," assailed Cassie. She hadn't always liked the dresses or shirts Margaret had made, and remembered complaining that the other girls in her class bought their clothes at trendy boutiques.

Thinking back, Cassie now realized how difficult it must have been financially for Margaret. She knew from the first year she'd worked how precarious it could be with only one paycheck between herself and homelessness. And Margaret hadn't worked outside the home. She'd had a small stipend from her father's estate and the allowance she received from the state for Cassie, Fiona and Piper.

She hadn't had to make dresses for them, Cassie thought, running her fingertips lightly over the textured material. She'd done it out of love.

Cassie felt a pang at how ungrateful she'd been. Taking things for granted, complaining when she couldn't have what the other girls in her class had.

She set the dress aside and pulled out another one. How many hours had Margaret labored to make these, hoping to bring a smile to a young girl's face, instead of scorn or derision?

Cassie felt two inches high. Why hadn't she been a better person as a teenager? Margaret had shown her nothing but kindness, despite the hard time Cassie had given her.

Somehow she had to let Margaret know how much she appreciated all she'd done for her.

Reaching farther inside the box, she pulled out a folder of school papers. They were all As. Smiling, Cassie scanned a few. Margaret had thought enough of her to keep these papers, along with her posters and books, without knowing if she'd ever see Cassie again. Touched at the gesture, Cassie went through the entire box. Here was the program from her first play. A yearbook from high school, more photographs. And a pressed rose, from the small bouquet Matt had given her for some long-forgotten occasion.

When she was finished, she carefully repacked it. There was also a box marked Fiona, and one for Piper.

Cassie stood up and headed back downstairs, feeling both nostalgic and lonesome. She'd never appreciated what she'd had when she was living here. She had focused on what she didn't have. How stupid could one kid be?

She'd give anything for another chance. Staying until Margaret was on her feet was the best she could offer. Today strengthened her resolve to do just that.

Heading for the kitchen, she began to grow anxious about what she was going to say to Allen McLennon when she met with him tomorrow. She was also worried about Stephen's reaction to her plans, and curious as to how Matt would view her decision to stay. How had life become so complicated?

Cassie decided to wait until after her visit with Allen McLennon to tell Stephen about her catering assignments. She wanted to know what she was up against on Margaret's behalf.

Stephen was a lawyer. He liked facts, not supposition or speculation. She wanted to have answers to his questions.

Dressed in her suit despite the heat of the Mississippi morning, Cassie was prepared to do her best. She'd already talked to her bank in Boston about transferring funds as soon as she opened an account in Bradford.

She picked up Edith and they arrived at the bank shortly after it opened. Cassie quickly established a checking account for herself. She would need it for her new business venture, as well. After calling her bank in Boston with the new account number, she asked to see Mr. McLennon.

"Miss Harper, Miss Hodges. What can I do for you ladies?" Allen asked when his secretary showed them into his office a short time later.

"We're here to discuss Margaret's outstanding loan and the payments that are in arrears," Cassie said. "I've talked things over with Edith Harper, who as you probably know has power of attorney for Margaret while she's incapacitated."

Edith pulled out a sheet of paper and laid it on the edge of the desk. "I'm acting for Margaret until she's well again."

Allen glanced at the paper, then looked at Cassie. "Ordinarily I don't discuss a client's business affairs with anyone other than the client or the legal representative, but in this case, I can tell you the bank is starting foreclosure proceedings. The loan payments are months behind. And given Margaret's current situation, I don't expect to see her resuming payments. Business is business."

"I'm able to make a substantial payment toward the arrearage. Matt Bennett will be here this afternoon with another payment. That should bring the account fully current. Next we'll see how to get the loan paid in full."

Allen frowned. "We've already started the process."

"Then stop it," Edith said.

Cassie nodded.

"I wouldn't think the *bank*," she emphasized the word, knowing full well Allen was the one with the power, "would want the bad publicity that would arise from taking an ill woman's home away from her—all for a few thousand dollars. Especially when that house and the acreage surrounding it are worth much more than the loan amount. Just think of the speculation if the bank then sold the house and left the woman homeless. Sounds like unfair business practices to me. I wonder what government agency regulates that."

"Business is business," he said testily. "The consequences of falling delinquent on the loan were clearly stated in the agreement. Now, if there is nothing else."

He rose.

Cassie remained seated.

"My fiancé is an attorney. I'll have him look into the various options we have at this time. Perhaps through him I can get another loan and pay this one in full. Or, worse case, we could sell some of the land ourselves and pay off the loan that way. At least we would know we'd made the best deal and Margaret wouldn't lose her home."

Allen sat back down and glared at Cassie. It was another moment before he spoke.

"You girls were nothing but trouble when you were here and I see that hasn't changed."

Cassie gave him a bright smile.

"If trouble means rallying around when family needs help, then you bet I'm trouble, more than you'll be able to handle."

"Family! You were nothing but a bunch of no-account orphans Margaret took on for some foolish reason. I told her so at the time."

"Allen!" Edith was shocked.

"That was when we all thought you cared for Margaret," Cassie said, wondering again what had happened between them.

"I'm not discussing the past with anyone—especially you," he said.

"Perhaps you should. In the meantime, I'll see what my fiancé says and will be back in touch."

"All right," Allen said with poor grace. "I'll see to it the bank holds off on calling the note until the end of the month. Does that give you time to come current? Otherwise, it'll be out of my hands."

"It's more than enough time. Thank you."

Cassie stood and helped Edith to her feet. As they left, she realized her knees were shaking. She had no intention of calling Stephen. Given Margaret's circumstances he'd probably advise that Edith sell the house, pay the loan and invest the balance for Margaret's retirement.

"You did it," Edith said, smiling happily. "You saved Margaret's house for her."

"We're still not out of the woods entirely," Cassie cautioned. "We have to find a way to make the monthly payments."

But she felt flushed with victory.

"You're a good girl, Cassie. You did right to come home. Margaret's very proud of you, you know."

Cassie smiled, warmed by the compliment. "I'm glad this part is settled at least. Can I drive you someplace?"

"No, I have my gentleman friend Mr. Evans waiting."

Edith waved to an elderly man sitting in a large sedan. He got out of the car and came to meet them.

"Cassie Hodges, this is Mr. Michael Evans, my dear friend. Michael, this is one of Margaret's girls, Cassie."

"How do you do? I'm delighted to meet you. How did the meeting go?" he asked.

Cassie smiled. "It went well. Edith can tell you all about it. Thanks, Edith, for the support."

"Margaret's my best friend. Of course I want to help!"

Once Michael and Edith drove off, Cassie walked over to the park. She opened her cell phone to call Matt.

He answered on the second ring.

"The bank is holding off until the end of the month," she said in a rush. "I've arranged to have my money transferred. I don't see any problem in clearing the overdue amount. We will still have to figure out how we'll meet the monthly payments in the future."

"I'll have the necessary money by the time it's due. We'll keep the wolf from the door. Good work, Cassie."

She felt pleased with his praise. He'd always been positive about her accomplishments at school, too.

"I don't think Allen McLennon's too happy with me," she said, wanting to keep talking with Matt, to share the morning's events.

She told him how the banker had reacted, and the comments he'd made about Piper, Fiona and her.

"Did the entire town think we were no-accounts?" she asked.

"I never heard that. In fact, I always thought Allen McLennon had an eye for the ladies, no matter what their age or background. He's never married, though, so maybe he only likes to look. I never pictured him a snob."

"He was over at the house a lot that last year. I thought for sure he and Margaret would marry. Maybe the prospect of taking on three no-account orphans kept him from popping the question. But then he should have been happy when we left. Oh well, I'm glad she didn't hook up with him. He's a sleazoid if he would take possession of Margaret's house when she's too ill to fight him."

"I don't think he would have acted so fast if that consortium wasn't pressuring for a golf course," Matt said.

The sound of heavy machinery could be heard over the line.

"Where are you?" Cassie asked.

"I stopped by a new housing development that's going up near my project. I have some concerns about runoff and wanted to talk to the construction manager here. Why?"

"I could hear the equipment, that's all."

She hesitated, then decided to tell him about her new venture.

"I'm catering another couple of parties. That way I'll have more money to balance out not having my salary while I'm on leave."

"When?"

"One this coming Thursday, another on the weekend. Two more the following weekend."

"Just how long do you plan to remain in Bradford?" he asked.

Did she detect suspicion in his tone?

"I don't know. I have to talk to my head chef in Boston to see if I can get an extended leave. Then call my neighbor and ask her to get some things from my apartment to send to me. I'm staying another few weeks anyway. Until Margaret's on her feet."

"I thought you had to rush back to Boston."

"I've had a change of heart."

"And what does Stephen think about this?" Matt asked.

"He doesn't know yet. I'm not sure what his reaction will be."

That was a lie. She knew he'd be upset with her, frustrated she wasn't doing things his way. But it definitely wasn't any of Matt's business.

"If he doesn't mind, then he's a stronger man than I would be," he said.

"What do you mean?"

"I wouldn't want the woman I was going to marry traipsing off a thousand miles away and then staying indefinitely. It could take Margaret months to recover."

"Maybe, but they've already started physical therapy and speech therapy. She could be back home sooner than we expect. Anyway, I owe her. We were a family. I was too young and self-centered back then to realize it, but with maturity comes some wisdom. She's my foster mother, the only mother I really remember. I'm staying."

"What about your other foster parents? Wasn't the woman a mother figure?"

"Not really. By then I was almost seventeen, and too old to latch on to her the same way. But we're good friends. More like sisters. I keep in touch with them and have visited them in California. But it's not the same as with Margaret. She really raised me. Dottie Johnson just polished me up a bit. I shouldn't have to justify why I want to stay to help Margaret."

"Hey, I didn't say it wasn't a good idea, only that if you were mine, I'd be more than annoyed."

If you were mine. Once she had been.

"I've got to go. I told Allen you'd be sending in your share of the payment soon. Bye."

She hung up, more than annoyed that Matt hadn't been happier she was staying. At least he could have been a little grateful. Her help that morning put him a little closer to starting that group home he wanted.

She frowned. His comments about Stephen added to her feelings of guilt. She should have discussed her plans with him first. She really hated it when he made plans without consulting her and now she'd done that very thing. What did that say about her? About them?

Cassie leaned back on the warm wooden bench and tried to relax. The soft sounds of birds trilling in the trees, of children laughing in the playground were like a soothing balm. The sun was hot. She wouldn't stay long or she'd be cooked through. But just for a few moments, she wanted to empty her mind and let the sweet ambience of the sleepy town embrace her. She felt like she'd come home.

She knew every inch of Bradford. Knew more people than she'd remembered. Liked the fact people waved to her as she passed or greeted her on the sidewalk. It was peaceful and friendly, and she felt connected in a way she hadn't for the last decade. She wished she could capture the feeling, bottle it and carry it with her wherever she went.

Knowing she couldn't put off the moment, she flipped open her phone again and dialed Stephen's number at the law firm.

"Cassie, I'm glad you called. How are you doing? Have an arrival time for me?"

"No, Stephen, actually, I'm not sure when I'm coming back, but it won't be for a while."

"What does that mean?" he asked, perplexed.

"I want to stay to help Margaret get back on her feet."

"That could take months or longer, sweetheart. Sometimes stroke patients never fully recover."

"I know. Or she may bounce right back. I'll know more after I talk again with her doctor."

"What about the restaurant?"

"I have to call Thomas and discuss that," she said cautiously.

"He needs you. I need you. If you remember, I wanted to discuss our wedding date last weekend. Instead, I feel you're farther away than ever—and I don't mean just physically. Is anything wrong?"

Cassie didn't know what to say. She closed her eyes, trying to envision Stephen. He'd be sitting at his desk, briefs and files surrounding him.

But to her dismay, Matt Bennett's face was the one that came to mind. Standing in the middle of a construction site, a hard hat on his head, his arms brown and muscular in the spring sunshine.

She opened her eyes and focused on the storefront across the street.

"Don't be silly. Nothing's wrong. I'm needed here, that's all."

"You haven't seen the woman in twelve years. I'm sure she has friends around to help. She's managed without you all this time, she can again."

"I was wrong to stay away, Stephen. I love Margaret. I want to make up for that neglect. She's the only mother I've really known. You'd stay for your mother if she needed help."

"Technically she was your foster mother. And not such a good one, from what you've said."

"That was before," Cassie said slowly.

"Before what?"

"Before I took a good look at the life we had here and remembered all she did for us. Before I saw the dresses she made for us and recalled the late nights she stayed up hemming them. Or found out she'd saved the projects we made for her at school. She was a single woman, doing the best she could for three homeless girls. I owe her."

She heard Stephen draw in a deep breath. She knew an argument was brewing.

"As I see it, the state paid her to provide for you

and the other girls. Technically you don't owe her anything."

Cassie was taken aback by his unfeeling attitude.

"She was much more than some paid care giver. She gave us her values, taught us how to behave, instilled pride in us to achieve what we wanted. I'm not going to argue with you. If you don't think I owe her, then let's just say I want to stay."

"Have you made up your mind?" he asked.

"I guess. I wanted to talk it over with you."

"But if your mind is made up, what's the point of talking it over with me?" he asked reasonably.

"Oh, Stephen, I want to stay, but I want you to be supportive."

"Maybe I want you to be supportive, as well."

"What does that mean? I've always supported you."

"When you could."

"You knew when we started dating what my working hours would be. I've made arrangements to swap shifts several times to accommodate your schedule. When was the last time you arranged your work schedule to accommodate me?"

"It's hardly the same thing. Social events are usually scheduled for weekends and evenings."

"Which I work," she said stubbornly, annoyed by the unfairness of his complaint.

She didn't want to argue with him. Or was she trying to pick a fight—to justify her decision to stay longer?

"What's really going on down there, Cassie?"

His quiet question caught her by surprise.

She thought for a moment, then replied, "I think I'm finding out who I am."

"You're a talented chef with a wonderful job and you're engaged to a terrific man, what's more to know?"

She forced a laugh, as she knew he expected. But it struck her that she was serious about finding out who she was, and that was something Stephen wouldn't understand. He knew who he was.

"Be patient," she pleaded.

"I'm not such a patient guy. I want you back home."

Home. Where was home? Cassie wasn't sure she knew.

"I'll call you later in the week," she said.

Disconnecting, she rose and headed back to the old house. She felt restless and uncertain. She wasn't sure how much help she could be to Margaret, especially while she was still in the hospital.

Cassie had another call to make—to her boss. If he didn't extend her leave, she would have no choice but to return to Boston.

Entering the kitchen a little later, Cassie relished the coolness after her walk in the sun. She studied the old room, wondering if she could actually use it as her base. She knew Margaret would be delighted someone was cooking in the kitchen again.

Maybe Cassie would reorganize it a bit. She was full of ideas, and she still had to make an inventory of every piece of equipment, including plates and service dishes. She'd also have to inventory basic supplies from baking soda to cooking wines. What she didn't have, she'd see about getting.

She was bubbling with energy and excitement when she sat down to write out her plans for the first two events scheduled this week. When that was done, she rose with determination. She'd clean this kitchen from top to bottom!

Her spirits lifted.

She loved bringing order out of chaos and plunged right into the project.

By late afternoon, she'd wiped down every cupboard, washed every utensil, plate, pot and pan in the kitchen. She'd rearranged the place to suit herself, and began an inventory of supplies. She'd replace any she used before Margaret returned, but it was a waste not to use what was on hand.

She glanced at the clock, shocked to see it was after four. She hadn't even stopped for lunch.

No time for that now—she had a call to make.

She dialed the restaurant and asked to speak to Thomas. The conversation did not go as she wished. He demanded she return by the weekend. One of the other chefs had quit and he needed her expertise.

Cassie tried to explain, but Thomas was in no mood to listen.

"I'll let you know," she said.

"What are you saying? I expect you Friday night."

"And if I don't make it?" she asked, knowing the answer.

"Then you're history and I'll look for a reliable replacement."

"I have always been reliable. Check my record—no sickness, only the vacation I was due and I'm never late."

"I need you here, Cassie. Or someone else." He hung up.

Cassie had a childish urge to throw the phone across the room. She hated ultimatums.

She had until Friday to get back to Boston or lose her job.

Fuming at the unfairness of it all, she prepared herself a sandwich and a glass of iced tea. She wanted to stay, but no one else seemed to want her to stay. Not Stephen, or Thomas, or Matt.

Only Margaret.

That was enough for her.

After she ate her hasty meal, she went to get the paperwork she'd put aside about the private detective. She called the number listed.

The woman who answered didn't even screen the call but put Cassie right through to Roger Lloyd.

"I'm calling on behalf of Madeline Nunes," Cassie said.

"Is there something wrong that she can't call herself?" he asked.

"She's had a stroke. This is Cassie Hodges. I'm trying to find Piper Jeffries and Fiona Hunter. You were looking for them at Margaret's request. Did you find them?"

"My business is with my client. I don't divulge that kind of information to anyone else."

Cassie took a breath, trying to think.

"Margaret's not capable of speech right now or I'm sure she'd tell you it would be all right to give me that information."

"Maybe, but I wouldn't do it over the phone."

"Will you tell me what you've found if I come to New Orleans?"

"Where are you now?"

"In Margaret's house in Bradford. I was one of her foster children."

"Bring documentation so I know who you are. Can't be too careful these days."

Cassie took down directions to his office before she finished the call. She then dialed Edith to see if she would go with Cassie—bringing her power of attorney.

The two of them arranged to meet early the next morning to head off to New Orleans.

Twilight was settling over the town. The birds had quieted down some time ago, but the crickets could be heard beginning their nighttime serenade. Cassie sat on the porch reveling in the coolness of the evening and the sounds she remembered from childhood.

Matt's truck drove up the driveway and stopped near the house. He climbed out and looked around. Cassie had visited Margaret earlier this evening and had hoped to relax a little before going off to bed, but it didn't seem as if that was going to happen now. The faint starlight gave enough illumination for Matt to see her on the porch and he headed her way.

"I thought you were only planning to stay a couple of weeks," he said, climbing the three steps and stopping at the top, a sheet of paper in one hand.

"I said I'd stay however long it took for Margaret to recover."

She didn't want anyone telling her what she should do. She'd had enough of that.

He waved the paper.

"This doesn't sound to me like a few weeks. It sounds more like a permanent business."

"What are you waving around?"

"This! As if you didn't know." He thrust the paper at her.

Cassie grasped it and straightened it out. It was a poster advertising catering—by her!

9

"I didn't print this," Cassie said.

Elegant Events by Cassie was the caption. No Catering Job Too Big or Small, it promised, then gave the phone number at the house.

"Then who did?" Matt asked.

"My guess would be Betsy. She's so enthusiastic about the idea of my doing a few events. But I told her I wouldn't be home for that long. I do have a life in Boston to get back to. Maybe sooner than I'd like."

"Go now," he said. "I'll watch out for Margaret. You don't need to stay. Why disrupt your life there when you don't need to?"

She continued looking at the flier. It wasn't fancy, but elegant and simple. It gave her a thrill. Betsy had really jumped the gun on this, but it was a lovely idea. Maybe she could use the name when she ventured out into a real business.

"Where did you find it?" she asked.

"At the café. They could be plastered over the entire town for all I know."

"I'll call and ask."

Cassie felt a frisson of excitement as she traced the

fancy script Betsy had used. Elegant Events by Cassie. It had a nice ring to it.

The house phone rang.

"Go back to Boston, Cassie," Matt said.

"When I'm ready," she replied, heading inside to answer the phone.

It was Edith Harper.

"I'm afraid I won't be able to go with you tomorrow, Cassie," she said. "I'm feeling poorly and I just don't think I'm up to making the trip to New Orleans. I can give you a letter saying you have my permission to obtain any information the detective has, as well as a copy of Margaret's power of attorney. Will that work?"

"I'm sorry you're not feeling well. But I think that'll work. I'm willing to try, anyway. I'll swing by your house in the morning and get everything. Can I do anything for you tonight?"

Cassie had counted on Edith being her ace in the hole. She hoped having the paperwork would be enough for Roger Lloyd.

"No. I'll just take my medicine and go to bed. Getting old is awful sometimes."

"I'll see you in the morning," Cassie said.

"Who was that?" Matt stood in the doorway.

The light from the hall showed lines around his mouth and face. She couldn't remember him ever looking so tired. Had he had a tough day?

"Edith Harper. She's not feeling well. She was going with me—"

Cassie stopped abruptly. She didn't have to tell him everything.

"Going where?"

"It's not important. Now, if you've said all you have to say, you can leave."

He shook his head.

"I'm waiting to hear more about this catering business you're starting."

"I'm not starting a business per se, just doing a few events for some friends of Betsy's. It's no big deal. But I do need to make some money while I'm here. I transferred all my savings to the bank in town, and I've used most of it for Margaret's loan."

"That flier suggests you *are* staying indefinitely. Why are you still here, Cassie? Why not go home?"

"I'll return to Boston on my own timetable. I need to get to bed, so if you'll kindly shut the door—with you on the other side—I'd appreciate it."

"Don't you want to know what happened when I delivered my payment on Margaret's loan?"

"I assume you paid it and got a receipt. What else would have happened?"

"One of the representatives of the golf club group was at the bank. He offered to cut me into the deal."

"No. What did you say?"

He crossed his arms over his chest.

"Well, now," he drawled, "as Allen pointed out, business is business."

"If you dare go in with those people, I'll make your life so miserable you won't know what hit you," she said, stepping closer. "What did you tell them?"

"What do you think?"

She hesitated a moment, then said slowly, "I believe you told them to forget about it. You're too committed to the idea of this home to let anything get in the way."

"Good guess."

She smiled, feeling relief.

She hadn't seen him in years, but she still knew a lot about Matt Bennett.

"You're sure Margaret likes the idea?"

"Actually, I was surprised at how quickly she warmed up to it. She's from a different generation. I thought she'd view young girls who get pregnant without being married in a negative light. But she's surprisingly sympathetic. And I think she liked the idea of being needed again."

"She's not so young."

"She's not so old, either. Besides, it's not a lot of physical work. As I see it, she'd be more of a house mother."

Cassie smiled.

"If you had suggested that to me a few weeks ago, I would have said Margaret had no motherly traits, but I was wrong. She did her best for us, and it was more than good enough. My values came from Margaret. My manners and social skills, not to mention cooking skills—they all came from her teachings."

Matt nodded.

"I picked up a few things from her myself growing up."

Cassie wondered if they were going to move into a let's-remember-the-good-parts-of-our-childhood mode. She didn't want that. Matt had no reason to like her. He'd said that over and over. And their discussion the other day hadn't seemed to do much to change his mind.

Or had it? She wished she was brave enough to ask.

"Where were you and Edith going tomorrow?" he asked.

The nostalgic mood vanished.

"New Orleans, to see the detective Margaret hired. I can't get any information from him over the phone, so Edith was bringing her power of attorney to see if that would work. Now she's not feeling well and can't go."

Cassie shrugged her shoulders, but apparently didn't hide her disappointment.

"I can give you a ride into New Orleans, if you like," he offered.

She stared at him a moment. What was he up to? She didn't trust Matt a bit.

"Why would you?"

"Why not? I'm going in, save you driving in a strange city. Or do you know New Orleans better than I think?"

She shook her head. She hadn't been to the city since that last day with Travis. She pushed the memory from her mind.

"Okay, I'll be ready in the morning. Eight-thirty okay?"

She had until Friday to find Piper and Fiona, and maybe arrange for Margaret's care. Then she had to return to Boston to keep her job—and her fiancé happy.

Who was keeping Cassie happy? she grumbled, heading up to bed.

Matt stood for a moment on the dark porch after Cassie closed the front door. She didn't appear to be in any hurry to leave Bradford.

He didn't want her around. Seeing her, listening to her, reminded him of the passion they'd shared twelve years ago. He'd loved Cassie with every part of his being. Apparently she'd never loved him as much or she wouldn't have spent the day with Travis.

Unless her story was true. Or she believed it to be true.

Had Dolores lied?

Had Cassie really been hurt and wanted to pay him back?

That was her story. It held a kernel of truth.

He walked down to his truck, looking back at the dark house. Only a dim light showed through the front door glass. Did Cassie leave the light on all night? As if in answer, it flicked out. Her room was in the back, so he wouldn't see that light when it went on.

Climbing into the truck, he started the engine and headed for home. He didn't understand his offer of a ride. If she'd lived in Boston all these years, she could get around New Orleans.

He didn't like admitting to himself that she still

tempted him. Her hair was shorter than she used to wear it, only brushing her shoulders now. It was still glossy and shiny in the light. The yearning to touch the soft strands was almost a physical pain. He used to comb his fingers through her long hair, feeling the silky texture, the warmth near her scalp.

Of course it was usually a prelude to a kiss—something he wouldn't mind repeating.

No one had ever made him feel like Cassie had. Despite the pain of the years, he could remember that. Remember the special bond they'd once shared.

Was that the reason for his offer—to recapture the past?

It'd never happen. Dolores stood firmly in the way.

He frowned. It was easier to keep blaming Cassie than take the blame himself.

Acting on impulse, he turned the truck toward the town cemetery. Dating back to the late 1800s, it was neither scary nor decrepit. Old Hiram McGee kept it immaculate.

When Matt got there, he took a flashlight and headed for the plots he knew so well. One simple stone for his sister. It had been all he and his mother could afford. The one for his mother was a bit more elaborate—placed on her grave three years ago, when he'd had the money.

Cassie had been right. His mother should have been the parent in the family. Instead, she'd drunk herself into a stupor nightly, leaving Dolores and him to fend for themselves.

He'd found something special with Cassie and had turned to her to fill the void left by his dysfunctional family.

But whom had Dolores turned to? His fault had been to leave his sister behind.

In a normal family, it wouldn't have mattered so much. His mother would have taken care of Dolores, and when she was old enough, she'd have found her own way.

But that hadn't been the case and he had to live with all the old baggage.

"What really happened that last day, Dolores?" he asked the silent stone.

Only the crickets responded.

He let his mind drift to the past, thinking about his sister and her many obsessions. If he were honest, he knew her dependence on him wasn't normal. She'd been demanding and whining and had constantly played on his emotions. He'd let her, thinking he was doing his best for her.

Things changed when Dolores started high school. He didn't know why, but she'd become clinging, jealous even of his friends. She'd wanted him all for herself.

Cassie had been right, Dolores hadn't liked any of the girls he'd dated.

"You were my sister, kid," he said softly. "I still miss you. You would have been a knockout, wowing the boys. What would you have been when you grew up?"

He'd never know. At sixteen, Dolores had never voiced any longings for the future. She had been firmly established in the present. Had she known somehow there was no future for her?

When Matt reached home some time later, he called Edith Harper.

"I'm sorry to phone so late," he began.

"I'm up. My arthritis is bothering me something fierce. Can't sleep when that happens."

"Did Cassie tell you I'm taking her into New Orleans tomorrow?"

"No. I'm glad she has someone to go with her. I told her I couldn't make it."

"You have Margaret's power of attorney, right?" Matt asked.

"Yes. Cassie figured we needed it to get the information from the private detective."

"I'll swing by in the morning and pick it up, and a note from you giving us permission to receive the information on your behalf."

"You'll have to write it," Edith said. "I'll sign it, but that's about as much as my hands will allow."

"Deal. See you in the morning," Matt said. "Sometime after eight. Do you know anything about this guy?"

"No. Cassie asked me that, too. I knew Margaret had consulted a private detective, but not who he was or the outcome. You know how closed-mouthed she can be. When she first heard from Cassie a couple of years ago, she said it was past time to find her girls. I guess that's what the loan and all was about. But she never said she'd heard from any of them except Cassie."

"Let's hope we learn more tomorrow," Matt said.

At eight-thirty the next morning, Matt pulled his car into the crushed-shell driveway of Bradford Hall. He stopped right behind Cassie's rental and climbed out. She should be ready to leave in a few minutes, so he leaned against his car and waited.

Cassie puzzled him. She'd virtually ignored Margaret, Bradford and everyone connected with the place for a decade. Then out of the blue a couple of years ago, she'd contacted Margaret. When she'd found out Margaret was ill, she'd flown down immediately. Why?

And why the push to find Piper and Fiona after all this time?. If they'd wanted to reconnect, they could have contacted Margaret as Cassie had done. Was something more going on? Had she come back to ingratiate herself in Margaret's good graces as he'd suggested when she'd first shown up?

He heard the back door open and looked up. She came down the short flight of stairs and started toward him. She was wearing a suit and high heels, and carried a tote bag. When she spotted him, she hesitated only a moment, then lifted her head higher and continued walking.

"Morning," he said easily.

"Good morning. I called Edith. She said you already arranged to stop by to get the papers we'll need."

"I did. Picked them up on my way here. Also some coffee. Hop in."

Cassie got into the car. Spotting the envelope from Edith, she took it and tucked it safely in her tote. She fastened her seat belt and graciously accepted the cup of coffee he offered when he climbed in behind the wheel.

As he pulled away from the house, he said, "I need an address."

She gave it to him.

They were ten minutes into the drive before Matt spoke again. He didn't like being the one to break the silence, but she was driving him crazy.

"What's the point in finding the others?" he asked.

"To connect," she said, sipping the last of her coffee.

"Not for some idea of an inheritance?"

She frowned and shook her head.

"We were as close as sisters. They were my best friends for all the years I was growing up. I want to know what happened to them. What if one of them needs help? Or just needs a friend?"

"They could have made the effort to find you."

"Maybe they did. Margaret didn't know where I had gone. Until I contacted her, she couldn't have passed on my address. I want to do this. You don't have to understand."

"I think I do."

"What do you mean?"

"You're looking for what you lost—your family," he said.

Cassie caught her breath, but didn't say anything.

"Right?" he probed.

"Maybe," she admitted a moment later.

"Three teenagers who didn't have anyone else. You told me how you became blood sisters. You probably want to share your good news with them."

"What news?"

"About your engagement." Matt glanced at her, but he couldn't read her expression.

"I guess," she said.

"You guess? I'd figure you couldn't wait to get home—"

He stopped, thinking back over the last few days.

"You don't consider Boston your home," he said slowly.

"What are you talking about?" she asked.

"I've heard you say you're going home when you leave the hospital and return to Bradford Hall, but whenever you talk about going back north, you always say, going back to Boston, not going home."

"You're crazy. Of course Boston is my home. It's where I live."

"There's a difference. Where you live isn't necessarily home."

"Is Bradford home to you, even though you live in New Orleans these days?" she asked.

"It'll always be my hometown."

"It's mine, too."

"Are you looking for a home, Cassie? Is that what all this is about?"

"I have a perfectly good apartment in Boston. Don't try to psych me out. I'm not some needy girl you have to rescue."

"You never were."

She didn't respond. When he looked at her, she was fighting tears. That stopped him cold. He looked for a place to pull over. He couldn't concentrate on driving and find out what was going on with her at the same time.

"What did I say?" he asked.

Spotting a driveway, he swerved in and stopped.

"Why are you stopping?"

"I want to know what's wrong. Are you crying?"

"I'm not crying," she said fiercely.

"No? Sure looks that way."

She stared out the side window, her body held tightly, as if she was afraid if she relaxed, she'd collapse.

"Cassie?"

He reached for her chin, turning her face to his. Tears shimmered on her lashes.

"Dolores said I was needy and that you were such a knight in shining armor you had to rescue every female in sight. She said you didn't really care for me, you just wanted to play hero. Your comment brought it all back. I was so hurt. Why is it things that happen when we're teenagers have the power to wound so deeply?"

"We only get perspective as we age, I guess. Dolores was wrong. I did care. It wasn't about rescuing anyone. You gave me something I needed, as well. My sister had problems. I knew that, even when I tried to deny it. I'm sorry she was so awful to you."

Cassie jerked her chin away from his touch.

"She wasn't the only one."

Matt leaned back in his seat. He knew she meant his accusations after his sister had died. He still wasn't one-hundred-percent convinced Cassie couldn't have done something to prevent Dolores's death, but he hadn't a clue what that might have been.

As time went on, the anger he'd once felt was fading. She had explained. He believed her. He wished things could be different, but the damage was done.

The one thing that hadn't changed was the attraction he still felt for her.

Scowling, he started driving again. He was not going to get sucked into some kind of relationship that was destined to go nowhere. She was engaged, her life planned out. He had his own goals. All they shared were memories of a happier time.

The only sound for the rest of the drive into the Crescent City was soft jazz playing on the radio.

Cassie didn't want to admit Matt was right, but he sure gave her food for thought. Did she regard Boston as home? She'd lived there for the last several years. She'd gone to culinary school there, found her first chef's job, rented an apartment near Harvard, then had moved to her current one when her salary had increased.

Of course Boston was home.

Not like Bradford, though.

In Massachusetts she had a limited circle of friends. Of her own doing. She was cautious of making close ties after all her childhood bonds had been ripped apart.

And the saying was true: There were no friends like old friends. She and Betsy had reconnected immediately. She knew she and Piper and Fiona would as well.

She admitted she wasn't in a hurry to return to Boston.

She didn't even miss Stephen.

That thought shocked her. She was planning to marry the man, yet she didn't miss him when they were apart?

Maybe she needed to rethink that. She'd said yes when he'd proposed, but had she merely longed to belong again? To have a family, to know she had a place in the world?

She adored Adele. Loved the interplay between her and Stephen. She so wanted to be included, not forever on the outside looking in. Wasn't that enough of a reason for marriage?

Stephen loved her. Cassie loved him and his mother. It would work. She could make it work.

Yet, what if there was more? What if she could recapture the wild passion she had once felt for another man? Stephen was loving, but he didn't inspire wild passion. No one ever had except the man next to her.

Which had made the break all the harder when it had come.

She shivered, not wanting to remember how painful that had been. She had a life now that suited her. Best not to rock the boat and risk ending up alone again.

"So what do you plan to do if you find Fiona and Piper?" Matt asked as the miles sped by.

"Contact them. Tell them about Margaret. See what they've been doing over the last twelve years. Do you think Margaret *could* have located them?"

"From that scrapbook you found on Piper, my guess is Margaret probably knows where she is. But you didn't find anything about Fiona."

"No."

Cassie was pinning her hopes on the detective. What if he had located her foster sisters? Excitement began to build the closer they came to New Orleans.

When Matt stopped in front of a high-rise office building some time later, Cassie felt a slight letdown. She'd expected an old brick building, slightly shabby and neglected. This glass-and-steel edifice was modern and bland. What kind of agency had Margaret contacted?

They found out a few moments later when they opened the door on the eighth floor to a reception area that could have been in any office in America. Cream-colored walls, dark-gray carpet and standard oak furniture gave the place a staid, conservative feeling.

"I have an appointment with Mr. Lloyd," Cassie

said to the receptionist, a middle-aged woman with a friendly smile.

"He's ready to see you," she said, rising to show Cassie and Matt into another office.

When Cassie entered, Roger Lloyd stood and offered his hand. He was of medium height and build, with a thick head of salt-and-pepper hair—not at all the way Cassie had imagined a private detective would look.

She introduced herself and Matt, then glanced around the office as they were invited to sit in the visitor chairs. Computers, faxes and printers lined one wall. Another had a row of file cabinets. The view from the window overlooked New Orleans with a glimpse of the river to the right.

Cassie turned back to Roger Lloyd and reached into her purse for the papers Edith had sent.

Once formalities were dealt with, Roger straightened the two folders in front of him. One was thick and bulging. The other was thinner.

"I'll tell you what I related to Miss Nunes." He opened the thin file. "We've had no luck in locating Fiona Hunter. She ran away from the foster home she was sent to twelve years ago and was never heard from again. Sad to say, there wasn't as much of an effort to locate her at the time as there should have been. We have no idea where she went, or even if she's still alive."

"The sheriff in Bradford said he'd check driver's licenses in other states, if she's still using her maiden name," Cassie told him.

"Miss Nunes first contacted us about two years ago. Running a check of driver's licenses was one of the first things we did, that and marriage and death records. The good news is we never did find a death record under that name. The bad news is we never found *anything* connected to Fiona Hunter. She could have changed her name when she ran away. We even checked the Jane Doe deaths in Mississippi and neighboring states from that time. Nothing."

Cassie's excitement faded. She had had such hopes.

"What about Piper?"

"Now, she was difficult to trace, as well."

Closing the file, he put it to one side and opened the thick folder.

"It turns out that Piper Jeffries married and divorced before she was twenty, moved to New York, married again and moved to Paris. She's living there now. We don't often get international cases."

Cassie brought out the scrapbook from the tote bag and laid it on the desk.

"I found this in Margaret's things. It looks as if Piper's a model in France. I can't read the articles, but the photograph in one clipping shows her on a runway."

"Monique is the name she uses there. No last name professionally. She's quite the rage in Europe, I understand. We contacted a clipping service in Paris when we located her and they sent all those articles. I gave them to my client, of course, along with the address one of our operatives located for us."

"Can you read them?"

"No, I don't understand French. Didn't Miss Nunes have them translated?"

"If she did, I don't know about it. She can't talk. The stroke was quite serious and it looks as if recovery is going to be slow."

He nodded.

"I gave contact information to Miss Nunes once I received it from our counterpart in Paris. I can't tell you if she contacted Monique or not."

"I didn't find anything when I went through her papers," Cassie murmured, studying the foreign newspaper clippings. "I'd appreciate getting that info. I'll try to contact her myself. She'll want to know about Margaret's condition."

Roger Lloyd wrote out the address and phone number from the information in the file and slid the paper across the desk to Cassie.

"Are you continuing your search for Fiona?" Matt asked.

Cassie looked at him. She'd almost forgotten he was there.

"We have requests out," the P.I. told him. "Periodically we reissue them. So far in the two years we've been working on this case, we've had no response. The case remains active, if that's what you're asking, but I don't hold out much hope of anything turning up at this stage."

"Maybe we could advertise in newspapers for her," Cassie said.

Roger nodded.

"Which cities were you thinking of? Do you have any idea where she might have run off to as a teenager?"

Cassie shook her head. "I would have thought she'd return to Bradford. But maybe not. She was really angry no one believed her when she recanted and said Margaret had *not* beaten her. If she could have proved it, Fiona would have tried. She was stubborn to a fault and had an amazing sense of justice. Of course, she had a lot of anger, as well. I guess in a way we all did."

Roger nodded. "If you think of anything that would help us in our pursuit, we would act on it immediately. Unfortunately, I've exhausted my usual channels, and even a few extraordinary ones. It could be Fiona is dead."

Cassie wouldn't accept that. Fiona was too much a fighter to end up dead at a young age.

"Thank you, Mr. Lloyd, for all your help. If you do find Fiona, please let us know right away."

"I will. You're staying at Miss Nunes's home?"

Cassie nodded.

"It was my home as a child. I'll be there until Margaret doesn't need me any longer."

"She's lucky to have you," he said.

He bid them goodbye, and Cassie and Matt left, Cassie clutching the precious contact information for Piper.

"I want to call her right away," she said, fishing in her purse for her cell phone.

"Wait until you get to the car," Matt suggested. "You'll have more privacy."

Cassie agreed impatiently. She couldn't wait to call.

"There's a time difference of how many hours?" she asked. "I don't mind waking her up in the middle of the night, but I hope she's not at work."

"It's late afternoon there. She might be at work, or home. I'm betting a busy model has an answering machine," Matt said as they reached his car.

As soon as they were inside, Cassie began dialing.

"It's ringing," she cried.

After the fourth ring it switched to voice mail. Tears pricked Cassie's eyes as she heard Piper's voice for the first time in a dozen years. The message was in French, but Cassie knew that voice.

"Piper, it's Cassie. I'm in Mississippi. Call me at Margaret's place, please. I need to talk to you. You remember the number, I'm sure, but just in case—" Cassie rapidly recited the house's phone number, then gave Piper the one for her own cell.

"Call me right away."

10

Ending the call, Cassie felt let down. "No answer."

"She'll call you as soon as she gets in," Matt assured her.

He turned slightly in his seat, resting his arm along the back.

"I have to stop at the job site for a few minutes. Do you want to go with me?"

She looked at him.

"Actually, you can drop me off near a bus or trolley line. I want to go to Tulane University and see if someone there will translate these articles for me."

"I thought you were going to check at the high school."

"I considered it," she said, "but thought I'd better protect Margaret's privacy. I have no idea what these articles will say, and the less Bradford's grapevine knows, the better for all of us."

"I'll take you there now."

"I can manage on my own, if you have places to go," she said.

"No trouble. I brought you, I'll chauffeur you around."

"Thank you," she replied stiffly. "I'd like to see your job site after the university."

As they drove through the streets of the old city, Cassie looked around with interest. The last time she'd been in New Orleans had been the day she and Travis had skipped school for a wild adventure. They'd walked along the banks of the river, Travis trying to act like a big stud. She remembered fighting him off all day wishing he had been Matt instead.

At the university, they found an assistant professor of French in her office. She took the articles and scanned a few, smiling as she read.

"Fascinating. Your friend is a model. These articles talk about some of the fashion houses she's worked for. And she's been on the cover of *Elle* and another French magazine. Do you want a literal translation?"

"If you wouldn't mind," Cassie said. "I can't believe it. I always knew Piper was pretty, and she loved fussing with makeup and hair color, but she's really cashed in on her looks and made it to the top."

"I wonder how she ended up in France," Matt said.

"I don't have time right now to translate all the articles," the professor told them, "but I could make an assignment of this for my beginning class. I'll have each student translate one article completely. I could probably return them to you in a few days."

"That would be wonderful," Cassie said. "I appreciate your giving me the gist of them today."

"My pleasure. It'll be a fun project for my students—and show them some of the advantages of knowing another language and how they can actually use it in practical situations."

Leaving the building that housed the French department some time later, Cassie looked around at the campus.

"It's pretty. Did you like going here?"

"Yes," Matt answered.

"Would you care to elaborate?" she said, wishing to know more about Matt.

As teenagers they'd spent hours talking about the future. It had turned out so differently from what she'd once expected.

"Tulane's a great school. I wasn't able to participate in a lot of the social activities since I was working my way through, and every moment I wasn't studying, I was out hustling money. But overall my memories are good. Where did you go after high school?"

"I tried college in Jackson for a semester, but didn't like it. My foster family invited me to go with them when Al got transferred to Boston. I'd been trying to earn a living as a cook. I saw the culinary school there and knew I'd need more training, so I applied and was accepted. I love my work. It's creative, and satisfying—especially when customers send word back they loved a meal."

"What happened to those foster parents?"

"We still keep in touch. They live in L.A. now. I saw them a couple of years ago when I went to California for my vacation. They're always interested in what I'm doing."

"But it's not the same as with Margaret."

She shook her head.

"So your cooking now has you venturing into catering."

"I've been thinking about it for a while. It'd give me lots more creative freedom. I could pick and choose what events to cook for, how large a crowd, what to include on the menu. And keep my own hours. I don't usually get home until late at night, and weekends are the busiest times at the restaurant."

"I'd think weekends would also be busy in the catering business. That's when most people have parties."

"True, but I could plan ahead to take off a Saturday or Sunday. I don't know, somehow it seems like the perfect solution—especially since I'd be my own boss. You're in charge of your own company, don't you like that?"

"I do. I worked construction through school, learned all I could from some of the best men in the business. I saw different aspects that I felt I could improve. I'm not sure I've done that, but as you say, I'm in charge. If anything goes wrong, it's my responsibility since I'm the boss."

"Do things go wrong?"

"What kind of work doesn't have snafus?"

They reached the car and were soon on the road again.

"This site we're going to visit is behind schedule. I want to double check we're doing all we can to catch up. I hate being late."

"What kind of project?" Cassie asked.

She was enjoying this tentative truce they seemed to have reached, though she wished she knew if he still believed she'd contributed to Dolores's death.

"Luxury apartment complex. It's on the outskirts of an old section of the Quarter. Twenty-four apartments in a lush environment. Expensive as all get out, but the developer's already rented almost every unit, and they're asking a small fortune. It's centrally located, elegant, with all the amenities we could install. I wouldn't mind living in a unit myself, but the rent is exorbitant."

"Is that what your company does, build apartment buildings?"

"Not as a rule. I specialize more in single-family dwellings. We build duplexes sometimes. This is only my second multi-dwelling apartment building, and it's much larger than the first one. Mike McIver is the driving force behind the project."

"Do you ever regret not being an architect?"

"No. An engineering degree might have come in handy, but I don't do too badly. And I love construction, though it's a precarious business. I have several men who work for me, so I'm responsible for their salaries as well as my own. Insurance costs have skyrocketed recently, and all the regulations the parish puts down since Katrina drive me crazy. Not enough to quit and try something else, however."

When they reached the construction site, Matt asked her to wait in the car while he headed off to talk to his crew.

The building looked complete to Cassie. Red brick walls, dark-green trim. The landscape was spectacular. Mature trees dotted the grounds, with newly planted ones nearby. The flowers spilling from the circular beds were bright reds, blues and yellows. She wanted to get out and wander around, but not knowing how long Matt would be, she remained where she was.

She'd done what she wanted in New Orleans. She was ready to return home.

There was that word again. *Home.*

Was Bradford really home? What did that do to all her plans for a life in Boston? Could she scrap them and start over—this time back in Mississippi? When she'd left years ago, she'd thought she'd never come back. Now that she was here, she wondered if she could leave.

What was she going to do about Stephen? She closed her eyes, thinking about him. He was attentive and always concerned about her. She opened her eyes and frowned.

But he didn't share a lot of things. They didn't like the same movies. Didn't find humor in the same situations. And sometimes she felt excluded when he spoke of friends or events she wasn't familiar with.

But wouldn't that change over time? Once they lived together, they'd grow closer. And she definitely had no doubts about his mother.

That thought surprised her. Was she searching for a mother figure? She didn't need one, She had Margaret.

Being back in Bradford had shown her clearly that she had a mother. She had memories of her childhood. She had a family she could fall back on—if she could find them.

She checked her phone. It was on. No messages. Where was Piper?

When Matt returned, he asked her if she wanted to get something to eat before they returned to Bradford.

"I am hungry," she said, struck by the bitter sweetness of being with him. Once her world had revolved around him, but now she walked warily. She couldn't deny the pull of attraction. Maybe she was playing with fire, but she couldn't resist.

"Let's find some fabulous place in the French Quarter and splurge like tourists," she suggested. "I want to try something new."

"You mean, check out the menu to get ideas for your own," he commented dryly.

She laughed. He'd always read her better than Stephen had.

She wouldn't think about that right now. She would simply enjoy the afternoon.

On the drive back to Bradford, Matt glanced over at Cassie. She'd fallen asleep. Some company he was proving to be. He couldn't even keep her alert enough to talk.

Not that he could think of anything more to talk about. He wanted to know everything she'd done since he'd last seen her, but asking questions like that could lead to speculation about the future. She was engaged to a nice man—her own words. Her future was in Boston.

What did he want, for her to change her mind and move back to Bradford permanently? But he didn't live in their hometown anymore.

Would she consider moving to New Orleans?

Dumb idea. Yet he couldn't help thinking how right the day had felt. They'd always been good together, knowing what the other was thinking, how to make each other laugh.

Matt wondered how different their lives would be if Dolores hadn't intervened. Was he ever going to be emotionally free of the past? Had his sister known what she would consign him to with her irresponsible actions? Would she have cared?

When he reached Bradford, Matt was reluctant to drive Cassie to Margaret's. Instead he turned in at the hospital. She stirred.

"We're home?" she asked sleepily.

Matt felt a reaction down to his toes. He wanted to brush back that glossy hair and kiss her fully awake. Take her to his place and make love to her until dawn.

The thought shocked him. He'd gotten over Cassie years ago. This was lust, pure and simple. Or, maybe not so pure. But he was strong enough to resist.

"We're at the hospital. I thought you'd want to tell Margaret how today went and see how she's doing."

"I do."

She sat up and fussed with her hair for a moment. Matt clenched the steering wheel tightly to keep from reaching out to help. When she looked at him, he did his best to keep his expression from giving away any of his feelings.

"Are you coming up?"

"I'll wait here. When you're done, I'll drive you home."

"If you have things to do, I can walk. It's not far and it's a lot more pleasant in the evening hours than in the heat of the day."

"I'll take you home," he repeated.

"Then I'll keep the visit short."

She opened the door and soon was inside the hospital.

Cassie found Margaret awake. Sitting beside the bed, she began to tell her about the day in New Orleans. When she got to the part about contacting the detective, Margaret became agitated. She tried to talk, but the words were unintelligible.

Cassie quickly changed the subject without mentioning she'd already tried to contact Piper. She hadn't expected Margaret to be so upset.

Instead she talked about spending the day with Matt. The older woman gradually calmed down as Cassie described the apartment complex and their lunch. She knew she was making it seem almost as if they were friends again. Margaret hadn't approved of Cassie spending so much time with Matt when she was in high school, but maybe she viewed things differently now.

When the visit was over, Cassie returned to the

parking lot to find Matt where she'd left him. She got into the car.

"Margaret didn't take it well that I went to the detective's," she said. "She got so upset I thought the nurse might come over and ask me to leave. Why do you suppose she wouldn't want me to continue the search?"

"I have no idea."

He started the car and headed for Margaret's house.

"I checked my phone but Piper still hasn't called."

"Maybe she's away for a few days," he said.

"Or maybe she doesn't want to have anything to do with us," Cassie said slowly.

She'd expected Piper and Fiona to jump at the chance to reconnect.

"Why would you say that?" Matt asked.

"All three of us know where Margaret lives. Piper could have contacted her. I did. Maybe I'm wrong in thinking they'd want to reconnect."

"Give her some time. If she doesn't call you by the end of the week, then maybe you're right and she isn't interested. You don't know what she's doing these days."

He pulled up in front of the house.

"Want me to go in with you to make sure everything is secure?" he asked.

She shook her head. "There's no need."

She climbed out and headed for the back door.

She heard Matt get out.

"Cassie," he called.

Hesitating a moment, she turned around.

"Evelyn told me a year or so after Dolores's death that Dolores had told her I was still interested. That I was playing hard to get and trying to make her jealous by going out with you. The kiss you saw that day—it didn't mean what you thought. Evelyn was really testing the waters to see if Dolores was right."

Cassie stared at him. She remembered how crushed she'd felt when she'd seen Matt and Evelyn kissing.

Dolores again.

Instead of confronting Matt about it, instead of trusting him, Cassie had planned revenge by going out with Travis.

"I've been thinking about what you said. Dolores was my sister. I loved her. But I realize now she *was* manipulative and selfish and unbalanced." He hesitated a minute, then continued. "I think I would have thought the same as you did—that she was blowing smoke again."

For a long moment Cassie remained silent, unsure how she felt. Vindicated. Relieved. Hopeful. Sad. Instead of resolving the issue, she felt confused, unsure how to react.

"Thanks for telling me," she said.

With that, she went into the house.

Matt stood beside the truck for a moment longer until he saw the lights go on, then, settling behind the wheel, he headed for home.

He was a fair man. He'd blamed her for years. But he didn't anymore. It was only right to tell her. She could go back to Boston knowing he no longer hated her.

Driving through the darkened streets, he wondered how their future would have unfolded had his sister not wreaked such havoc.

Remembering their recent kiss, Matt wasn't entirely sure he knew the end of their story.

The next morning Cassie was up early. She hadn't told anyone of her plan, but she was returning her rental car and getting a van. She'd need the extra space. Then she planned to stop at Mabel Truscott's to review the menu for her niece's luncheon, and check out what serving pieces she might need. A shopping expedition for fresh produce would finish out her day.

Feeling upbeat, Cassie headed for the rental car agency at the New Orleans airport, her head full of plans.

Her cell phone rang halfway there.

"Hello?" she answered.

"Hi, sweetheart. It's me."

"Hi."

She couldn't keep the disappointment from her voice. If she'd been able to check who was calling, she'd have seen Stephen's number. She'd hoped for a split second it would be Piper.

"Expecting someone else?" he asked.

"Yesterday I got a phone number for Piper. I called and left her a message. She's living in Paris."

She'd told Stephen about Fiona and Piper months ago after they'd started getting serious. He hadn't been too interested, saying it was years since she'd seen them. Granted, it had been a long time since they'd had contact, but that didn't erase the ties.

"I hate to sound like a broken record, but when are you coming home? The Phillips have invited us to join them at that new play I wanted to see. It's a week from Friday. You will be back by then, won't you? Shall I accept for us both?"

"Stephen, this isn't a good time to talk," she said, stalling. "I'm driving on a freeway and there's a lot of traffic."

She wasn't sure when she was returning. Or even if she wanted to go back to Boston.

The realization shocked her and she forced herself to concentrate on driving. She'd deal with decisions about her future later.

"When would be a good time?"

The edge in his voice was hard to miss.

"Later. I'll call you later."

Darn it, she thought as she hung up. He was pressuring her and she didn't like it. If he wanted to go to the play with the Phillips, then he should go. Even if she were home by then, she'd probably have to work. She never begrudged him spending time with his friends. She wasn't all that sure she wanted to see the play anyway. She liked action-adventure movies, not esoteric theater productions that addressed the dark side of humanity.

She had to make up her mind about what she wanted.

And how she felt about Stephen. She owed him some kind of explanation. She just wasn't sure what it would be yet.

By early evening, Cassie was dead tired. She rented a panel van that could carry everything she needed for the scheduled catering events. The weekly cost was more than the rental car, but it was only temporary.

Mabel Truscott had been delighted with the proposed menu, and had shown Cassie all her serving plates and silverware. There were only a few items she'd need to buy herself for the luncheon.

Not a problem if she was starting up a business in Mississippi. Even if she ventured into catering in Massachusetts, she could take the new items she'd bought back with her.

She put the groceries away, then prepared a cup of tea and sat in the kitchen, reviewing the recipes she'd selected and jotting notes on the side. She needed to call Betsy and make sure—

Her phone rang again.

"Hello, dear. It's Adele. Is this a bad time to call?"

"Hi, Adele. Now is fine. I'm always glad to hear from you. What's up?"

"I haven't talked to you in several days so I thought

I'd call to see how you're doing. How is Margaret?"

"Doing better every day. I think the doctor is planning to move her out of of ICU soon. She's started therapy, but I don't see any change in her ability to sit up on her own or talk."

"And you? What are you up to?"

"I've been going through a lot of Margaret's papers and things, reminiscing a lot. I'm also planning to do some catering while I'm here."

What had Stephen told his mother?

"How exciting. What are you doing exactly?"

"It started last week when my friend Betsy needed help. I catered a bridge club party at the last minute. Several of the women there liked the luncheon so much, they asked if I'd do something for them."

"I thought you liked the restaurant end of things," Adele said.

"I do. But I've considered going into business for myself for some time now."

"A perfect solution to the work situation when you and Stephen marry. You can set your own hours and coordinate schedules better."

"Exactly. I'd still have to work some evenings, since a lot of functions are for dinners or evening receptions. But if we made plans ahead of time for a weekend, I could keep it open and not schedule anything."

It would work, though Cassie thought it a bit one-sided. It seemed more and more of her time was being arranged to suit Stephen's schedule.

"You haven't overextended yourself, have you?"

Adele asked. "How much longer will you be in Mississippi?"

"I'm not sure how long I'll stay. I have committed to a couple of events two weeks away. But it's only to fill in the time until Margaret can leave the hospital. I want to be here for her."

She didn't mention the ultimatum her boss had given her. Had she made up her mind not to return by Friday?

What would happen if she lost her job?

"Another two weeks. Dear me. I wish you would reconsider. Spring is bursting out everywhere and we were planning another weekend at the Cape. It's so much nicer there before the summer crowd arrives. I have an idea. Why don't you see if Stephen can arrange for Margaret to be brought to a convalescent hospital up here? That way you'd be back home and still able to visit her."

Cassie was taken aback. The expense would be enormous. Not that it would be too much for the Cabots, she imagined, though Stephen's financial status was something the two of them had never discussed.

How could she know so little about the man she'd agreed to marry?

"I don't know. Margaret's always lived here. Her friends are here. Taking her away might not be good for recovery."

"Just a thought. Think on it and we'll see what we can come up with from our end. We both miss you."

"I miss you, Adele. But this is important to me. I need to be near her."

"I understand, dear. I must run. Call me in another day or two and let me know about bringing Margaret up here."

Cassie's tea was cold. She pushed it away, frowning. What had that been about? Move Margaret to Boston? The woman would probably suffer a setback if Cassie even suggested it.

The one time Cassie had asked Margaret to visit, she had refused in no uncertain terms.

Yet for a moment, Cassie felt a warmth infusing her. Adele and Stephen cared for her and were concerned about her.

Cassie took the cup and saucer to the sink, dumping the tepid tea. She loved Stephen. And she loved Adele. They were going to be her family once she made up her mind when she wanted to get married.

How hard could that be? She should set the date. Tell Stephen she'd marry him as soon as Margaret was well.

Feeling overwhelmed, Cassie hurried away from the bright lights of the kitchen and out into the soft evening air. But she couldn't run from her thoughts. She had to decide what she wanted.

"It's not easy," she said to the evening stars. "I thought I had everything I wanted, but coming back is changing how I feel about things. What am I going to do?"

The stars remained silent. Cassie sighed and sat on

the porch steps. She was thrilled to have these catering events.

Oddly enough, she didn't miss the restaurant kitchen at all. How fickle was that? Only a few years ago she'd been so delighted to be hired there, and even more pleased when she moved up in the hierarchy. Now she felt constrained.

She knew she could do well in catering. If Betsy was committed to joining forces, she could take on the decorating and serving or coordinate hired help to work the larger events.

It was late by the time Cassie rose to go back inside. She had some hard decisions to make. Would starting her own business be as promising in Boston as here in Bradford? Would there be greater scope in the city, or would she find it more difficult starting out on her own without an established clientele?

The biggest decision, of course, was what to do about Stephen.

11

Friday afternoon Matt bagged up the last of his mother's clothes and carried them to the truck. Six bags to donate to the church rummage sale. He'd had her onetime friend Sadie Connors help him sort through the things. It had been ten years since she'd died, long past time to clear the room.

Sadie had an eye for what might bring the church some money and what was just rubbish. She'd sorted with Matt, reminiscing about his mother when they'd been girls together. Her memories were different from his. Sadie seemed to gloss over the breakup of his parents' marriage and his mother's alcoholism. That was primarily what Matt remembered.

He'd already carted off the rejects, and Sadie had finished washing the things for the church. Now that he'd dealt with the clothes, he turned to some of the other items in the bedroom.

He didn't remember his mother being attached to much of anything—except the bottle. The few knickknacks around the room held no sentimental meaning for him. He'd keep the furnishings, but not the linens. It would be easier to rent the place furnished than not.

When the room was as bare as a cheap motel, he stood in the doorway surveying it. Paint was called for. New curtains in the windows and new bedding. A rug on the hardwood floor would soften the austerity. Would the next person who occupied this house be happier than his mother had been?

Taking a break, he headed for the church. The annual rummage sale was in two weeks so his timing was good.

Sadie met him at the door.

"We sure do appreciate this, Matt. I know it's hard to part with your mother's things, but there will be a lot of women able to use them. That has to give you comfort."

"I'll be glad the things get used."

He felt like a hypocrite. He hadn't been attached to the items, just too caught up in other areas of life to bother dismantling the house and getting rid of things no longer needed.

But it was past time. He still hadn't decided whether to sell the place or rent it, but either way, once the deal with Margaret's place was complete, he didn't plan to return to Bradford if he could help it.

There were still several rooms to go through. Then he needed to paint and update the bathroom fixtures. It would be summer at least before the house would be ready for showing to prospective tenants or buyers.

He planned to combine his order for supplies along with the one he'd drawn up for Bradford Hall. Save on costs through economy of scale.

Swinging by Edith's place, he went in to discuss the situation with her. If she gave the go-ahead, he could continue with plans for the renovation of Margaret's house and not wait until Margaret was one hundred percent again.

An hour later, Matt turned into the driveway leading up to Bradford Hall. He hoped Cassie was home and amenable to letting him inside to finish estimates on the first phase of the project.

The McIver job was winding down, and his crew would be ready to start in less than a week. Supplies needed to be ordered and work schedules set. He had a short window of opportunity before his next project in New Orleans was scheduled to start. At least Edith had agreed to proceed. He didn't anticipate any problem from Cassie.

As soon as he parked, he went to the back door and knocked.

"Come in," Cassie yelled.

Entering the kitchen, he looked around at a scene of utter chaos. Pans were on the counter, two bowls were soaking in the sink. The table had been pulled into the middle of the room and Cassie was busy working with chocolate icing and thin slabs of cake. She stood barefoot in shorts and a sleeveless top. There was flour down the left side of her clothes and a dab of chocolate near her waist.

She glanced at him then went immediately back to work.

"What do you want?" she asked.

"To take some measurements of the house."

She looked up, frowning.

"For the group home? Can you get started already?"

"We stopped the foreclosure. Edith gave the go-ahead on Margaret's behalf. I'll drop by the hospital later and let Margaret know we're moving ahead. I have another project scheduled in New Orleans starting in June, so that gives us about six weeks to get this job done before my crew is tied up again."

"You're not touching the kitchen," she said, spreading a thin layer of frosting on the sheet of cake. "I need it for my work."

"Did the cake fall?" he asked, thinking it wasn't as high as most cakes he'd seen.

She shook her head. "I'm trying a new torte recipe. Thin layer of cake, thin layer of chocolate, alternating. I didn't specialize in pastries or desserts, so I need to make sure I know what I'm doing before going on an assignment."

"Should I volunteer to taste test?" he asked.

Her expression fascinated him. She was studying her work as critically as he did his, looking for any flaws or imperfections.

She smiled as she continued layering the torte.

"I might let you. It'll be great, you know."

Matt didn't doubt it. He had to almost force his gaze from her.

"I'll get started at the front of the house. Then the bedrooms."

"Whatever. Do you need any help holding the tape measure?"

"No."

Heading toward the front, Matt checked the notes he'd already made for the renovations. Before Margaret's stroke, the two of them had spent several days discussing proposed changes, keeping them to a minimum for the sake of cost and time. He knew what Margaret expected and he planned to deliver.

Sometime later he moved on to the upper floors. The old house had more bedrooms than Margaret or her father had ever used. The sole bathroom on the second floor would not be enough. Their budget wouldn't allow for a bathroom in every room, but where possible, he wanted two bedrooms to share one. New plumbing would be the largest single expense.

Matt was almost finished when he heard Cassie calling.

He went to the top of the stairs.

"What?" he said.

"Torte's ready and I want a piece, too. Come and test it."

He joined her in the kitchen a moment later. The place was still a jumble, totally unlike the Cassie he remembered. In the center of the table sat the torte. Six inches high, covered in hard chocolate with chocolate roses and embellishments on top, it was a work of art.

"That's too pretty to cut," he said.

She smiled in delight. Matt felt as if she'd slugged

him. He wanted to stare at her beautiful face, keep that smile in place and bask in its warmth.

"Now, if it just tastes as good. Betsy's coming over later to test it out. I think it does look good. Not bad for a first attempt without a lot of the right utensils. I need to get some proper baking pans and things."

She reached for a knife.

"I've been making lists like crazy. It's one thing to dream about opening a business, but something else to actually do it. There's so much more to it than I realized."

"Too much?" he asked, pulling out a chair and sitting at the end of the table.

He pushed away the crumpled waxed paper and dirty mixing bowl to clear a space.

"Sorry about the mess," she said, placing a plate with a generous slice of torte in front of him. "I need a scullery maid."

Stepping back, she watched him closely.

Matt took the fork, cut into the concoction and slowly studied it before lifting a bite to his mouth.

The tastes exploded on his tongue. Chocolate and almond. The cake was fresh and moist, and the rich chocolate icing melted in his mouth.

"Delicious," he said.

He couldn't remember when he'd had something so good.

Cassie smiled again, but Matt was ready for it this time. He quickly looked back at his slice of cake and scooped up another bite.

"And the decorations look all right?" she asked.

"Elegant."

"That's what Betsy insists on calling our company, Elegant Events by Cassie."

"You two are partners?" he asked.

Where did Boston and the fiancé fit into all this?

"Matt, this is only temporary. I'm only here until Margaret no longer needs me. Betsy's helping me with the few events I've committed to, and I only agreed to do them because she *is* helping. Yesterday we had the engagement luncheon for Mabel Truscott's niece. It went well, but without Betsy, I'd have fallen flat on my face."

Cassie cut herself a slice of the torte and went around to sit on the right of Matt, scooting away the mess. She took a bite.

"Umm. I love chocolate. I wanted to have this for tomorrow's dinner. It's different, don't you think?"

The blissful look on her face told Matt how much she liked it.

"Different, and good," he replied, taking another bite.

There was a knock on the back door.

"Come in," Cassie yelled.

A tall man stepped into the kitchen. Matt didn't recognize him, but from Cassie's gasp, he knew she did.

"Stephen, what are you doing here?" she asked.

Matt watched as Stephen's sweeping glance took in the setup. He had to admire the man's composure. A lesser man would have jumped to erroneous conclusions.

"I came to see you, of course," Stephen replied. "I tried to call you on your cell when I landed in New Orleans, but it's not in service."

"I forgot to recharge it," Cassie said lamely.

She glanced around as if seeing the kitchen for the first time.

"Want some torte?"

"What?"

"I'm practicing a dessert for one of my events. Matt was testing it for me. Want a piece?"

Stephen glanced at Matt and then looked at the table. The only two places to eat were the cleared spots where Cassie and he sat.

Matt's slice of torte was only partially eaten. But he knew what he had to do. Rising, he gestured to his chair.

"Have a seat. I have to go."

He nodded once to Cassie, then walked out the back door.

Cassie watched in dismay as Matt left and Stephen sat gingerly in his place.

"I have to tell you, Cassie, this isn't what I expected. I thought you might be at the hospital. How is Margaret?"

"She's improving—slowly but surely. I go a couple of times a day, but visitors are limited. Stephen, there was no need to come all this way."

"I'm beginning to see that."

"What does that mean?"

She rose and went to get another plate. Maybe a piece of cake would help. She wasn't sure what to say. She had a feeling the next few minutes weren't going to be happy ones.

"What exactly is going on?" he asked, looking at the plate in surprise.

"I told you everything on the phone."

"Not everything. Who was that man?"

"Matt Bennett."

She didn't think she'd ever told Stephen about Matt. Only some vague reference to a high-school sweetheart. She was glad she hadn't revealed the full story. She realized Stephen wouldn't understand.

"And why was he here?"

"He and Margaret have plans to renovate this old house into a home for unwed pregnant teens. He was here to measure walls and floors so he can order supplies."

"So you offered him dessert?"

"He's someone I knew in high school. He was getting ready to leave when the torte was ready, so I asked him to give me his feedback. I'd like yours, as well."

She looked at the untouched cake on his plate.

"I don't understand you, Cassie. You blithely ignore your job, which is important to you, to come to a place you haven't set foot in for over twelve years. And I can't pin you down as to when you'll be coming home."

Cassie bit her lip. That was the whole crux of the matter, wasn't it? Where exactly was her home?

"Where's your ring?" Stephen asked abruptly.

Guiltily she looked at her left hand.

"On the bathroom shelf. I don't like to wear it while I'm cooking. I'm afraid it'll get damaged."

She knew he thought she meant the bathroom upstairs. With any luck, he wouldn't push the issue. She didn't want to hurt his feelings. He was the nicest man she knew. And none of her doubts and anxieties were his fault.

"How long are you staying?" she asked.

"For the weekend. And I hope to get a better idea of when you're coming back before I leave."

"The thing is, I'm not at all sure at this point," she said. "I recently got a phone number for Piper and left her a message a couple of days ago. She hasn't responded yet, but every time the phone rings I hope it's her. I've had no luck with Fiona. Then I have these catering engagements to fulfill."

"That's another thing I don't understand. Why in the world did you accept any assignments?"

Stephen was obviously trying to hold on to his emotions, but a glimmer of frustration showed.

"For the experience and the money. As you pointed out, I'm not working right now. I need some income."

She hated sounding so defensive. Anyone in her right mind would be reassured Margaret was doing well and return to Boston. Stephen would really think her crazy if he knew she hadn't returned by Thomas's deadline. She could consider herself unemployed now, except for her catering events.

"If you decide to go out on your own, there are plenty of opportunities in Boston."

He glanced around the shabby kitchen and the chaos that reigned.

"This is nothing like you, Cassie. You have state-of-the-art equipment at the restaurant, and I've never seen you in such a messy kitchen. You're usually the epitome of order."

"I'm still orderly. I'll have this place cleaned up in no time."

"That's not the real issue. I want you to come home with me. Now. This weekend."

Cassie looked at the man she'd once thought she could spend her life with. She admired him tremendously, but seeing him today, she knew clearly that she could never marry him. He was too nice to keep leading on. She had to tell him now.

She didn't love him enough to marry him.

The knowledge lifted a burden she hadn't known she was carrying.

"I am so sorry, Stephen," she blurted out. "I can't marry you."

She felt regret for the loss of the future they'd planned, but she was surprisingly certain of her feelings.

"What? What are you talking about?"

He looked baffled.

"Coming back to Bradford has been like coming

home. I have old friends here, a past we all shared. If I can locate Piper and Fiona, I'll have my family back again. It's what I want."

She took a deep breath.

"I've been doing a lot of thinking while I've been sitting with Margaret or alone in this house. I had a lovely life in Boston, but I never felt truly whole there."

"That will change once we're married." He leaned forward. "What's going on? Why the change of heart? Was it that man who was here when I came in? What's he to you?"

Cassie shook her head.

"There's nothing between us. But there is a connection I feel here that I don't feel in Boston. It's not you, Stephen, it's me. You are a perfectly wonderful man. But not for me. I have to stay here in Bradford."

"Cassie, I love you. You love me. We're getting married."

He spoke as if he were talking to a child.

"But I've never—"

She stopped suddenly. How could she possibly tell him that she had never felt the passion for him that she had for Matt. That seeing Matt made her realize what she felt for Stephen wasn't enough to sustain her for the rest of her life. She'd been blinded by the promise of a family, by the comfortable feeling she had around Stephen. But married love should be more than warm friendship.

She couldn't do that to Stephen. Or to herself.

"Never felt for me what you felt for that boy in high school," he finished for her.

She froze. She didn't want him to think she had taken up with Matt since she'd returned. It was true he'd kissed her once, but that was all. She pushed away the memory of the exquisite feelings that one kiss had evoked.

"But that was some childish infatuation you had as a teenager, not real love," Stephen said. "You're grown up now, Cassie. Act like it."

Cassie didn't respond, but she began to think her feelings for Matt were real love. The kind that might take a back seat for a while, but never go away. Seeing Matt had awakened dormant emotions in her. It wouldn't be fair to commit to another man in marriage until she sorted out exactly what those feelings were.

"I'm sorry, Stephen. You deserve more than I can give. Find some wonderful woman who will adore you forever and snap her up."

He just looked at her. For a moment Cassie saw the hurt in his eyes, but he quickly masked it.

"I'm not giving you up so easily."

"It's not easy. Oh, Stephen, I've been thinking about this ever since I arrived. I feel like I've come home, and it's such a sweet feeling. I've reconnected with old friends as if we've only been apart for a few months. Margaret is here and I never fully realized how much I missed her. I think I can make a go of this catering business—especially since I already have an established network of references and referrals. And that way I can be nearby when Margaret needs me."

"I need you," he said, sounding almost desperate.

"You're too self-sufficient to need anyone. But Margaret truly needs me. She loved us. She kept all these things from our time together—school reports, homemade gifts—just like a real mother would. She even took out a large loan on this property to finance an extensive search for Piper and Fiona. Private detectives don't come cheap. She opened her home to three little girls who had nowhere else to go. She did her best for all of us and we owe her big-time. I want to stay here."

"For how long? Until she recovers? And then what? She won't need you. She's managed fine all the time you've been away. You'll chafe at the limitations of a small town. You've been in Boston too long to accept the slow pace of life in a Mississippi backwater."

"There speaks a true Bostonian. Honestly, I love it here, Stephen. If I get antsy for a big city, New Orleans is only about ninety minutes away. I tried the big city. It's exciting, stimulating, invigorating. But it's also lonely and impersonal."

"But you have me—"

"I'm sorry. I can't marry you."

She felt mean, but she knew it was the right decision.

"I'm booked until Sunday morning at the motel in town," Stephen told her. "There's only one in this town, so you'll know where to find me."

He got up and glanced around, shaking his head.

"I don't understand this at all, Cassie. I know I want to marry you. We're good together. Don't let some misplaced sense of obligation ruin both our lives."

She went to stand beside him.

"It's not a sense of obligation that makes me want to stay. Stephen, think. You must have known I had doubts the way I kept putting off setting a date. If we were madly, passionately in love, we would have zipped off to Atlantic City or Las Vegas and gotten married right away."

"I doubt that. What would Mother have thought?"

"You know what I mean. I've had doubts since I accepted your proposal. I thought they'd fade, but coming here has put things in a different perspective."

"Temporarily. What will you do when Margaret recovers and life resumes its normal course? You have a good job in Boston, an apartment you like. And me. Cassie, I don't want you staying here. Come back with me."

"I can't."

He had family, connections, friends up the ying-yang, and he had asked her to share that life. She'd so wanted to belong. But now she knew she belonged here. The last thing she wanted was to hurt him, but she could not marry him.

"If you change your mind, you know where to find me," he said stiffly.

She touched his arm lightly.

"Don't stay, Stephen. I'm not going to change my

mind. Go home. You know I really treasure your friendship and your mother's."

It wasn't much, but she didn't want to end their relationship on a hostile note. She'd had enough of that in her life.

"Mother will be shocked and upset. She loves you like a daughter."

"I love her."

But not as a mother. Not the way she loved Margaret.

"I'll call and tell your mother," Cassie said, dreading the task, but she knew if she left it to Stephen, he would likely say she was still undecided.

He paused at the door and kissed her gently.

Cassie remained still, not returning the kiss. She hoped he'd remain a friend, but he was not her lifelong mate.

She was afraid she might be a one-man woman— and that one man would never want to marry her.

Feeling guilty and sad about the way she had ended her engagement, Cassie flung herself into cleaning the kitchen. It took longer than she expected and it was early evening by the time the place sparkled again.

Betsy stopped by, sampled the torte and declared it a definite must for their menu. They discussed the plans for the dinner the next evening. Cassie told her about Stephen's visit. Betsy wanted to know all the details, but didn't comment when Cassie told her she simply knew they weren't right together.

She also told Betsy about the deadline Thomas had

given her. She was truly on her own now.

When her friend left, Cassie ran upstairs to take a quick shower and change into clean clothes. Then, wrapping the rest of the torte carefully, she headed for Matt's house.

She was shocked at the poor condition of the place. He'd said something about not visiting often, but she still couldn't imagine him letting the house fall into such disrepair, especially given his line of work.

She parked behind his truck and carried the cake up to the front door. Ringing the bell, she waited.

He opened the door a few minutes later, but just looked at her without saying a word.

"I brought you the rest of the torte. I don't want to have it around in case I nibble it to death. You liked it, right?"

He nodded and took the cake from her.

"Want to come in?" he asked.

"For a few minutes."

When she stepped inside, she was surprised to see boxes stacked against one wall. Furniture had been pushed into the center of the room.

"Are you getting ready to move?" she asked.

"I'm renovating this place while I'm in Bradford."

"Going to sell it?" she asked, walking around the living room. Patches of faded paint revealed where pictures had once hung.

"Don't know yet. Sell it or rent it."

"But not live here yourself?"

"My home's in New Orleans now."

She nodded.

"Can I see the rest of the house?"

He shrugged and gestured toward the hallway. She led the way, not knowing where she was going. She'd never been inside Matt's house before. His sister made her feel too unwelcome.

The first room on the left was a bedroom, stripped bare except for a few furnishings.

"This was my mother's room. I just finished clearing it out. Sadie Connors took most of her things to the rummage sale at the Catholic Church."

Cassie didn't say anything, but she wanted to ask why he'd waited so long after his mother's death to clear her room.

"That's my room across the hall," he said, moving down to the next room on the left. "This was Dolores's."

Cassie stopped in the doorway. Dust covered every surface. Pinned to the wall were posters of a rock band that was popular when they were in high school. Two photos of Matt were thumbtacked to a bulletin board cluttered with notes and school papers important only to Dolores.

"My mother refused to let me clear this out," Matt explained. "Once she died, I didn't come home much."

"It's been twelve years since Dolores's death. That's a long time."

"Too long. I'll tackle this room next."

Cassie wondered if she should offer to help. But the thought held no appeal. Dolores hadn't liked her, and she didn't want to disturb any ghosts by invading her space.

"Where's the fiancé?" Matt asked.

Cassie turned and headed back down the hall. She hadn't seen the kitchen or dining room, but she'd seen more than she wanted. The house was depressing. She was ready to leave.

"Stephen's at the motel."

"He isn't staying with you?" Matt asked in surprise.

Cassie bit her lip. This was proving more awkward than she'd anticipated.

"Actually, he and I are no longer engaged."

If she'd expected some kind of reaction from Matt, she was in for a disappointment. He said nothing for a long moment.

Then he responded, "That was fast. What happened? He wasn't unreasonable about my being there when he walked in, was he?"

She made her way out onto the porch. The yard was a tangled mess. If he wanted to sell the house, or even find tenants to rent it, there was a lot of work to be done.

"Stephen's never unreasonable," she said, avoiding a direct answer.

"So why the breakup?

She leaned against the railing, wondering exactly how to explain what she wasn't even sure of herself.

"I don't want to stay in Boston," she said finally. "You nailed it. Being here in Bradford, I feel as if I've come home. I didn't appreciate what I had when I was

230 | Barbara McMahon

a girl, but I do now. Ever since I was taken away, I've felt as if I were floating around, never putting down roots, never finding my niche. I don't feel that way anymore."

"Don't let the moment color your entire future. It's fun to visit a hometown, but that doesn't mean you're meant to come back here for good. I remember you wanted out in the worst way when we were teenagers."

"Piper, Fiona and I had such great dreams. We were going to go to college, have fabulous careers and live extravagant lives. In those days, Atlanta looked exciting. But I've lived in Boston—I've had enough of cities."

"Maybe Stephen could move," Matt said, coming to stand near her.

Cassie shook her head. "It's not just a matter of where we would live. It's complicated. I don't think I'd make him a good wife."

She couldn't tell Matt he was the benchmark against which all other men were measured.

Matt was silent for a moment. "If it was about that kiss—"

Cassie looked at him. "Partly."

"I kissed you."

"And I liked it."

"Cut yourself some slack. What's a kiss between old friends?"

"A woman passionately in love with her fiancé wouldn't tolerate being kissed like that."

"Maybe you're just caught up in the nostalgia of being back home."

"You think?"

"One way to find out," he said, slowly pulling her closer.

When he leaned over to kiss her, Cassie closed her eyes, yearning for his kiss with a surprising intensity. The touch of his lips against hers fulfilled her wildest dreams. She smiled and pressed up against him, kissing him in return.

Feeling her response, Matt deepened the kiss. It wasn't nostalgia, it wasn't anything except pure lust. She had missed him terribly over the years. Felt at one time as if a part of her had been cut out.

She didn't analyze the past, or think about a future. The moment was enough. The delight of kissing him brought a new realization. It would take very little effort to fall back in love with Matt Bennett.

12

"So there you have it," Cassie told Margaret later that evening. "The trials and tribulations of Cassie Hodges. I don't know if I'm doing the right thing by leaving Boston, but I feel I am. I want to explore the possibility at least. And if laterI decide I don't like living here, then I'll find another place. I've done that before."

Margaret appeared more alert than Cassie remembered before.

"I feel badly about Stephen. But I can't keep his hopes up. I know I can't marry him. That's enough about me. The nurse tells me you're being moved to a different floor tomorrow, no more intensive care. That's so cool. And visiting hours will be a lot more lax on the medical ward. Not that I'll be able to come more often on the days I'm working. I did tell you Betsy has found two more events for us, right?"

Margaret squeezed her hand once. They had settled on that limited method of communication. One squeeze was a yes and two was a no. Margaret wasn't strong enough yet for lengthy conversations, and Cassie found it difficult to formulate her statements so they needed a yes or no answer, but it was the best they could do. She hoped the therapy Margaret was doing would soon enable her to talk.

"I have to go back to Boston to arrange to move my things and close my apartment. I thought I'd fly up right before the first of the month, if I can manage it. Then I won't have another month's rent to pay. So that gives me a couple more weeks here before I go. Is it all right with you if I stay in your house until you come home?"

Margaret squeezed her hand once.

"I told you Matt came by to measure the rest of the space so he could order supplies. I haven't heard anything from Allen McLennon since Edith and I went to the bank. Edith's in charge of that for now. She's been such a help. You're lucky to have her for a friend."

Margaret squeezed again.

"I wish I had such a good friend who had known me all my life," Cassie said wistfully. "I thought at one time Piper and Fiona would always be there for me, but being split up sure changed that. I've known Betsy since high school, but we're not really heart-to-heart friends. Do you know what I mean?"

Margaret responded yes.

Cassie looked at their linked hands. Margaret's were old and frail. The tendons stood out. The wrinkled skin was soft and thin. Her own hand was strong and capable of all the tasks she had ahead of her. But she remembered when Margaret's hands were strong—held out to her in love.

"I want you to know I appreciate all you did for me."

Cassie looked her square in the eye.

"I love you, Margaret. I'm sorry I wasn't the best daughter to you I could have been. You were the best mom for me. I want us to be closer in the future."

At Cassie's words, Margaret grew agitated, rolling her head from side to side on her pillow.

"I didn't mean to make you upset," Cassie said, jumping up. "Shh. I'm here now and I plan to stay."

As Margaret gradually quieted, Cassie sat back down, afraid to say anything in case it evoked another reaction like that one. She glanced up guiltily as a nurse left the station and headed for their room.

Cassie was sure Margaret wanted her to stay in Bradford, so she was perplexed by her reaction.

The nurse hurried in.

"What happened?" she asked, checking the monitors, assessing her patient.

Had Margaret's reaction triggered an alarm?

"I don't know. I was telling her how grateful I am for all she's done for me and she got upset."

"Miss Margaret, you calm down," the nurse said. "It's not good for you to get all riled up about things. We'll work on communication and you can tell us exactly how you feel. But until then, calm down."

Margaret grew still, her eyes were wide with emotion.

"Maybe we should cut this visit short," the nurse said.

Cassie nodded, squeezing Margaret's hand.

"I'll be back in the morning. I hope you're happy with my decision to stay in Bradford."

She kissed Margaret's cheek and left.

There were a myriad things to do for tomorrow's dinner party. Cassie had to make another torte, make sure the butcher gave her the best pieces of beef, check out the vegetable section of the local store. She'd been pleased with the produce she'd found for the luncheon and wanted to make sure she continued to use only the finest ingredients. That made all the difference.

She and Betsy had discussed the dinner on the phone and had everything covered. Still, anticipation filled her.

Mabel Truscott's luncheon for her niece had gone off without a hitch. A few more flawlessly presented events and Cassie felt certain her business would grow through word of mouth.

But as she tried to review her lists later that night, her thoughts centered on Matt instead. His kiss had been magical. She'd thought returning to Bradford had been coming home, but she knew now that coming home meant being held by Matt again. Kissed by him.

For a few moments she'd been able to forget his scathing words from the past. She was once again sixteen, in love with the most wonderful guy in the world. The future was bright with promise and she knew they'd conquer any obstacles.

Foolishness. He'd ended the kiss and left her on the porch. Obviously it hadn't been as magical for him as for her.

She read the next item on the list and checked it off.

The phone rang, and Cassie made her way down the dark hall to answer it. In the morning she was buying a cordless that she could take with her. Why hadn't Margaret done so at some point over the years? She also needed to give her cell number to everyone who called.

"Hello?"

"I thought I'd give you a call to see if you're going to be home tomorrow," Matt said, getting directly to the point.

"I'm home until about four. Then Betsy and I have a dinner to fix for Suzanne Canaday. We're going there to cook."

"I want to finish up on the measurements so I can get the order in. My foreman tells me we should get the final inspection on the McIver project on Tuesday. I can rotate some of my crew up here to start work on the house next week."

"Isn't that rushing things? Shouldn't you wait for Margaret?"

"I don't need to wait. I know what she wants. We've got provisional approval from the planning department, so I want to move ahead as fast as I can before they change their mind."

"Why would they do that?"

"If enough pressure comes to bear, I think one or two could be swayed to change their votes. Allen

McLennon carries a lot of weight in this town. Don't forget he's fully behind the consortium's proposal for a golf course and country club. He can stir up trouble even if the loan is taken care of. And not everyone in town is behind the group home. Some people don't want those girls in Bradford."

"It's not as if you're bringing in druggies. These are likely girls who have no place else to go and don't know what to do. Are you planning on having counseling available?"

"Yes. I've worked it out with Social Services and the local churches. Margaret had the idea of teaching them home skills. She said too few girls learn basic homemaking tasks these days."

"Sounds like Margaret. She was forever drilling those skills into us when we lived here. That's how I first learned to cook."

"I hope she recovers by the time the first girl arrives," he said.

"Is there someone already lined up?" Cassie hadn't thought through the logistics of a home like the one Matt proposed.

"No, but I want to have the place up and running by summer. Then we'll put the word out to agencies, ob-gyns and schools."

"Do you think Dolores would have gone to a home like the one you're proposing?" she asked.

"Of course not. She had me. I would have watched out for her, helped her. I don't know what she was

238 | B<small>ARBARA</small> M<small>C</small>M<small>AHON</small>

thinking those last moments. For some reason, she must have felt desperate, with nowhere to turn."

"Teenagers have enough problems dealing with life without the added screw up of hormones from pregnancy. She might not have felt she could turn to you or your mother."

"Not Mom," he said bitterly. "She'd have just poured another shot."

"Your mother must have been very unhappy to drink so much. Maybe she really loved your father and his leaving left her with a hole that never healed," Cassie said gently.

She could understand Mrs. Bennett better if that was the case. The gap inside her when she'd left Matt had never fully healed.

"Excuses."

"Some people are less capable of dealing with life than others. I always wonder why they're often the ones to get all the hard luck."

"Such a philosophical discussion deserves more time and attention than I have right now," Matt said, but his tone was light. "I'll be over in the morning."

"Come early and I'll fix you some Belgian waffles that are to die for," she invited.

Almost holding her breath for his reply, Cassie wondered what she was doing. She had told Stephen there was nothing between her and Matt. And there wasn't. But still.

Cassie hung up, smiling wryly. She was fooling

herself if she believed that friendship was all she wanted from Matt.

Matt leaned back on the sofa. Was he crazy? He'd responded to that invitation like a dog to a bone. He didn't want to rekindle old feelings. What they'd had was in the past. So why had he so quickly accepted an invitation to breakfast?

Closing his eyes, he tried to rationalize what he'd done, but the picture of Cassie in his arms made that impossible. Kissing her had been dumb.

Kissing her had been amazing.

He'd forgotten how sweet she tasted. How fast his desire exploded when he touched her. He had wanted more than steamy kisses. If reason hadn't taken hold, he'd have swept her up to his room and made love to her right then and there.

He remembered the months they'd dated in high school. At first he'd been drawn to her looks, the shiny dark hair, the blue of her eyes. That smile could still knock him out. But soon afterward, he'd begun to notice how smart she was, how entertaining.

By Christmas of his senior year he'd been hopelessly in love with her, and she with him. They'd been inseparable. Dating, studying together.

And rushing home whenever Dolores had demanded it.

He didn't want to go there. No matter what, all roads led back to Dolores and that final act.

He got up from the couch and went to her room, looking around at the things he'd soon have to get rid of to paint. There was nothing he valued here. He'd have Sadie choose what might be of interest to others for the sale. The rest would go to the dump.

His beautiful sister wasn't in the room anymore.

There had been few pictures of his family—money had been too tight. But he had a school picture of Dolores from that year.

Such a waste of a life. She could have done so much. She'd had him to help her. Why hadn't she let him?

Turning, Matt went to the back porch. He was tired, but too keyed up to sleep. Sitting on the steps, he chased the memories away and focused on the projects ahead of him.

Cassie hummed as she set the table for breakfast. The batter was made, the strawberries cut and dusted lightly with sugar. She'd whip the cream when she and Matt were ready to eat. Fresh fragrant coffee dripped into the pot. It was exactly eight o'clock. Matt would be arriving any moment.

She heard the sound of the truck in the driveway. Feeling as giddy as a schoolgirl, she surveyed the kitchen. It looked much better than yesterday. The table was cleared except for the two place settings. The counters shone in the light.

With a perfunctory knock, he entered. Cassie felt as if he brought in the sunshine.

"Good morning," she said, smiling brightly.

He held out a bouquet of flowers. "For you. In appreciation of a home-cooked meal."

"Thank you, they're lovely."

Her heart skipped a beat. She'd never received flowers from him before.

She took them and touched the bright blossoms lightly.

"I'll put them in water. Ready for coffee? It's just about done."

"I'll get it."

He went to the pot and filled the two mugs she had sitting beside it. He added some cream to one and carried them both to the table.

Cassie found a vase and filled it halfway with water, then placed the spring bouquet in it. Carrying the flowers to the table, she set them down and smiled again.

"I love them."

She glanced at Matt to find his dark gaze fixed on her. Feeling flustered, she grabbed her coffee mug and moved to the counter.

"I'll have those waffles in a jiffy," she promised, glad for something to do.

"The coffee's good," he said a moment later.

"Much richer than what I was used to in Boston."

She tested the heat of the waffle iron.

"It's the chicory, I think. I didn't start drinking coffee much before I left Mississippi, but I find coffee elsewhere blah."

Great, she was rambling on about coffee.

"You could have come back to Bradford when you finished high school."

"To what? I didn't think I could live with Margaret anymore. There was nothing else for me here."

"I know you were angry at being sent away," Matt said. "Especially since you knew it was for the wrong reasons."

"I think we were all railroaded out of town," she told him.

Switching on the electric mixer, she began to whip the heavy cream.

"Pretty strong term," he said over the noise of the beaters.

She didn't answer him for a few minutes until the cream formed soft peaks.

"I know there weren't a lot of foster families in Bradford," she said, removing the mixer, "but I had friends whose parents would probably have let me stay with them to finish high school. No one asked and no one offered. I felt it was whoosh—get them out of town. Looking back, I wonder if there was a reason we were separated and not allowed to keep in touch."

Matt didn't say anything. She knew he was thinking about his own family problems at the time.

Her cell phone rang.

"Darn. This waffle is just about done. I can't leave it now. Can you answer it for me? I keep hoping Piper will call. It's been almost a week. Even if she was working, she'd be home by the weekend, don't you think? I think it's in the living room. I should have brought it here."

Matt rose and went to get her phone. She heard the murmur of his voice as she lifted the lid of the griddle. The waffle was perfectly brown, its deep pockets waiting for the strawberries and cream.

He came to the door, holding out her phone.

"It's your ex-fiancé. He wants to know if you'll have lunch with him."

"Jeez," she murmured.

She lifted the waffle from the griddle and placed it on the warmed plate, topping it with the cream and strawberries. Swiftly she set it down at Matt's place.

"Thanks."

She took the phone. She should have let it ring, but she didn't want to risk missing Piper's call.

"Hi, Stephen," she said stepping out of the kitchen for privacy.

"Am I interrupting something?" he asked.

"No. Matt's here to finish taking measurements."

"Does that include measuring the depth of the Belgian waffles?"

Oops, Matt must have told him. Darn it!

"Well, I was fixing them and he was here. Anyway, he said you wanted to get together for lunch?"

She really didn't have time for a leisurely lunch. She had a million things to do for her dinner that evening. But Stephen had come all this way to see her. It wasn't his fault she'd broken the engagement. Guilt lay heavy on her shoulders. She should have told

Stephen she couldn't marry him much sooner. Still, he had always been so good to her.

"I thought I'd take you someplace nice, where we can talk."

"I'm short on time today, I have an event to cater this evening. But lunch would be great."

She tried to infuse her voice with enthusiasm, but felt her stress level rise a notch.

"I'll pick you up—"

"I'll meet you in town. I have shopping to do this morning and some other errands. I also want to stop by the hospital and check on Margaret."

"It's not as if Bradford is some huge metropolis. I can swing by and pick you up. What time?"

"I'll meet you at noon at Ruby's Café, the one in the center of town. But I won't have a lot of time, Stephen. I'm sorry."

"I'll take what I can get. See you at noon."

Cassie hung up, annoyed with herself. Why hadn't she just said she couldn't do lunch and leave it at that? Now she was going to be pressed for time to get everything ready for the dinner.

"Problem?" Matt asked when she returned to the kitchen.

"No."

"The waffle is delicious."

"Want another one?"

"Why did you invite me for breakfast?" he asked.

"I have to eat. You do, too," she said, parroting his remark from the other night.

"Nothing more?"

"I like to cook, and it's not as much fun cooking for one."

"Stephen would have loved breakfast with you."

"That wouldn't be fair. Our engagement is over. I'm not trying to send mixed messages."

"And what message are you trying to send me by inviting me for breakfast?" Matt asked, a slight edge to his voice.

"That I make wonderful food for any occasion, so you'll talk me up to all your friends and I'll be flooded with requests."

She went over to the counter to cook another waffle. She didn't need him analyzing her every move, but she said nothing. Their relationship was tenuous. She wasn't going to rock that boat today.

When the waffle was in the griddle, she leaned against the counter, sipping her cool coffee.

"What are your plans for upstairs?" she asked.

"Margaret and I discussed adding a couple of bathrooms. That's the biggest part of the project. The rest is primarily cosmetic. We also need to bring the wiring and plumbing up to current code. Once we get certified from the state, we can apply for grant money to keep the home running."

Cassie asked more questions as they ate, impressed with the planning Matt and Margaret had done. This was not some quick scheme they'd just thought up. They'd obviously been working on it for many months. She wondered why Margaret had never mentioned it to her in any of her letters. Probably because it involved Matt, and she knew the history between the two of them.

"You've thought of everything," she said as she began to clear the dishes.

"I've been thinking about it for years. When Margaret approached me last year, I was that far ahead of the game."

"She approached you?"

He nodded, rising to get another cup of coffee.

"She said she wanted to feel useful again."

Cassie ran hot water over the dishes as Matt stepped beside her.

"She talked about you," he said. "She was really proud of all you've accomplished."

"I invited her to Boston several times. She never came."

"She's an odd woman. Never married. On her own since her father died. Yet she took on three homeless girls. And she stayed around even after the accusation Fiona made. I always thought I'd have left Bradford if something like that happened to me," he added thoughtfully.

"It must have been hard to stay," Cassie mused. "Gossip would have been rampant."

"I expect most of the people in town knew she'd never have done such a thing."

"Then why was it handled the way it was?"

"Interesting question. Wonder if Sam could look up the old records and see if there's something we didn't know at the time."

"Do you think he would?"

"I can ask."

Matt was standing too close. Cassie felt as if he were crowding her space. Yet the tingling awareness that shot through her was too delicious to miss. She held her ground, wondering if he planned to step even closer.

"I'd appreciate any insights he could give," she said breathlessly, all too aware of Matt's powerful presence.

"Me, too," he said. Slowly, his eyes never leaving hers, Matt took her into his arms and pulled her closer still. "Tell me to stop," he said.

"Why ever would I say such a thing?" Cassie asked, standing on tiptoes to kiss him.

Third time's the charm echoed in her mind as he opened his mouth over hers. Heat poured through her and she sought to get even closer. She wanted the loving they'd shared as teens. Maybe they'd been young, but it had been hot and honest, and she knew with certainty she'd never feel this way with anyone but Matt.

Things had gone wrong. Their lives had been derailed. But the feelings wouldn't go away.

His hands traced the contours of her back, roaming up to her neck, where he threaded his fingers through her hair, tilting her head back to trail kisses down her neck to that rapidly beating pulse point at her throat.

Suddenly she heard a car.

13

"Betsy's here," Cassie said, pushing away. "She's coming to help with the dinner tonight."

"Then I'll get the measurements and get out of your way."

So no after kiss discussion.

She'd think about that later.

She glanced around the kitchen and took the dishes, stacking them quickly in the sink.

"Hey," Betsy said as she pulled open the screen door.

Her hands had several plastic bags dangling.

"I think I got everything you needed."

She placed the groceries on the table.

Cassie smiled broadly.

"You're a lifesaver."

"Naw, easy enough to do. What next?"

"I need to get started on the torte or it won't have a chance to chill. How about flowers for the centerpiece?"

She couldn't believe she was switching to business mode. Part of her was still tingling from Matt's kisses.

"I'm going to pick them up later and take them

directly to Suzanne's. I'll arrange them in whatever vases she has." Betsy looked at her closely. "You all right?"

"Yes, why?" Cassie resisted the urge to finger comb her hair. She hoped she didn't look as if she'd just been kissed like never before.

"You're flushed. It's going to be a hot day, but it's not that hot yet."

"Feels like it to me. I guess I've been too long in Boston."

Cassie turned to get the bowls for the torte. Her ears strained for sounds of Matt.

"Where's Matt?" Betsy asked, taking the produce from the bags and putting it by the sink for washing.

"Upstairs somewhere. He's measuring for the renovations," Cassie said, hoping she sounded sufficiently disinterested. The last thing she wanted was to give rise to gossip.

"I guess he wants to move as quickly as he can before more obstacles come up," Betsy said.

Cassie was relieved Betsy didn't seem suspicious of Matt's presence at the house.

"Like what?" she prompted.

If she could get Betsy talking, maybe she could concentrate on the task at hand.

"The planning commission, the town council's reluctance to make a final decision. There's a lot going on. I think Allen McLennon's behind most of it. Rumor has it he wanted the country club."

"With free membership for himself, I'm sure," Cassie said.

"How else can he throw his weight around? He's the president of the bank, as you know. Isn't that enough?"

"If he wants more power, he should try a larger city. Bradford isn't exactly New Orleans."

"Or even Jackson."

"I wonder why he never married," Cassie said. "I thought he'd marry Margaret, but I'm glad that didn't come to anything. He's a jerk. But I wish Margaret had met someone else and gotten married. She's so alone."

"Not anymore. She has you."

"And maybe Piper if she'd ever call back."

"You found her? You didn't tell me. Where is she?"

Cassie brought Betsy up to date.

"So I left a message, but Piper hasn't returned my call. I clearly gave her both Margaret's phone number and my cell. Matt suggested she might be away on vacation or something."

"Or off on some exotic photo shoot modeling bathing suits," Betsy said dreamily. "She always loved messing with her hair and wearing dramatic makeup."

"Remember how Ms. Tomlin in PE made her wash her face before every class?"

"I think she was jealous. Piper was such a beauty and Ms. Tomlin was rather plain."

Cassie heard Matt's truck start up. In a moment the sound of the engine faded as he drove away.

"Guess Matt finished what he came for," she said.

"Wonder why he didn't stop in here before he left," Betsy said. "He can't still be mad at you, is he?"

Cassie thought about the kisses, the caresses and the soft words whispered in her ear. "I don't think so. But he took Dolores's death hard."

"He blamed himself for not saving her."

"As if anyone's totally responsible for another person."

"What next?" Betsy asked as she shook the water from the vegetables and placed them in a colander to drain.

Cassie reviewed the dinner plans and she and Betsy worked companionably together until it was time for her to shower and change for her lunch with Stephen. She wished she hadn't agreed to it–time was pressing. But she felt guilty about ending their relationship, after he'd come all the way from Boston to be with her.

He was waiting at the café as she'd suggested. She entered and headed toward him.

"Hi," she said, slipping opposite him in the booth he'd chosen.

"Cassie."

He smiled at her, reaching for her hand.

Cassie took her napkin and placed it in her lap to avoid contact.

"You look radiant," he said, studying her.

She felt a prickle of guilt.

"Thank you. I've been getting ready for tonight's catering event. Betsy was with me at the house helping with preliminary work, and we're planning to meet at the event location at four. I need to do a few things before that, so I apologize, but lunch has to be short."

"Why was Matt at your house today?" he asked, ignoring her comment about a short lunch.

"He's going to be there a lot as I understand it. He's remodeling the house in preparation for a home for unwed teenagers. Margaret's working with him. Or she was before the stroke."

"You're not planning to step in for her, are you?" he asked.

"What do you mean? I'm not interested in running a home for pregnant teens."

"You might cook for them or something."

Cassie shook her head.

"No. I'm merely staying there while Margaret's in the hospital. I'll have to find a place of my own soon."

"I think you've let the entire situation play havoc with your life," Stephen said. "You have a solid career in Boston. We were planning to marry and make a life together. You're throwing it all away for a backwater town and a woman you haven't seen in twelve years."

"If your mother needed help, wouldn't you rally around her?" she asked.

"My mother is hardly a paid care giver with a tarnished reputation."

Cassie tilted her head slightly as she looked at Stephen.

"I never said her reputation was tarnished."

"After what happened, how could it not be?"

"Is that how it looks to an outsider? I'm surprised at you, I'd expect you to weigh all the evidence before passing any judgment. Instead, you seem to have tapped into town gossip and made a decision based on things you don't even know about."

"I know enough. People are very friendly to strangers in this town. I've also heard about Matt Bennett, that you two were quite an item in high school. He's the man you told me about. Only you didn't tell me he blames you for his sister's death."

She shrugged and picked up the menu.

"Old news. I think I'll have a chicken salad. What are you having?"

"I'm having a hard time accepting your breaking our engagement," Stephen said heatedly. "I want you back in Boston."

She laid down the menu carefully and looked him directly in the eye.

"I have made up my mind and plan to live my life as I choose. You've always had your family behind you. I've had so little during my life. But one thing I did have and threw away was the love of a wonderful woman. She needs help now and I'm going to be here to give it."

Cassie got up and leaned over the table.

"I'll always remember your kindness and love with warm feelings, Stephen. Thank you for asking me to be your wife, but I'm so sorry I can't do it. Have a nice trip back to Boston and give your mother my love."

She kissed him on the cheek.

"Goodbye, Stephen."

She turned to leave before he could make a scene. Not that Stephen was likely to do so.

Head held high, she walked out of the café. She'd never done such a thing before, but she was not going to subject herself to a lunch full of recriminations.

She hesitated when she reached the sidewalk. Now what? She guessed she'd go back home and have something to eat and then get ready for her evening's assignment.

Matt's truck stopped across from her.

"Want a lift?" he called.

She nodded and hopped into the cab.

"Where to?" he asked as he drove off

"Home, I guess."

"Coming from lunch?" he guessed.

"Coming from the café, there was no lunch."

"Why not?"

"Stephen didn't want to eat, he wanted to talk me into going back to Boston and marrying him. I didn't want to listen to that, so I left."

Matt was silent as he drove along Main Street. When he came to the turnoff for Bradford Hall, he slowed.

"Since you missed lunch, want to come to my place to eat?"

"Only if you're not going to try to talk me into anything."

"Only into eating the sandwiches I make," he promised.

"Deal."

Cassie wondered if Matt was going to bring up what had happened that morning. She wasn't sure she wanted to talk about it, but not talking about it seemed odd, too. She decided to let him take the initiative. Leaning back in the seat, she felt the cool air blow over her heated skin.

"Hear from Piper yet?" he asked.

"No. I thought I'd call again tomorrow. Maybe something happened and the answering machine didn't record the message."

"Or she doesn't want the contact."

"There is that possibility. But I'd like to think there are other reasons. Let me have my dreams as long as possible."

"Can't hide from reality."

"I guess not." Cassie sat up. Was there a hidden meaning in his comment?

"I can make the sandwiches, if you like," she offered when they reached the Bennett house.

"Because you're the cook?"

"Because you're feeding me and I want to pull my own weight."

"I'll make them. You can critique. Ever want to be one of those restaurant critics?"

"No. I like to enjoy a meal, not rip it apart. I don't even read them. Thomas, the head chef at the restaurant where I work, once told me I got a rave review on my veal Marsala. That was nice to know, but I'd probably be upset by a bad review. I'd rather get feedback from clients."

Matt stopped the car near the front of the house.

"How are you coming with the cleanup?" she asked, not moving.

"Slowly. Lots of memories."

"A few good ones, I hope?"

"Some. Actually, more than I expected. In recent years I've seemed to focus on the bad ones. But we did have some happy times here."

"That's the way I feel about my years in Bradford. For some reason I only remembered those last few days, but I lived with Margaret from the time I was four until I was sixteen. There were lots of happy memories."

"So for today, we'll only remember the happy ones," Matt said, climbing out of the truck and coming around to open the passenger side door for Cassie.

Matt wished they could only remember the happier memories forever. But life wasn't like that. There was good mixed in with bad, and he'd had his share of both. It was what he decided to do with them that was his call. He could learn from the past, and try not to repeat any mistakes.

Like getting too involved with Cassie? How far was he willing to go?

And how far did Cassie want to go?

He let them into the house and headed straight for the kitchen. He'd started painting his mother's old room, and the house smelled of new paint.

"We'll eat outside," he said. "The smell can be overwhelming."

"Are you using any of your crew to help with this place?" she asked as Matt began fixing the sandwiches. He had plenty of cold cuts and fresh bread. He piled the meat and cheese high on the slices of bread and then added pickles to the plates.

"Cokes or beer in the fridge," he said, lifting the two plates.

"I'll have a Coke, what do you want?"

"Same."

He led the way to the backyard. Two benches flanked a weathered picnic table. Matt had built the set in woodworking class back in high school. He'd been so proud of the result. His mother had shrugged and said eating inside was good enough for her. Dolores had loved it, though. She'd wanted to eat outside all the time.

He put the plates down. Cassie sat opposite him and popped open her cola. "Looks good," she murmured, taking one half of her sandwich.

They ate in silence for a while. He watched her. She looked around as she ate, taking in the overgrown yard, the stand of trees at the far back. Beyond was the meadow old man Stanford owned. He grazed sheep there sometimes, mostly to keep the growth down, Matt figured.

"You were lucky you had this house," Cassie said thoughtfully. "We were lucky Margaret took us in and had her house. Her daddy left it to her. From what I heard, he was a real bastard."

"Strong-willed, that's for sure. I never knew him. Seems to me I heard he died around the time I was born. At least he stayed around. My father bought this place, then took off. Somehow Mom was always able to make the payments. I paid the rest off a few years back. It's not worth that much, but if it's fixed up, it'll bring something."

"You could rent it out in case you want to live in it some day," she said.

"My home's in New Orleans. I have no intention of returning to Bradford to live."

"You're living here now."

"I'm staying here temporarily. Same as you."

"Oh, no, I'm here for good," Cassie said. "I plan to find a place of my own and make a terrific success of Elegant Events by Cassie."

"More scope in a bigger city."

She shrugged.

"I want to earn enough to have a comfortable life. I don't intend to work myself to a frazzle and have no time for friends or fun. Besides, I'd have to compete with established firms in another locale. And I've already made contacts through Betsy."

"I remember the girl who was dying to get away from Bradford," he said.

"We had big dreams back then. And I've been away. I'm glad I lived in Boston all these years. That gave me my big-city experience, but now I like what I find here. Though I'd like to travel—maybe go visit Piper if she ever responds."

"Darn, I forgot. Tulane University called. The professor we spoke with has your translations. She said there wasn't much more than what she told us, but her students had fun doing the work. Two of them want to meet Monique if she ever comes back for a visit."

"Why'd she call you?"

"I don't know. Want to run in to New Orleans tomorrow and pick them up?"

"Tomorrow's Sunday," she said.

"I told her to courier the translations to my office today. Someone will be there. We can swing by and pick them up in the morning if you want."

"Yes, I do. Now if we could only find Fiona."

"Did the sheriff have any luck?

"Last time I spoke with him about it, he said they'd listed hundreds of Hunters, with combinations of Fiona, Feeona, Pheeonah and other variations. He's trying to narrow the field, but he doesn't hold out a lot of hope we're going to find her."

"Maybe she'll just show up one day. You did."

"Because I subscribe to the local paper and saw the article about Margaret."

"Maybe Fiona subscribes as well."

Cassie's face lit up.

"I never considered that. We could ask the paper to check for us. Do you think they would?"

Matt didn't think Fiona was the type to subscribe to a paper from a town that couldn't possibly hold fond memories for her, but he had no wish to shoot down Cassie's hopes.

"Worth a try," he said.

"We'll probably have to wait until Monday. This waiting business is so hard!"

"You're impatient. It's been a dozen years since you saw her, another day or two won't hurt."

"Especially since the chances of finding her are slim to none," she said wryly. "I should count myself lucky we got a lead with Piper. Time enough to search for Fiona if I can make the French connection."

He nodded. "What are you going to do if Piper doesn't want to come back to visit?"

"I'll deal with that when it happens. I can at least catch up with what she's been doing." Cassie held up a finger and showed him the tiny scar. "We're blood sisters."

He laughed.

"I remember."

Matt began to see the bigger picture. She really did consider those women her family. She had no photos of her real mother, no memories of her father. Her only family had been two girls in similar circumstances and a woman with no family of her own.

Nothing wrong with that, Matt thought.

They talked for awhile about changes in the town, who had left and who had stayed from their high school friends.

"Oops, I've got to go," Cassie said, checking her watch. "I've got to meet Betsy at the café at four and I have to pick up some things from the house."

"I'll take you home then," he said, reluctant to have the afternoon end.

It had been pleasant to sit at the picnic table and

talk with Cassie. They hadn't done a lot of that in the past. Why talk if he could kiss her or touch her?

The dinner went perfectly. Cassie was flushed with excitement when Suzanne Canaday came in right before she and Betsy were leaving to compliment her on how well everything had gone, and how much the guests had enjoyed the food—especially the torte. Suzanne paid with a check for ten percent above the agreed price.

"I put in a little extra," Suzanne said with a warm smile. "You far exceeded my expectations. I suspect Georgina will be calling you this week for a dinner party she wants to put on. Don't be sharing that torte with anyone else, now."

Betsy laughed softly when she left. She packed up the last of their things and headed for the door.

"That can be your specialty—create a unique dessert for each client. If they don't have you back within a few months, you share the dessert with some other client."

"Can you imagine keeping all that straight?" Cassie asked.

"That's what a computer's for. Which you'll need anyway to keep track of supplies, dates, costs, staffing. Honey, you're going to move into the big time now, so I'd say let's get organized from the get-go."

"I'll do the cooking, you can do the rest," Cassie said.

"Deal," Betsy said. "Dexter can help me."

The house was dark when Cassie arrived back at Margaret's. She let herself in. She was tired, but so pleased the dinner had gone well. And if Suzanne Canaday was right, she would have future bookings from some of tonight's guests.

Heading for her room, she noticed the blinking light on the message machine.

"Hi, it's Matt. How did it go? Call me."

She didn't hesitate a moment, but quickly dialed the number.

"Bennett," his deep voice answered.

"It was great. The torte was a hit, and Suzanne doesn't want me to serve it to anyone else. Betsy thinks that could be a gimmick—exclusive fancy desserts for clients. If they don't use my services regularly, then the dessert passes on to another client."

"Betsy has marketing genius. Keep her on."

"I plan to."

"I'll pick you up at nine. We'll be in New Orleans in time for lunch."

"Thank you, Matt." She hung up, wishing he'd come by in person to see how the dinner had gone.

"Oh well, we have tomorrow," she said as she climbed the stairs.

Cassie was ready long before Matt arrived the next morning. She wished she had given the professor her email so she could have sent her the results directly.

Anticipation brimmed. She could hardly wait to see what the articles said.

It was time to leave another message for Piper, Cassie thought, dialing the overseas number again. When she heard Piper's voice, even speaking French, she smiled.

"I'm still waiting for a call, Piper. Things have changed since my last message. I'm staying in Bradford. Come home for a visit. *Call me!*"

After repeating the phone numbers, Cassie hung up. Even though Piper wasn't home, she'd felt a tenuous connection being on the phone to France.

A car was coming up the driveway. Grabbing her purse, Cassie ran outside, anxious to see him. And to find out what was in the articles that Margaret had so lovingly pasted in a scrapbook.

14

"Thanks for driving," she said when she got into the car. "I don't have a car of my own. It's so easy to take public transportation in Boston, I never bothered with the expense. The rental is getting pricey, though, so I need to see about getting something of my own soon. Probably a van like I have now, to carry things around."

"Won't you need it specially fitted to accommodate your catering business?" he asked.

"Probably. I wonder if I can find a carpenter who could build me some shelving and maybe put in a small refrigerator that could be connected to the engine. Without costing an arm and a leg, of course."

"I know several carpenters," Matt said.

"I'll keep that in mind."

The sun shone from a cloudless sky. Speeding along the highway, Matt cranked up the air conditioner. The oaks dripped Spanish moss and the median was a colorful blur of wild flowers sown by a civic group.

Sunday morning wasn't a busy time and the interstate was almost empty. Cassie felt as if everything was going perfectly. She'd hear from Piper soon, she had a feeling.

And the sheriff would find Fiona and she'd come back for a visit.

Cassie wondered if they would recapture the closeness they'd once had. She hoped so.

She thought of her and Matt. Twelve years ago he'd been her soul mate, or so she'd believed. But the bond had not held. The first crisis had severed it completely.

She wished with all her heart she could find that feeling of closeness again.

"You're quiet," Matt said.

"I'm just thinking. I wonder if Margaret tried to contact Piper and she didn't respond. She sure isn't answering my phone calls. I tried again before you arrived."

"It seems to me she'd return your call, even to say don't bother me again."

"Maybe she figures if she ignores me, I'll give up. But I'm not going to give up. I want to talk to her. And Margaret does, too. She kept all those clippings. I also found my letters I've sent over the last couple of years."

"I found three letters from my father," Matt told her unexpectedly. "When I was going through my mother's things. They were all written shortly after he left. In one he gave an address, he'd found work in Miami. Then apparently he sent her some money in the next one, and in the last he asked her to please write and tell him about me and Dolores."

Cassie looked at him.

"Really? So you have an address? You can try to find him. Maybe your mother wrote back and said she didn't want him to contact her. Oh, Matt, maybe he didn't abandon you after all. Maybe your mother told him to stay away."

"Not much of a man if a letter from his wife keeps him away from his kids," Matt argued.

"I think you should try to contact him. Hear his side of the story."

"Why?"

"To find out. I'd give anything to know more about my parents. My mother showed up in Bradford saying she was a widow. She worked at the grocery store as a clerk, got pneumonia and died. I can only remember bits and pieces about her. Mostly her laughter and her smell. She always wore one kind of scent. If I come across it unexpectedly, I'm immediately reminded of her."

"You never learned anything else?"

"As a project when I was in ninth grade, I tried to find out more about my family. Margaret had some basic information and she helped me search for my father's obituary in the Jackson paper. It didn't say much, just gave his age and death information and that he was survived by a wife and daughter. My mother's death notice was about as informative. Margaret had saved it for me and dug it out when I was doing that project."

"There are ways to get more info."

"I guess. But I've never had the burning need that

Piper did. She never even knew who her parents were and always wanted to find out. I wonder if she ever pursued that."

They were silent a moment, then Cassie spoke again.

"I really think you should find out about your dad."

"Maybe."

"I even know a detective who could help you," she said with a smile.

When they reached the outskirts of New Orleans, Matt circumvented the city and headed for the McIver job site. The big trailer that served as the construction office was open, and there were workers on the site and in the office. Cassie went in with Matt, surprised at the activity on a Sunday.

"We're pushing to get it finished," Matt explained when she commented on the activity. "The final inspection is this week and I want it to pass the first time."

"Hey, boss."

A middle-aged woman with bright red hair called out to Matt from behind a desk piled high with papers, folders and rolled blueprints.

"Thought only we peons worked on Sunday," she teased.

"I stopped by to pick up a packet sent here yesterday," Matt told her.

He introduced Cassie to Sally Harmon.

Sally pulled out the thick manila envelope and the scrap book and handed them to him.

"How are things going?" Matt asked, passing the envelope and book to Cassie.

"Shipshape. We'll pass with flying colors. Want to check in with Joe?"

"Yeah."

He turned to Cassie. "I'll only be a moment."

Donning a hard hat, he left for the construction site.

"Have a seat. Important papers?"

Sally looked curious.

"A translation of some newspaper articles," Cassie replied.

"I'd love to visit," Sally said, pointing at the mound of papers surrounding her, "but I've got a pile of work to do."

"That's okay, I want to read these right away."

Cassie sat down, grateful for the chance to see what the clippings said.

The transcriptions had been typed, and each article clearly referenced. Someone had photocopied the articles so the scrapbook was intact.

She began to read. The first few items were short, brief accounts of a new model in Paris, Monique, an American who was taking the fashion industry by storm. That had been seven years ago.

The more recent articles revealed more about her career, the designers she worked for, and tidbits about her connection to playboy Jean-Paul Santain. Apparently Piper had been married to him at one time.

Cassie remembered the detective telling them

Piper had remarried after her divorce from Billy Bob. She wondered about this second husband. A dashing Frenchman sounded just like Piper.

As she continued, she smiled at the gossipy nature of some of the articles, which reported Monique's attendance at gala events and whom she was dating. So marriage number two hadn't lasted, either.

There were a few from a trade magazine, the most recent only three months old. These focused on her career, which seemed to be skyrocketing. She was in high demand.

Cassie loved reading about Piper's life over the last seven years. Her foster sister had definitely made it big. Cassie just hoped she could take time to come home for a visit.

Matt walked back into the trailer.

"Interesting reading?"

"Not much more than what the professor told us the other day, but lots more details. It seems she's really a big model in Europe. No wonder she doesn't want to be reminded of her roots."

"You coming in this week, boss?" Sally asked.

"I'll be here Tuesday for the inspection. I'll call you tomorrow and give you my schedule."

He placed the hard hat on the rack and gestured to the door.

"Ready?"

"Sure," Cassie said, and after saying goodbye to Sally, they headed back to the car.

"Lunch?" Matt asked.

"Sounds good. I didn't eat much breakfast."

As they drove through the city, recently built homes gave way to older ones. They were heading toward the Garden District, an area of lovely old houses with beautifully landscaped grounds.

When Matt turned into a high-rise complex near the District, she was surprised.

"This looks like apartments, not restaurants," Cassie said.

"Condos," he replied, pulling into the parking area. "I live here."

"Fancy," she murmured.

"It suits me."

Five minutes later he ushered her into his home. It was on the river side of the complex, high enough for an unobstructed view of the Mississippi. The wide windows along the outside wall were uncovered, allowing the spectacular setting to be visible at all times.

"Wow, this is amazing," Cassie said, going to the window and looking out.

After getting her fill, she turned and studied the furnishings. Modern, yet comfortable looking. The walls held tasteful paintings. The hardwood floors had expensive-looking rugs to soften the stark effect.

Matt stood near the door watching her.

"A far cry from the house in Bradford."

"Only because you let it fall into disrepair. But this is the real you, right?"

He nodded.

"I like the sleek look. Yet I bet it's comfortable to kick back and watch TV."

She glanced at the large-screen television dominating one wall.

"Which you must love."

"It's good for football games."

He headed for the kitchen area.

Cassie followed, surprised at the signs of wealth she saw. Even Stephen's apartment wasn't as expensively decorated.

"You must make a killing in construction," she said sitting on one of the bar stools at the black granite counter that separated the eating area from the kitchen.

He opened the refrigerator and withdrew some containers.

"I also get a deep discount on architectural supplies," he told her.

Looking over the opened door, he shook his head.

"Construction is as iffy as farming. We're dependent on the weather and the fickle fortunes of men. Sometimes I'm flush, other times I'm living on peanut-butter-and-jelly sandwiches."

"I like PBJs," Cassie said.

He reached in for a jar of jelly and held it up.

"Want one today?"

"Why not?"

Cassie didn't care much what she ate, she liked being with Matt. Tension rose as she watched him preparing their lunch. She couldn't remember a time when Stephen had ever fixed her a meal. He contended he could never do it as well as a professional chef.

But Matt wasn't bothered by things like that. He cut the sandwiches on the diagonal and slid her plate over to her.

She kept her eyes on his hands. Broad, with long fingers, they were scarred here and there from work-related accidents she guessed.

She remembered the feel of them on her skin, a little rough, strong, warm. And every touch inflaming her when they were randy teenagers in the throes of passion.

Swallowing hard, she tried to concentrate on her sandwich. He poured her a glass of milk and she smiled.

"I feel like a little kid again."

"Comfort food."

"Exactly. I should be celebrating. I now know lots more details about Piper. I wish she'd call."

"Maybe she's traveling."

"Could be. Anyway, I hope she gets home soon, if that's the case."

She took another bite.

"This is good. How long have you had this place?"

"About four years. It was a foreclosure and I got it at a low price. Otherwise I'd still be living near the student housing for Tulane."

"I have an apartment that overlooks the Charles River. It's small, but cozy and I like it. But it was only after my last raise that I could afford it."

"No big regrets to be leaving it behind if you move?"

"When I move. And no regrets. It's just an apartment. How big is this place?"

"Two bedrooms. One I use as an office. Want the grand tour after we eat?"

"Sure."

She carefully refrained from looking at him. She didn't want him to guess how much she wanted to see his home, to get a better idea of the man he had become. He'd made his dreams come true, in a way. He had left Bradford behind and was a successful builder.

So three for three, she thought whimsically. Piper had done well, she herself had, and so had Matt. What about Fiona?

"Tell me about your business," she said.

Matt looked at her for a moment.

"What do you want to know?"

"How you got started, what you like about it. Why here? Why not farther away?"

"My roots are in this area. I went to college here and stayed."

He told her of his early jobs, how the company gradually expanded. And how he was now branching out into small apartments as well as luxury homes. Not only was Cassie fascinated by his account, she plain liked to hear his voice.

She could have stayed there forever, listening to him, but Matt finally rose and carried their plates over to the sink. Running water over them, he looked at her over his shoulder.

"I'll show you the rest of the apartment then we can leave."

"I'm in no hurry," she said.

His look intensified. "Meaning?"

Instantly Cassie realized how provocative that might have sounded.

"Meaning, that would be fine. I don't have any other plans today except to visit Margaret and tell her what I learned about Piper."

He couldn't read minds, she knew that. But if he could, would he be pleased at what she was thinking?

Like she wanted to be with him. She wanted to recapture the feelings that had so filled her with love when she'd been a teenager

Matt led the way to the living room again, then down the short hall. There was a guest bathroom and a good-size room he'd made into an office.

Finally he opened the door to the master bedroom. It was huge and sparsely furnished, but as in the living room, the view from the window dominated.

"Nice," she said, her eyes on the king-size bed. Quite a change from her narrow twin bed.

"One great feature," he said, going into the wall near the bed and flicking a switch. Slowly, blackout curtains closed across the window, plunging the room into twilight.

"So you can nap during the day," she said.

It set the light perfectly for napping..

Cassie looked at Matt. He was staring at her.

"Want to try the bed?" he asked.

She laughed nervously. "I was thinking it was lots larger than my twin. Time to get going?" she asked.

"If you want to visit Margaret, we'd better start back."

"Thank you for bringing me today."

"The pleasure was all mine," he said.

Cassie sighed, wishing she could hold on to the afternoon forever.

Yet Matt never gave a hint that his feelings about her part in his sister's death had changed. Never said a word about a future together. Was he willing to give them a chance?

Matt drove straight to the hospital at Cassie's request.

"I can walk home," she said.

"I'll go up with you."

"She may already know everything I found out, but if not, what fun to tell her about Piper," Cassie said.

Matt had his own worries. Mainly, what the heck he thought he was doing. He didn't want a relationship with Cassie. There was no future for them. Yet they would always have that bond from their high-school romance. And even if he sold the house, he'd still have a tie to Bradford with the teen home.

Spending the day with her, sharing meals, wasn't the way he thought their relationship would end up. Was this all? Or dare he even think about a different future?

Margaret was asleep when they walked into her room. Not wanting to waken her, Cassie chose to go home and come back early in the morning.

Matt drove her the short distance.

"Come in for coffee?" Cassie invited when they reached the house.

"Sure."

The wiser move would be to drop her off and head for home. Showed how unwise he could be as he followed her into the house.

She flicked on the lights in the kitchen as they entered. She glanced out to the hall from habit. The light was blinking on the answering machine.

Cassie rushed to the foot of the stairs. Pressing the button, she listened as Sara Lightfoot requested her to call regarding a luncheon she wanted to have catered. Betsy had phoned to rehash the dinner at the Canadays'. And Piper had called from Paris.

"Matt, Piper called," Cassie shrieked, picking up the phone to dial her number.

"'Lo?" a sleepy voice responded when the call went through.

"Piper? It's Cassie."

"Cassie? I called as soon as I got in, but only got the machine. What's going on there?" She sounded tired.

"I've been trying to reach you to see if you can come back to Bradford. Margaret had a stroke. I found out and came here right away. I haven't been back in years, but not a lot has changed. How is Paris? Can you come?"

"I'd like to, but can't right away. I'm sick as a dog. I was on a shoot in Marrakech and had to fly home last night. I was in the hospital in Morocco for two days. I still feel sick as can be, but I'm so loaded up on antibiotics and anti-diarrhea medicines I can hardly stay awake. What are you doing there?"

Quickly Cassie filled her in on what had been happening, ending by saying, "Come as soon as you can. Oh, Piper, I've missed you so much through the years."

"Hey, I missed you, too. Tell Margaret to hang in there, I'll be there as soon as I feel well enough to fly."

"I knew you would. Any idea where Fiona is?"

"No. You lost touch with her, too?"

"Everyone but Margaret. But I've reconnected with some friends here in Bradford since I came back. I can't wait to see you. I just learned today what a big success you are."

"Yeah, until the next blond babe comes along and knocks me off my pedestal."

They talked for a couple of more minutes, then Cassie said goodbye and hung up, feeling giddy with excitement.

Matt was leaning against the doorjamb to the kitchen.

"So you reached her."

"I did, and you were right, she was away—in Morocco. She's sick, sounded terrible. But as soon as she's well enough to fly, she's coming here. It was so great to talk to her. She sounded just like she always did. I can't wait to see her again! Now if I can only locate Fiona."

"Try the detective again tomorrow."

"Good idea." She almost danced over to him. "It's been so long. I could have talked longer, but she sounded so awful. Maybe she'll feel better tomorrow and I can call again. Want some coffee?"

"No. I'm heading out. I'll take a rain-check on the coffee."

15

Cassie was feeling frustrated. It had been three days since she'd seen or talked to Matt. After Sunday, she thought they might be drawing closer. She knew he had hang-ups about Dolores, but had hoped he might be moving beyond them.

Wishful thinking.

Stephen had called her once from Boston, again asking her to let him know when she was returning. Cassie had been as kind as she knew how, but firm. She thought they shouldn't speak to each other for a while.

Adele had also called, urging her to think things over carefully and not be swayed by emotions as a result of Margaret's brush with death.

The longer Cassie was in Bradford, the more certain she was of her desire to stay. It'd be different now. She was no longer a teenager railing against fate. No longer so desperate for acceptance and a feeling of belonging that she threw herself on others.

She'd made a niche for herself in Boston and could do the same in Bradford. She already had a good friend in Betsy. The Monday she'd had coffee with another woman she knew from high school. Her business looked as if it might actually take off. She had received a new commission as a result of Saturday's dinner.

There was Piper's visit to look forward to. Cassie had called her on Monday and they'd talked for a half hour.

And most important of all, Margaret was recovering. She no longer needed the close nursing monitoring that she once needed. She was pronounced out of immediate danger of another stroke. She could sit up for a limited period of time, and she was alert and always anxious to participate in her physical therapy.

Cassie caught Dr. Pendarvis on his rounds Wednesday and questioned him about Margaret's progress.

"She's doing well. We've started her on a new regimen of blood pressure medication. With proper diet, some exercises and the medication, I don't think she'll have another stroke. She needs to continue the PT to get back her strength and mobility. Once she's mobile, the rest of her care can be given at home, if someone is there to look after her."

"I'm moving back to Bradford. I need to get to Boston and pack, sublet my apartment, and formally quit my job there. How much time do I have before she'll be able to come home?"

"We'll be transferring her to a convalescent hospital in another week or so, I think. We'll see how well she responds to the physical therapy. She may be there for a few weeks."

"And her speech?"

"Aphasia is a tricky thing. She should regain most of her facility in that area, but may always have trouble finding the right words. Or she may not recover. That's harder to predict."

Cassie thanked the doctor for his frankness and went to see Margaret.

"I spoke with your doctor," she said when she was seated by Margaret's bed.

Cassie was happy to see how well Margaret looked. The bandage was gone and her hair had been washed. It looked soft and white, not lackluster as it had a few weeks ago. Her eyes sparkled, and she looked more like the Margaret Cassie had known a dozen years ago.

"Your prognosis is excellent. And you can go home as soon as you're mobile. So when you go to physical therapy, be sure to apply yourself!"

Cassie smiled, remembering how often Margaret had told her girls to apply themselves. It was odd to have the shoe on the other foot.

"I have to return to Boston to close up my place and arrange to have my things moved," she said.

Margaret reached for her hand and squeezed it once.

"I'll put the things in storage until I find a place here in Bradford."

Margaret squeezed twice.

"I don't want to get rid of them."

She shook her head slightly.

"There's no room at the house. Besides, Matt is

moving ahead with his plans for the teen home. You need to get ready for that, as well."

Margaret squeezed twice.

"What do you mean, no? He's depending on you."

Margaret moved her eyes to her body, shaking her head slightly.

"You're going to have a complete recovery," Cassie said, guessing her thoughts. "You have a lot of years left yet, and we all need you."

Margaret withdrew her hand.

"I found Piper," Cassie said.

Margaret's eyes grew wide.

"I didn't tell you before because I wanted to know for sure when she's coming. She's sick with some flu bug and doesn't know her exact arrival date, but she's planning to fly to Bradford to see you. I can't wait. I've missed her as much as I've missed you over the years. Just think, you'll have two of your girls back together."

The smile that lit Margaret's face filled Cassie with happiness.

She smiled in return.

"We haven't given up hope of finding Fiona. Wouldn't that be something, the three girls from Bradford Hall back in Bradford. Think the town can stand it?"

Margaret nodded slightly.

"You're making such good progress," Cassie said, recognizing the effort the older woman was putting forth. "You'll be back home in no time."

Cassie planned to be there when Margaret came

home. With any luck, Piper would be as well.

When she was back at the house, Cassie took a calendar and checked when her next catering event was scheduled. She then called the airline and made a reservation. She had time to fly to Boston, pack and be back in time for the next event.

Matt finished emptying the old dresser. He'd gone through the closet and packed up the bedding and the clothes to donate. The knickknacks Dolores had acquired had little meaning for him. He kept a couple of pieces, wrapping the rest in newspaper and packing them in a box for the church. School papers were skimmed. He kept a couple where she'd done well. Her grades had always been erratic. Sometimes she got As, other times she barely passed.

Knowing more about learning disabilities now that he was an adult, Matt wondered why no one at school had done more to help his sister.

When he pulled the empty dresser away from the wall, he heard a thunk. Dragging it into the middle of the room, he looked behind it. A book had fallen onto the floor. Stooping to pick it up, he realized it was a journal. Had his sister kept a diary?

Opening the cover, he recognized Dolores's handwriting. He read the first few sentences. She wrote that she was starting a journal on the recommendation of one of her teachers, who had suggested writing out her feelings might help her clarify how she felt about things and discover what made her angry and what made her happy. She said she would try it for a few months, but she figured it was just a trick to get her to improve her writing skills.

Matt smiled at that. His sister had resisted anyone who tried to help her.

He went to sit on the side of the bed, leafing through the pages. Dolores hadn't dated them, so he had no idea when she'd written it. Reading a bit more, he picked up on her frustration with their mother, her devotion to the rock band she idolized, and her love for Stewart, as well as her jealousy about Cassie.

That gave him pause. Cassie had told him Dolores hadn't liked her, and here it was in black and white. This page had been written sometime in the last few months before her death.

He read on, wincing when he came to the section about how her brother had let her down by his interest in other girls. She wanted their family to be close, but the three of them kept going their separate ways.

When he read the account of her first thoughts of suicide, he wanted to gather his sister in his arms and keep her safe forever. She'd initially talked about it to get attention. A mixture of triumph and shame mingled in the words she'd written. She hated doing such a low thing, but it had worked—it had brought her brother to her and proved he loved her more than Cassie.

As he read on, he learned things about his sister

he'd never suspected. His attention really perked up when she talked about Stewart. She poured her teenaged heart on the pages. She was totally in love with the guy, Matt realized.

Then the tone changed. Something had happened. She just referred to "the incident." She wanted Stewart to marry her, but he was pulling away. She hated some guy she referred to as "A," and as Matt read more about the way he'd been pushing Dolores into a more intimate relationship than she wanted, he felt his anger grow. Matt wondered if he could find out who the guy was.

The last entry was written after she'd found out she was pregnant. She was horrified.

She couldn't go on the way things were. She hated herself and "A." She hated the fact her brother liked someone better than her. Finding out Stewart was seeing someone else made her panic. If she could make Matt believe Cassie was the cause of her death, that would end any chance of her brother staying with Cassie. Dolores wanted Matt to mourn her, to know at last that she was the most important person in his life, even if it would be too late by then.

After that, the journal had only blank pages.

Matt felt his sister's anguish. Felt the emotional intensity that only teenagers were capable of, even when it was out of proportion to reality. There had been so many options for Dolores, but she couldn't see them, couldn't imagine any other one.

It hadn't been about Cassie after all. It had been about Dolores's life and the fear of having a baby. The anguish of her boyfriend turning away and the pressure from "A."

Matt remembered talking to Stewart at the funeral. The entire high-school class had shown up. The guy had denied he'd gotten Dolores pregnant. He was seeing someone else. Had been for a while. Matt knew that.

Was it Stewart's betrayal that had pushed Dolores over the edge? Matt had blamed Cassie for telling her. What was hard to believe was that someone else had not already told her.

It was obvious Dolores had planned her suicide. Even the call to Cassie had been designed to place blame and guilt. His sister had been a mixed up, unhappy, troubled teen. And her meticulous plans had played out as she'd intended. Including his reaction.

He closed the book, feeling as hurt and sad as he had when they'd arrived at the hospital to discover Dolores was already gone.

That evening, Matt dialed Cassie's number. It went to voice mail.

"Call me," he said.

When he awoke the next morning, Matt lay in bed thinking over the revelations of his sister's diary. He had been unfair to Cassie. She'd tried to explain. He needed to tell her the truth.

He wondered again who "A" was.

After he showered and dressed, he went to the library, asking to see the high-school yearbooks for the time he and Dolores had been at school.

Leafing through them, he was surprised at the number of boys' names starting with *A*. Aaron Phelps was in Dolores's grade. Matt stared at the photograph, not recognizing the boy. Andrew Harper was a junior that year. Alex Carpenter, another junior. Had Matt seen him hanging around Dolores? Abner Sinclair, Abe Cohen, Adam Price.

Matt studied each photo in turn, trying to remember seeing Dolores with any of them. He hadn't paid a lot of attention to what she'd been doing in those days—he'd been too caught up with Cassie.

The fact his sister had been several weeks pregnant when she'd died had come as a complete surprise to him. Which of these guys was the father? Had the boy known he'd impregnated her? Had she turned to the guy for help and been rejected?

Matt jotted down all the names. He had somewhere to start, at least. He'd look them up one by one.

He'd also look up Brittany Barstow; she'd been Dolores's closest friend. Maybe she'd be willing to tell him more now than she had back then.

Closing the book, he headed for Cassie's. No time like the present to apologize.

The house was empty, the rental van gone. Was she at the hospital? Did she have an event? Just his luck—

when he was ready to resolve things between them, she wasn't available.

Cassie was surprised how little time it took to pack up her apartment. She signed up the first moving company she called and soon had large boxes full of her belongings ready to be transported to Mississippi along with her furniture.

Two days after she'd arrived, Cassie was the proud owner of a used van. She packed her suitcases and all the boxes containing her kitchen utensils and cookbooks into the back and headed south. She'd debated waiting until she got back to Mississippi to buy a vehicle, but had found the perfect one in the paper. And it made transporting all her cooking utensils much easier than trying to get them on the plane with her.

The drive also gave her plenty of time to think and plan. She was in constant contact with Betsy, who must be beating the bushes for jobs. They were booked for every weekend through June and a couple of Saturdays had both afternoon and evening events.

How she was going to manage those was a problem, but one she was happy to solve.

She hadn't heard from Matt. Was there a reason for that? Was he regretting the time he'd spent with her? She'd be sick at heart if that were the case.

Was she deluding herself that he was softening his stance? She wanted a return of the closeness they'd once shared so badly she thought she'd rationalize anything to get it again. But what if he didn't feel the same way?

She stopped in Washington to spend the night. Calling Piper from her motel, Cassie was sorry to hear she was still sick. But she'd made her plane reservation for two weeks later. No matter if she was sick or well, she promised she'd be in Mississippi the first of June.

"Don't come if you're sick," Cassie said. "Margaret wouldn't be able to see you right away if you're still ill and she was so excited when I told her you were coming."

"How is she?" Piper asked.

"Getting better all the time. The doctor thinks she'll be mobile before long. Then she'll be able to return home. That's where you can help. I've got a bunch of catering events lined up so I can't be home all the time with her. I'm sure her friend Edith will come to stay with her when she can, but she's plagued with arthritis and doesn't get around as much as she once did."

"I'm not much of a nurse," Piper said.

"She won't need nursing, just someone there in case she falls or something."

"Whatever happened with you and Matt?" Piper asked. "I always thought you two were the great love story of the ages, but in all our conversations, you haven't mentioned him once."

"Long story, I'll fill you in when you get here. I've got to go. This call will cost the earth, and I'm self-employed now. Can't count on a steady income."

"I know all about that. I'll fill you in on the ups and downs of self-employment when I see you. Bye."

It was late when Cassie arrived in Bradford. She drove straight home, not stopping by the hospital. Time enough to see Margaret in the morning. Now she just wanted to get to bed.

Unpacking only the bare necessities, she fell into bed and quickly went to sleep.

A short time later the phone woke her.

Fearing an emergency, she dashed down the stairs. "Hello?"

"Don't you listen to your messages?" Matt asked.

Cassie sat on the bottom step, leaning against the railing. Her glance took in the answering machine's blinking lights.

"I just got in from driving all day and half the night. I haven't even been asleep a half hour and you wake me up. I haven't checked the mail, listened to messages or anything else. And I don't plan to tonight, either."

She hung up and went back upstairs.

The next morning, Cassie awoke refreshed and raring to go. Her first plan of action was to make a complete inventory of all the cooking utensils she and Margaret had between them, and jot down any she needed. She'd purchase what she could today. She also needed to restock her supplies of flour, sugar, spices, condiments and oils in large quantities.

As she stepped from her shower a few minutes later, she sniffed appreciatively. The aroma of fresh coffee wafted on the air.

Was someone in the house?

Dressing quickly, she hurried downstairs and into the kitchen. Coffee brewed in the machine. Matt sat at the table, a white bag sitting in front of him.

He was reading the newspaper, but looked up when she entered.

"Good morning. I brought bagels and cream cheese. I figured you might not have anything in the house if you've been gone."

"I was only gone a few days."

"I didn't know you were planning to be away," he said, rising and crossing to the coffee machine.

He took the carafe and filled two mugs, adding cream to hers and turning to hand it to her.

Cassie took a deep breath. She wasn't sure why he was here, and equally uncertain whether she wanted him here or not. She had things to do that didn't include Matt.

"I went to Boston to pack up," she said, taking the offered mug, then sitting down at the table.

She pulled the bag toward herself. Opening it, she took one of the fresh bagels and the container of cream cheese. She spread cheese on half the bagel and took a bite. Heavenly.

"That was fast," he said, returning with his own mug. He sat opposite her. "I saw the Massachusetts plates on that van in your driveway this morning."

"I bought it in Boston and drove it home. It's full of stuff. The rest is coming with movers in a few weeks. I'm in no rush, since I need to find a place to stay by the time it arrives and I haven't even started looking."

"Thought you were staying here."

"For a while," she said, taking another bite. "What are you doing here?"

"I came to see you. I called several times, as you'll see once you do listen to the answering machine."

"Must have been after I left."

"I should have called earlier."

"Forget it. I don't want to hear shoulds. Thanks for breakfast."

"I cleared Dolores's room," he told her. "And found her diary."

Cassie looked at him. "She kept a diary?"

"Yes, one of her teachers suggested it might help her sort out her feelings. She was a troubled kid."

"Weren't we all back then?" Cassie asked.

"Do you know how many boys there were in school whose names started with *A*?"

Cassie shook her head. "Probably more than one. And don't forget nicknames. Remember Arnie?"

"Reginald Pettigrew. How did he get the nickname Arnie?"

"I have no idea, but I remember how funny it was. Why do you want to know about boys' names?"

"I think some guy whose name started with *A* got her pregnant, not Stewart," Matt said. "Who could it have been?"

Cassie didn't remember Dolores dating anyone except Stewart.

"I don't know. She and I weren't friends."

He took a long drink of the hot coffee, placing the cup down with a thump.

"Well, I want to find out."

"What else did her diary say?"

He looked at her for a long moment.

"She planned her death, to the last detail. And it wasn't totally because she'd found out Stewart was seeing someone else."

Cassie stared at him. After all this time—vindication. Matt knew beyond a shadow of a doubt that she had not been the cause of his sister's death.

She should feel relief or something.

Instead, she felt sadness—that the boy she'd loved so much had never given her a chance. That the man he had become must have still harbored uncertainty even after she'd explained. It had taken a voice from the grave to convince him.

"Thank you for telling me. I think you should go now."

Matt looked taken aback.

"Go? I just told you I know you weren't the cause of Dolores's death. I thought you'd want to talk about it or something."

Cassie shook her head.

"I tried so hard back then to have you believe me. When we talked a few weeks ago, and I told you the entire story, you never fully accepted it, did you? You needed to hear from Dolores herself to believe."

"The fact is I do believe you," he said.

She forced a smile.

"Because you read Dolores's diary. I wanted you to believe me because you trusted me. Because you knew anything I said to you would be the truth."

"And the truth is you want me to leave?"

She nodded. She wasn't sure exactly how she felt, but not vindicated. More battered and sad than happy he finally believed her.

Why couldn't he have had faith in her all those years ago?

Why couldn't he have loved her as she'd wanted him to?

Matt got up and put his cup in the sink, then headed for the back door.

"The McIver project got its sign-off," he said, pausing in the doorway. "The money is being transferred to my account and I'll be ready to roll on this house next week."

"I'll make sure I stay out of your way."

She didn't look at him. She suddenly felt old and tired. Maybe she wouldn't do that inventory today after all. Maybe she'd go back to bed and hide under the covers.

Cassie heard his truck leave. She sipped her cooling coffee and eyed the journal he'd left. How dare he not believe her. Dolores had been determined to end their relationship and she had succeeded not once, but twice.

Matt drove to town and headed for the café. He hadn't eaten and wasn't going back to Cassie's to demand a bagel. He parked near the café and walked in. Glancing around, he saw some empty tables and a couple of empty stools at the counter.

Sam Witt sat beside one. Matt walked over and sat down beside the sheriff. Sam had come to Bradford after Matt moved to New Orleans, but they'd met at the café a few times, and usually struck up a conversation.

Their friendship was growing as Matt spent more time in Bradford.

"Good morning," the waitress behind the counter said cheerfully. "Coffee?"

Matt nodded but didn't return her greeting.

"How about you, Sheriff? Ready for a refill?"

"Sure thing, Darlene. Bring some more sugar, will you?"

Matt looked at Sam as he stirred in two heaping spoonfuls of sugar.

"That looks disgusting."

"Coffee tastes disgusting—I'm trying to disguise the taste," Sam said easily. "What's riding you?"

"Women!"

Sam laughed. "Can't live with them, can't live without them."

Matt didn't find humor in the situation.

"It's Cassie. I found a diary from Dolores that proved to me Cassie wasn't the reason for my sister's suicide. I told her so and she kicked me out of the house."

"Uh-huh."

"What does that mean?"

"She probably wanted you to believe her without proof," Sam said. "Women are funny that way."

"I did believe her."

"When? From what you told me when Cassie first came back here, you blamed her for Dolores's death, end of discussion."

"Now I know that was wrong. Nothing she did could have caused Dolores's death. My sister was a mixed-up teenager with some serious problems that were ignored."

Sam didn't say anything for a few moments.

"Did you ever marry?" he asked at last.

Matt looked at him.

"No. What does that have to do with anything? Given my family history, the best thing for me is to avoid marriage. At least I won't cause all the havoc in people's lives my parents did."

"If you were married and had kids, would you leave them?"

"No way."

"Drink yourself silly?"

Matt gave him a disgusted look.

"Get real."

"So you aren't your father. Or your mother, come to that. Why not give marriage a try?"

"You married?"

"Was."

"Oh." Matt shrugged. "I never wanted to risk it."

"I think you never found anyone to measure up to Cassie. I've talked to a few people in town while I've been trying to track down Fiona. Everyone thought the two of you were set to live happily ever after."

"Shows how wrong people can be."

"Or how pigheaded some men are. Cassie didn't cause your sister's death. She hasn't married in all these years and neither have you. Makes a man wonder."

Sam drained his cup and retrieved his hat.

"I'm off to make my rounds. Nice place, Bradford. Not a lot of crime, which is a good change from New Orleans. Wish I'd found this town and this job a few years back."

Matt watched him leave, then turned to his breakfast, which was just being served.

Was there some wisdom in Sam's comments?

He wasn't his father. He might make mistakes in the future, but they wouldn't be the ones his old man had made. He'd never leave a wife and children and walk away without a backward look.

Whoa, wife and children?

He slowly ate the eggs and bacon, thinking about Cassie as his wife. They'd have breakfast together every morning. Could he expect elaborate meals from a chef? Or something hastily thrown together because she preferred cooking for crowds?

How could he think of marrying someone when he didn't know much about that person? They'd been apart for twelve years. Was the teenager he'd so loved still a major part of the adult Cassie?

He finished his breakfast in record time. He was going to find out.

Cassie found Margaret sitting up in bed, watching the wall-mounted television in her new room. An elderly woman recovering from a broken leg was in the bed across from her, asleep. Cassie tiptoed to Margaret's bed. She could see the improvement in her foster mother over the few days she'd been gone.

"How are you feeling?" she asked, giving her a kiss on the cheek then sitting beside her and taking her hand. "Better today?"

Margaret squeezed an affirmative.

"I got back last night and went right to bed. I bought a van in Boston and drove it here. It'll be perfect for catering. I need a carpenter to build me some shelves, and other storage compartments. I want something that has a lip so trays won't slide off."

Mentioning the carpenter reminded Cassie of Matt's offer when she'd brought it up before.

Margaret tugged on her hand, a questioning look in her eyes.

"It's Matt," Cassie said, guessing Margaret wanted to know why she was down in the dumps.

"He found a diary from Dolores. It changed his

opinion of me and my actions the day of her death."

Margaret squeezed her hand, a lopsided smile on her face.

"It's so complicated. Why couldn't he have believed me when I told him?"

Margaret tugged on her hand again.

"Okay, I'll tell you the full story. Maybe you can help me."

Cassie related all that had transpired between her and Matt since she'd been back in Bradford.

"So there you are," she concluded. "I don't know what to do. He once meant the world to me, but then he let me down so badly, I didn't know how I'd survive. Now, after all this time, what do I do? Risk my heart again or take the safe road and cut him out of my life?"

Margaret squeezed again, several times.

"I do wish you could talk. I'd love to hear your advice. So here's the deal. I'm staying here in Bradford."

One squeeze.

"I'm starting my catering business with Betsy, and we're booked for several weeks now. It might just fly."

Another single squeeze.

"I'm staying in your house until you're home and back to normal."

Margaret nodded slightly.

"I'm staying away from Matt."

Double squeeze and a half frown from Margaret.

"I'm seeing where a relationship between me and Matt might lead?" she said hesitantly.

Margaret smiled, squeezed her hand and nodded once.

"I love him, you know," Cassie said.

Margaret nodded.

"I think I always have and always will. And that was why it was so devastating when he turned on me. How could he not believe me? I would have believed him."

Margaret tried to talk, but the sounds were unintelligible.

"Okay, okay, I'll see where this leads, but you and I are going to have a long heart-to-heart talk when you're up to it. I think I'm taking a huge risk here."

Despite her brave words to Margaret, Cassie wasn't sure she could face dealing with Matt any time soon. She felt hurt to her core. Was it unreasonable to expect someone she loved to trust her in return?

Or was what had happened so long ago best left in the past? Matt was no longer a teenager devastated by his sister's tragic death. He had matured, and so had she. If they both wanted it enough, they could find a middle ground.

It might not be the soaring elation she'd felt before, but they could build a lasting commitment. Build a family that would be strong and weather any crises together.

Or could they?

That was the major part of the problem. She didn't trust Matt to stand by her in tough times. What if some other tragedy happened in the future and he blamed her?

She couldn't live through that a second time. Better to go through life alone than risk that kind of hurt again.

She drove to the old house and went to the kitchen. Cassie thought best when she cooked. She decided to make some plain and simple chocolate-chip cookies. Maybe she'd call Betsy to see if she wanted to come over to help her eat them.

She wished Piper had been well enough to fly over sooner. Waiting seemed doubly hard now. The few phone calls they'd shared had left Cassie wanting to know so much more about Piper's life since they'd last seen each other.

Cassie took the second batch of cookies from the oven a little while later. As she placed them on the counter, she heard a car in the drive. Sliding the next batch in to bake, she went to the door.

Matt was walking up the steps.

"Are you here about the renovation?" she asked, annoyed she felt glad to see him.

Her attraction hadn't waned even if her good sense had convinced her he wasn't the man for her.

"I need to talk to you," he said.

"About what?"

"About what an ass I've been. What a colossal mistake I made twelve years ago. About what I want from life."

"Oh."

She didn't know what to say.

"Can I come in?"

She stepped aside and he entered the kitchen.

He saw the cookies and smiled.

"Nothing like warm cookies and cold milk."

"Then sit down and I'll get the milk."

It gave her something to do. She felt as skittish as a newborn colt, not daring to hope anything positive would come from their talk, yet wishing deep inside that everything would turn out right.

She piled cookies on a plate and put them on the table, then poured two tall glasses of milk.

She sat two seats away from Matt.

He was already eating one of the cookies.

"Mmm, they're great straight from the oven. I think these are the best I've ever had."

All cooks liked praise for their work. Cassie smiled.

"Thank you."

She waited silently. He seemed more intent on eating the cookies than talking. But this was his idea, so she'd let him speak first.

Draining his glass, he put it down, pushed it away and looked at her.

"I'd understand if you never spoke to me again. I was wrong about everything. Wrong in my assuming you would deliberately withhold help from Dolores. Wrong in the way I dealt with the situation back then. Wrong in the way I've handled things since you've been back."

Cassie wasn't going to argue with him. The hurt still lingered.

"I'm sorry. That's all I can say. I know I let you

down in the worst way possible, and I have no excuse except my own pigheadedness, as was recently pointed out to me. I ask your forgiveness."

She blinked. She hadn't expected so eloquent an appeal.

He reached out his hand.

"Please, Cassie, forgive me."

She looked at his strong hand, then slowly placed her own in his, palm to palm.

"It's hard," she said. "I was so hurt I didn't know what to do. The one person I thought I could count on let me down."

He squeezed her hand. "I'm sorry."

She looked at him, seeing the contrition in his eyes.

"I know. I'm sorry, too. Yes, I forgive you. You were a kid, too, I have to remember. You were so badly hurt by your sister's death and you had no support from your mother. We were both suffering."

"Only you handled it differently from me," he said, drawing her from her chair and settling her on his lap.

"The best thing in the world would have been to have you with me throughout all the weeks that followed," he said slowly. "I lost Dolores, but I lost my best friend, too. The girl I loved."

"You could have fallen in love with someone else."

"I don't think so. Neither of us married anyone else. Doesn't that tell you something?"

"We didn't want to get married?"

"We didn't want to marry anyone but each other."

Cassie's heart rate sped up. Was Matt saying he wanted to marry her?

"Will you let me spend the rest of our lives making you as happy as I can? Will you marry me?"

She hesitated.

Matt frowned. "Am I reading things wrong? Don't you love me?"

She nodded.

"I love you, but I'm afraid. What if something else happens and you turn on me again. How would I endure that a second time?"

"It's been a hard lesson, but I've learned not to jump to conclusions. I also know what's been missing in my life for years. Love from a special person. I'd never do anything in the future to jeopardize that love. I promise you that, Cassie. Whatever happens, I will never do that again. Give me that chance to show you how much I love you."

It was a risk. But she already knew what life was like without Matt. What would it be like with him?

She thought back to the glorious year she was sixteen. How could she pass up a chance to be that happy again?

"Matt Bennett, I'd love to marry you!"

He whooped in happiness and kissed her.

The buzzer sounded for the cookies.

"Darn, just when we were getting to the good part," Cassie said, rising from his lap.

"I'm hoping there are only good parts to come," Matt said, following her to the oven.

She put the baking sheet on the counter.

"That's the last batch."

Flicking off the oven, she turned and smiled at Matt.

"I love you, Matt. I don't think I ever stopped. The agony I felt when we were separated was almost unbearable. The distance I thought could never be crossed had me so hurt I could hardly make it through the days. I loved you so much that year. And now, and I believe I always will."

"I'll do everything in my power to keep you safe and happy," he promised, taking her into his arms to seal the bargain with a kiss.

When they came up for air, Cassie leaned back in his arms.

"I have obligations. I need to make sure Margaret's okay before getting married. She'll want to be at the wedding, you know."

"Of course. And we have to talk about where we'll live. My work's in New Orleans, and I don't want to live in Bradford."

"You've made that clear."

"Can you come live with me in New Orleans?" he asked.

"I suppose so, eventually. But for the next few months, I'll make Bradford home. Let me get some experience in catering here so I can take New Orleans by storm."

"And spend time with your family, once Piper arrives," Matt said.

"Yes," Cassie said with a happy smile. "I'll have my family—Margaret and Piper—around me. And the man I love. Now, if we could only find Fiona..."

If you liked **Cassie's Return**,
you may enjoy *Billionaire's Betrothal*,
book 1 in the *Gold Gate Romance* series.

If you enjoyed **Cassie's Return**,
please consider leaving a review.

More books by Barbara McMahon

Bradford Hall
Cassie's Return

Golden Gate Romance Series

Billionaire's Betrothal
Dakota's Hero
Finding a Wife for Tanner
Love Times Three

Her Not So Empty Nest
One Special Kiss
The CEO's Baby
Office Charade

Cowboys of Wildcat Creek

Valentine's Cowboy Rescue
Shelly and the Cowboy
Kristi's Cowboy Hero

Holly's Reluctant Cowboy
A Cowboy for Eliza

Sweet Reunion Romance Collection

Unexpected Reunion
Unpredictable Reunion

Unanticipated Reunion

The Talmadge Sisters

Letters to Caroline
Michelle's Marriage Deal

Trusting Abby

The Harts of Texas Series

Rebel Heart
Tangled Hearts

Reckless Heart

A Sweet Clean Christmas Romance Collection

The Christmas Cop
The Cowboy's Special Christmas
A Soldier's Christmas

A Teaspoon of Mistletoe
The Christmas Locket
A Key West Christmas

Cowboy Heroes Series

The Cowboy Next Door
Cowboy's Bride
One Stubborn Cowboy
Crazy About a Cowboy
Never Doubt a Cowboy

Cowboy Marshal
Summer Cowboy
Second Chance Cowboy
Movie Star Cowboy

Tropical Escape Series

Island Rendezvous
Come into the Sun

Island Paradise

Rocky Point Series

Rocky Point Legacy
Rocky Point Reunion
Rocky Point Promise

Rocky Point Hero
Rocky Point Inn
Rocky Point Dawn

The Ultimate Billionaires

The Cynical Sheikh
Falling for the Sheikh

A Sheikh of Her Own
The Unforgettable Sheikh

Sweet Romance Stand-alone Collection

Because of You
Cowboy Charade
I'll Take Forever
Jared's Promise
Mail Order Bride
Not Really Married

Sweet Meant To Be
The Cowboy Comes Home
The Paper Marriage
Trusting Jake
The Banished Bride